Dancing In The Shadows

By

Len Russell

Published by **Nun the Wiser Books** a division of
Dancing Tree Productions Limited

7 Ridge Road, Weston, Connecticut 06883 USA

ISBN 978-1-7803560-8-2

For Samantha, Lenny, Eliot, Hunter,
Benjamin, Lucas and Nathan

Live all you can: it's a mistake not to.
It doesn't matter what you do in particular,
So long as you have had your life.
If you haven't had that, what have you had?

Henry James from *The Ambassadors*

Hey, Englebert Humperdinck is in town!

Hamming it up with good mate Carole Spencer in the Four Canoes Restaurant in Rotorua. We were celebrating something, I forget what, about 1975.

PROLOGUE

I found in writing Book one, *The Man Who Cast Two Shadows,* a glorious opportunity to almost relive my life, the good and the bad of it. Writing it was nowhere near the daunting task I had imagined it to be, in fact it has been a pleasure. I first felt the need to write after a visit to family in Bristol in the summer of 2010. Now, some one hundred and sixty thousand words later and with more to come, I find myself enjoying one of life's greatest pleasures. I have been happy to receive many kind words and compliments from readers of book one. I hope book two, *Dancing in the Shadows* gives the same pleasure.

For those of you who haven't read the first book and are joining us midway through the story and are sufficiently entertained by these pages, I suggest you purchase book one to find out about the formative years of the roguish leading character in this story. I am now working on the final book of this trilogy, which should be released in early 2014. It will take the story from where it leaves off in Sydney in late 1981 to the present day.

I started out on the adventure of writing my story, not as a result of any vanity or wish to impress, but solely to leave a thirty-page record for my grandchildren so they'd know how they came to have the great good fortune to be born in New Zealand and to have British nationality. I regard both these to be great blessings in our troubled world. However, the story refused to be dealt with so briefly and has grown into more than a thousand pages. They record the passage of a guileless boy from Rickmansworth in the UK, who was seldom less than a few jumps ahead of the police in many countries. He lived a charmed life in the down under underworld amongst chancers, characters, madmen and madder women and with the aid of highly competent legal council and a dose of Bargee cunning, made it through and lived to tell the tale.

Left to right; The Stornaway Islander, Me, Colin and Merv on the Athenic.

HOW IT ALL STARTED

On the Athenic, Christmas 1956 and first trip to New Zealand.
Left to right, Colin Mayhew, Merv and me, all aged 18.

TROUBLED WATERS AHEAD
AFTER A QUIET START

In a time of emails and texting we easily forget how important phone calls used to be. They were the only way you could send an immediate and urgent message. If you wanted to tell a friend to get the hell out of Dodge and you were on the way out of there yourself then you picked up the phone.

"Lenny my friend," I immediately recognised the easy tone and accent of Roberto Fiona, the joint owner with "Diamond Jim Shepherd" of Tati's restaurant in Oxford Street, Paddington. I had not seen him since he asked me to travel to Fiji for a meeting, in April 1981.

He had asked me to go there, amongst other things, to host his new American girlfriend's family until he arrived. Then to escort them to Sydney, organise some top class accommodation for them, and generally make them feel at home. Though he did not say it, it was glaringly obvious that he may not be coming back to Australia. Subsequent developments, and news announcements, caused me to understand why. Sometime later, I got a phone call from him, asking me to pass on a message to someone.

"Lenny thanks for your help" he was a very polite

man; "The family are over here with me now" He didn't say where, I didn't ask. "Lenny, I give you some good advice; you have been very good with me. Lenny, leave Sydney, leave Australia, it is going to be very dangerous. Don't worry about your business, just get out, I know you are a police target, believe me it is dangerous for you. Same for me; I am not coming back" His soft Latin tones did not hide the anxiety in his voice.

This was from a man with international underworld contacts. A man whose father had been a General in the Argentine army until assassinated in one of the power plays that swept the country. Only a fool would not take heed. Lady Luck was with me; she must have been worried that I would ignore the warning, as this follow up occurred two days later. The phone rang, I sensed it was important, in those situations you do.

"Get out mate, get out of Sydney; go back to New Zealand; the shit is hitting the fan big time." The caller was a good guy; I had known him in Auckland when he was a hairdresser, come illegal bookie. It was Malcolm Wynn. He was now a high-flying lawyer in Sydney. He acted for Jimmy Shepherd (Diamond Jim) in property conveyancing matters.

"Lenny I'm telling you, the games up over here. I know you're not involved with the other business, but the cops won't care. They will want to know where all the cash has come from to start the Bathhouse and bet your bottom dollar your protection on that will be gone. They are grabbing anybody close to Jimmy. Everybody they really want has disappeared. They have to have some collars to cover themselves. I know they think they can fit you up. It's a no-win one mate. They crashed my office yesterday. I've just got out. This is serious shit mate; they are not fucking around. Get out while you can." This was Malcolm's breathless, but timely, warning.

The papers and TV news had been full of stories about a gang of downunder criminals arrested in London. It was Sinclair and the Mr Asia Syndicate. Australia had got too hot for them. They were shifting their operations to the UK, starting with a massive cocaine import. The original leader was Martin Johnstone, an Aucklander and he had started the whole thing off with an import of Thai Buddha sticks. From that beginning this murderous group had grown. For various reasons, Sinclair had ordered Marty killed. His body had been discovered. The British police had caught the local murderers Sinclair had used and they had led the police straight back to the Syndicate. From there the trail led back to Australia. The corruption became exposed and as Malcolm had so ineloquently put it: the shit really had hit the fan.

I had always respected my instincts more than

money; it was time to go, which I did. That decision was reinforced as, later that week, three burly cops smashed into my flat in Double Bay, followed by two heavies the next night. The word was out; Jimmy was gone and wasn't coming back. I had allowed myself to become a hostage to fortune. However, all this would unfold in the early 1980s. Let's regroup where book one ended and follow the events that led me to the nightmare in Sydney.

My trip back from the UK and my sojourn in Hong Kong had aroused in me an insatiable urge to start something else. I felt like a cowboy who had fallen and had to get back on his horse. Alternatively, maybe an explorer who had been home, become bored and had the urge, the need, to return to the unknown and explore once again. I make no claim to be anything as noble as an explorer, but I was feeling similar urges.

It was now summer and I was back in Auckland. My head was bursting with new projects; most of them as a result of my last trip to Sydney. My wife, Mary, and the kids were fine and had really enjoyed their time at the Orewa Beach motor camp.

One morning found me enjoying my usual start to the day. I was in one of Auckland's best-known meeting spots. To Aucklanders it was comparable to the legendary, 'meet me under the clock' in New York's Grand Central Station. I was having a leisurely al fresco breakfast in a waterfront café in the old, but iconic, downtown Ferry Building.

There was almost a carnival atmosphere. The colourful ferries were discharging incoming passengers and loading outgoing passengers and tourists eager to explore the magnificent Hauraki Gulf. The morning sun was casting warm rays. The water agitated by the ferries was lapping against the wharf piles yards from my feet. The bubbly waiter had just served my plate of scrambled eggs and salmon. All was well with my world. I was engrossed in my paper when from behind me I heard, "How are you Lenny?"

It was my old friend, the Tottenham hard nut, Keith Morgan. He was one of the first friends I had made in New Zealand. Keith had many plusses in his life, particularly in the underworld circle that I seemed to move in and out of as my life required. He was a major player in the 'gang who couldn't shoot straight'. Though that was the put down nickname I had bestowed on them, they were a very successful team of Pommie safe breakers who had plagued the authorities for many years. Keith was an all-round good guy and a staunch friend.

"Mate, how are you? Come and sit down, have some breckie with me; what's been happening?" I asked.

Keith smiled slyly.

"I heard you've been turning them over in Sydney

for a good earn and you just got out in front of the Jacks is the word on the street," he said with a warm smile.

News travels fast, I thought.

"Something like that mate, anyway how are your folks?"

By this time our respective parents had made contact with each other in London and had become friends.

"They're good mate; they're coming out next year."

"That's great. So what's cooking since I've been away?"

"Well as a matter of fact I've been looking for you. I heard you were using this place, so here I am, caught you," he said with another smile.

"Look Lenny, it's like this, remember that Wellington geezer, the big time money lender who had his safe done a while ago?

"Sure do. He's still squealing I heard."

"Well so would you be if it was you."

He had my interest.

"Okay, what's the drum?"

"Have you ever had any Bearer Bonds? Do you know anything about them?"

"No, never had them and don't know anything about them."

"Well some came from that geezer's safe. There's twenty grand worth in Sterling," he paused, "can you do anything with them, move them on or something?"

I was not surprised to hear this proposition from him; he always had other fiddles on the go. Keith had run sly grog gambling joints. I'd been a partner in a similarly successful one with the Bay Boys, Sammy and Gary Duffty in the Council social rooms in Napier St. They made good money, but they died out with the extension of the licensing hours.

Keith's joint was popular with the crowd and he always attracted a full house. His gambling was fair; well, as fair as Crown and Anchor could be. He enjoyed a good name and gamblers were safe in his house. The last one he had run was a very good one in a toff street in Parnell. It had operated under the grandiose title of the 'The Last Chance Saloon'. In that enterprise, he had an interesting partner, Marty Nunn, another London boy. Marty was a member of the safe breaking gang.

A few years later, after the sly grog joints had finished, Marty earned his spurs the hard way. He was a frail sort, not the type you would ever think of as a member of a successful safe breakers gang. He was no tough guy and no threat to anybody violence wise. As was bound to happen, the gang were rumbled; two of them were picked up and detained for questioning. In the 'interview', shall we call it that, poor old Marty received a real beating. It was at the hands of a notorious tough cop and one of his henchmen. Marty earned the respect of many people, over that. The cops and others thought he would crack and cough; but he didn't.

There was another odd twist to this story. Back in my home town, Rickmansworth, in the UK, some forty-two years later and while I was writing this second book, a friend, George, an old villain himself, had bought the first book. After reading it, he asked me to meet a friend of his, a chap who had 'history' in New Zealand. I was flabbergasted on meeting him to find that this chap was probably the most prominent member of 'the gang who couldn't shoot straight'. He was another Londoner. For obvious reasons he has to remain nameless as he is now a law-abiding and successful citizen. He was the other guy arrested in the same sweep as Marty. He was sentenced to a year in Auckland's very tough Mt. Eden Prison. On completing his sentence, he was up for immediate deportation back to England. By coincidence (oh yeah) he was escorted onto the plane by the same police officer who had battered him and Marty. A variety of choice words were exchanged by the pair on the tarmac. There were no warm handshakes and wish-you-well platitudes. Oh no, these were two hard men that circumstances had caused to be on opposite sides of life's fences.

The amazing thing about this story is that forty-two years ago I was close to those events. Then from my friend George, simply showing my book to his friend, this story came to life once again. It happened this way. On seeing, the book, George's friend had gone straight to its picture gallery. He was astounded to recognize in one of the photos, his old sparring partner, the tough cop. It stretches the imagination that twelve thousand miles and forty-two years later this almost forgotten story emerged less than two miles from where I now live and at the time of recording it. It certainly is a strange world.

Back in the Ferry Building café, Keith carried on cajoling me into helping him move the bonds. I thanked him for the opportunity, but refused it, as I knew they would cause trouble. I'd already heard that the money lender had commissioned some very heavy Wellington villains to retrieve his bonds and punish the robbers. I knew of the Wellington mob; they were ruthless and dangerous. It wouldn't take them long to track the miscreants down. They would achieve that quicker than the police could and then it would get very nasty. Because of the underworld interest in recovering the bonds, it was open season on the gang.

I MEET JASPER,
AN INCREDIBLE CHARACTER

Me with Jasper, King of the Gypsies and a girlfriend cruising
the Hauraki, what a life, I was 45.

Because of that troublesome Wellington job I met a
very interesting person called Jasper, who was to
figure quite prominently in my life. Jasper was a
genuine Romany Gypsy and acknowledged as the

Gypsy King in New Zealand and Australia. In certain circles on both sides of the Tasman he was a man who commanded respect. When I met him for the first time he was close to sixty-years-old. The cause of our meeting was an extension of the Bearer Bonds incident. Jasper was the intermediary, the fixer on behalf of the irate moneylender and the posse of Wellington villains hired in the quest to return the bonds and certain personal embarrassing items. Plus to dish out some punishment to the culprits.

I knew of him by reputation, so I was a little apprehensive when he approached me about them. He suspected correctly that I might have knowledge of them. His first approach was by a phone call asking me for a meeting, which I agreed to. We met the next day in a secluded but beautiful spot. It was a little lookout parking lay-by just before the Parnell Rose Gardens on St Georges Bay Road. It had breathtaking views over the working harbour, Devonport and out across the Hauraki Gulf. This was the spot where Jasper parked his Volkswagen camper when he was overnighting in Auckland. What fantastic views to wake up to. People paid massive prices for houses in this area for that pleasure. The old gypsy stayed true to his roots and enjoyed it as his right.

"Lenny, I'm really pleased to meet you," he said. He had been sitting, calm as you like, in a folding canvas chair enjoying the view as if it was his back yard; which to his way of thinking it was. I had driven in and parked alongside him. We shook hands; I was impressed by the strength of his shake. It wasn't exaggerated for my benefit; it was just the way he was.

He was a short, squat, very strong build. His skin reminded me of my old Bargee Aunt Ruby's, a nutmeg tan that the harshest winters could never completely shift. His eyes twinkled; they signalled alertness to everything happening around him. He had a little, short, grey beard that suited his appearance. His face reflected a lifetime of experiences, but was friendly and welcoming. In spite of all that I had heard about him, I felt very comfortable in his company.

"Jasper, I'm very pleased to meet you too, it's probably about time." We both smiled at the innuendo in that comment. We chatted about associates and friends common to us both. It was a rite of passage, a mutual declaration of where we stood in the company we spoke of.
"How's Duncan? He hasn't been around for a while, not in Auckland anyway." I was talking of Duncan McFarlane, an old acquaintance from Wellington. Duncan was a well-respected crim character from the Windy City. (When Duncan died, his Obituary was headed, "Shadowy figure on edge of crime dies.")

"He's good Lenny, really good; the bookie business is doing well, plus other things." I didn't enquire about the other things.

"Anyway, that brings me to what I want to talk to you about, he'll be up here shortly if I don't sort a certain matter out. Look Lenny, let's cut to the chase. That okay with you?"

"Sure, go ahead, let's hear it."

"Well mate, it's over that safe job in Wellington; you probably know the one, the moneylender geezer. It's like this; he didn't go to the cops or insurance companies. Apart from the black cash, he had some very personal stuff in the tank, embarrassing stuff that he wanted kept quiet about, if you get my drift. That's why it didn't get any press, but I am sure you know about it." He looked at me quizzically.

"Yes mate, I did hear about it on the grapevine, but that's all, I was in the UK about that time; I only heard a whisper when I got back."

"Well mate, the geezer is spewing over it. He's commissioned me to try to get the bonds and the other personal things that he doesn't want floating around back. In the meantime, he's lining up Duncan and a couple of tasty lads to come up here and do the team who did it. I think it's going to get very nasty. It's as simple as that, Lenny. And no offence, but I have to ask you, do you have the bonds, have you been offered them, or know where they are?" He looked me straight in the eye as he said this. I took my time in answering him; this was major action, a wrong word or blink, could easily be misinterpreted and the results become calamitous.

"Jasper this sounds like it's going to get very heavy. I'm pleased to tell you I haven't had them offered to me. I don't know where they are or who's got them, or even whether they're in Auckland, I don't know about it, Jasper. It's not the area I'm in. Scotty and I do our deals around the country, mind our business, don't poke into anybody else's and that's about it; Jasper, there isn't anything else I can say."

"Okay, Lenny, that's about what I thought. I have a couple of other avenues to check out. One with that Pat McSweeny; I think he's out now. He's probably the best safe man in the country. He always works alone so he'd need help with the bonds. Maybe old Toofats, I'd better speak to him. He could handle the bonds. Looks like I've got a lot of work to do."

I took that as my chance to scarper. I put my hand out and went to leave.

"Good luck with the dig then mate, I better go now."

"Hang on a minute, c'mon, why not stay for a cuppa?" Without waiting for a reply he called out to his girlfriend, Dawn, "hey sweetheart, make a cuppa for us."

I hadn't seen Dawn until then, she came out smiling. The rumours were true, she was stunning; a very natural little eighteen year old blonde. As always, the world is a strange place.

"Oh yeah, Lenny, there was something else I meant to tell you. I was talking to an old mate last week down in Gisborne; he said if I saw you to say hello and he wants to catch up next week; he's coming up to Auckland." I knew immediately who he meant. It was a legendary character named Kimball Robert Brisco Johnson. Jasper had obviously been discussing me with Kimball.

Jasper had seemingly accepted my protestations about the bonds. We stayed talking for another hour and agreed to stay in touch. We had many mutual, shall we say, colleagues. It had been inevitable that our paths would cross.

I was relieved that Jasper had accepted that I could not help him. I hasten to add that Jasper was reputed to have caused the abrupt disappearance of two or three individuals who had crossed his path. It was a fact that was never far from my thoughts in the meeting. Whether he really believed me or not, I was never sure; in any event he appeared to want to accept my protestations. We struck up an association that years later turned into a close friendship.

Jasper's living arrangements were rudimentary. His gypsy breeding was still very much a part of him; it was ingrained. He found it impossible to live in a house. He spent his time between singlehandedly sailing a forty-foot catamaran he owned and his Volkswagen Combi van fitted out as a sleeper. He would travel the length and breadth of New

Zealand, sometimes disappearing for months. He was always on the move, buying and selling anything from cars to caravans and trucks; he was a genuine wheeler-dealer.

Years later I was out with him on his catamaran cruising around the gulf, when out of the blue he told me a very interesting story. He had left England as a young man under a dark cloud. It was at the time when the authorities did not cut the gypsies any slack. He said life was generally very tough on the gypsies. They were constantly being harassed or moved on by the police. Sometimes the police timed it just when they were about to settle for a meal or a rest after being on the road all day.

One evening Jasper and I were sitting chatting and enjoying an old fashioned cup of tea; he didn't drink alcohol and neither did I. He got a little sentimental and told me that his one remaining ambition was to sail the catamaran down to the Southern Ocean to 'the Roaring Forties' one of the most dangerous stretches of ocean in the world. As an ex-seaman I was familiar with its fearsome reputation. Jasper generously offered to take me along when he eventually undertook that dangerous adventure. I thanked him for the invitation and declined as gracefully as I could. I was still only in my very own, 'roaring-forties' with lots of living to do.

So, why did Jasper suddenly leave the old country, as he and many New Zealanders of a certain age sentimentally referred to England. Jasper will be long dead now and knowing him as I did, I feel sure he wouldn't mind me telling the story. Jasper's people were real Romanies, not just itinerant travellers. They lived as well as they could making and selling pegs house-to-house, fortune telling, sharpening knives, that sort of thing. They were rarely able to stay anywhere for more than two days before they were moved on.

For Jasper and his family, it came to a head one summer's evening by the side of a country lane near Windsor in Buckinghamshire. A violent fight occurred after they had suffered a long day on the road. His family were all very tired and they had been evicted from their previous site in a no nonsense manner. Jasper and his family had made camp and were settling down for a meal and a night's rest. Just then the police raided them again. Jasper swore the police timed the raid deliberately to interfere with their meal and rest. The police moved in aggressively to remove his family. According to Jasper, a bullying, gypsy-hating Sergeant led the police assault. A very violent fight ensued. At the time, Jasper was nineteen and was minded to fight for his family. The battle was brutal; the Sergeant was either badly injured, or might have been dying. There was only one option available. Jasper was facing a fourteen-year or longer jail sentence, or worse, a hanging should the Sergeant have died. Like many before him and many since, he took the only option and fled.

His escape route, assisted by gypsies in many countries, resulted in his reaching Australia. Once there he joined a travelling circus. He became proficient in many of the circus disciplines. He was a wall of death rider, a knife thrower; he even walked the high wire, from which he once fell. It had left him with a limp, which he tried to disguise. Shortly after I first met him, he disappeared for a few years. He never said where he had been; I never asked. What I did know was that most of the high-end crimes that took place, often in Australia, had Jaspers footprints all over them. They were mainly armed bank hold-ups. However, going back to the Wellington moneylender's Bonds, Jasper eventually negotiated a truce between Keith and the Wellington crew. I believe it suited everyone, there weren't going to be any winners.

It was not until the early eighties that I renewed my acquaintanceship with him, and we became firm friends. So much so, that when my mother came to visit on a holiday, we took her out sailing the Hauraki Gulf on his catamaran. It was a glorious cruise and we stopped off on the Islands of Waiheke and Motuihe on the way. It was a trip this untraveled Geordie woman from little old Mill End never forgot. Jasper was a magnificent host; he treated my mother as if she were his own. That trip taught me a lot about Jasper and I have to say, also about myself. I heard it said that Jasper was 'as slippery as grease on a door handle'. Maybe that was true, but in any event I was pleased to have known him. I have often wondered whether he make that trip to the Southern Ocean. I hope so.

A later cruise with Jasper, me, my mother and a girlfriend.

KIMBALL JOHNSON,
ONE IN A MILLION

It was interesting that Jasper passed on the greeting from Kimball to me. In the circumstances, there could have been an underlying reason, as I don't think he would have lightly disclosed that he had checked me out with Kimball.

Kimball was another unbelievable character. He enjoyed a reputation throughout the length and breadth of New Zealand as an old school, old-fashioned man's man. He may have been a crook; he may have had a deserved reputation for over-the-top violence to his enemies, but for very good reasons, he was feared by some, but conversely, loved and held in high regard by many. He was a huge man of immense strength and capable of extreme violence should it be needed. On the other hand, he was known to cry over a sad film or a crippled kitten. He was a jumble of contradictions, but it would have taken a brave man or a fool to tell him so. I cannot recall anyone ever attempting such a thing.

Kimball was one of a tough strain of white men that New Zealand breeds, and who are often to be found in remote country areas. Whether it was Maori gangs, bikers, crooks or desperadoes; at various times Kimball rubbed shoulders, and sometimes more, with them all, but always he commanded their respect.

For much of his life he had been a commercial fisherman. In Gisborne, his hometown, he had his own boats, retail fish shop and a successful wholesale fish distribution business. He was a very talented man. Strangely, like many before him, he was attracted to the underbelly of the criminal world. He was immensely strong and fearless, leading him to become a street fighter of renown, but only fighting if challenged, disrespected, or harried into it. However, his fighting was always with people in the same league. He had straighteners with challengers, or other heavies in the criminal fraternity who had a grievance, real or imagined against him. I knew him over a period of twenty years and never knew or heard of him being bested in that time. It has to be said of him, that unlike other big powerful men I have met in my lifetime, he was never a bully; in fact, he despised bullies. Dangerous as he could be, he could also be quite humble and capable of great kindness to strangers, or people he knew, who were down on their luck. His true passion in life was country music. He wrote and performed much of his own material. He played the guitar very well, he had a fine voice and I was always amazed that he didn't exploit that huge talent.

Now let me take you to the point of this story. In

the time I spent with Kimball, I was witness to many of his escapades, but the one that touched me the most also made me ashamed of myself for my poor judgement of the man. At the time I was living on Takapuna beach. There was a bit of a property boom on and Kimball and I went to inspect a property on Whangaparoa Peninsula with a view to buying it. It was a refurbishment job on an old house. We figured it wouldn't take long and should provide a quick capital gain. We made an offer on the spot to the agent who we met there on site. With that completed, we returned to Auckland. We had travelled up to the Peninsula in Kimball's vehicle; it was a bumpy ride in an old jeep. He was quite extroverted in his choice of cars. After about thirty minutes of a hair-raising return journey, we pulled up with a screech and smoking tyres outside my house.

"No Kimball, you can't come in."

"Why Lenny, why can't I come in? Jeez mate you can be a miserable little pommie prick."

"No I'm sorry Kimball, but it's best you don't."

"Shit you can be a strange bastard; I thought we were mates."

"We are mates, but I can't trust you. They're old ladies in there and you'll frighten them if you play up."

My problem was that I had my mother over from England for a holiday. I had left her at home with two other elderly women for company. They were mothers of friends of mine and also on holiday in

New Zealand with their sons and families. Both were mothers of characters you read of in the first book. One was Keith Morgan's mum; the other was Jerry Clayton's mum. They were all well into their sixties and had led sheltered lives. The thought of exposing them to Kimball's rough brand of humour, genuinely alarmed me.

"What the fuck are you worried about Lenny, what do you think I am gonna do?"

"That's just it Kimball, nobody ever knows what you are going to do next."

My refusal had started to annoy Kimball. I suppose you couldn't blame him.

"Okay Kimball, we'll go in, but mate, I'm telling you, any problems or you get carried away, you know I've got a loaded shotgun in there. Mate I'm sorry to talk like that, but you worry me."

He gave me a withering look, grabbed his guitar and said, "let's go then."

The next hour-and-a-half was the best time of my mother's holiday, and I'm sure that was the case for the other two elderly ladies.

Kimball sang to them, made a fuss of them, joked with them and he told them stories about his growing up in an East Coast village in the back country. He royally entertained them. He finished the afternoon by going into his wallet and giving each of them a hundred dollars to spend on their holiday. It was a wonderfully generous gift; I don't mean just the money. For my part I confess to feeling more than embarrassed; I think I felt a bit ashamed. I had said some ugly things and looking back on it they were a silly overreaction. I tried to apologise to Kimball, but he just said, "don't worry about it, these things happen."

My mother never forgot Kimball. "And how's that lovely Kiwi boy?" were the words that ran off my mother's tongue any time her trip to New Zealand came up for discussion. Kimball and I shared a good relationship for many years. I understand from my son-in-law who grew up in Gisborne with Kimball, that he did eventually release a country western album to considerable acclaim. Unfortunately, he has now left us. He fought a long and hard battle with the grim reaper; the only fight he ever lost.

TREVOR TOOFATS SMITH
WHAT A MISTAKE

This next story concerns an Auckland crim and character from the sixties and seventies; he was larger than life in many ways. He was six foot two and twenty-three stone and as I found out, mean with it. I don't know how, but I had become involved with him, despite the fact that he was the very heavy duty 'Toofats Smith'. Towards the end of our association there was a fall out which became very bitter. Because of it, I was forced into a street brawl with all twenty-three stone of him. Our connection ended up with me once more in the Auckland Supreme Court.

I was now meeting some very dodgy geezers. They were interesting individuals and they were characters who could have graced any of Damon Runyon's books. This particular one, Toofats, was an Englishman, a Londoner. Nobody ever knew how, or when, he got to New Zealand and he kept it a tight secret. He actually revelled in the nickname of Toofats. He was into every racket possible, from loan-sharking to laundering and receiving. Trevor Toofats was not only fearsomely big; he was one of those men in life who also had a scary manner. He had a fierce looking face, even when he smiled, which was not that often. He drove a large Ford Falcon station wagon and he drove in a way that seemed to command all other drivers to give way to him, which they did.

He had one of Australasia's top safe men on his team. This was Rex, a little Aussie who suffered from a permanent cough. He was nicknamed, 'The Speckled Hen' as it was his dream to make enough money from blowing safes to buy a chicken farm. Regrettably, this noble plan never bore fruit. The main reason being Rex had a weakness for fine wine, first class hotels and wild, wild women, whenever he was in funds from his latest strike. It was unfortunate for The Speckled Hen that this was a weakness well known to police forces on either side of the Tasman Ocean.

A year went by and Toofats and I got entangled in a couple of deals. This was a mistake as we were both headstrong and completely different types. Our relationship ended in a very dangerous public brawl, which took place in and outside his house in Richmond Road in Grey Lynn, early one Saturday morning. As I have previously pointed out, I was no fighter; well, not in this league anyway. My area of expertise was in a far different field. Unfortunately sometimes in life you have no choice, it is fight or flee. On this occasion there was not an option, it had to be fight. The amusing thing about it (though the brawl itself was not amusing; it was bloody painful) was the fact that his house was in a Pacific Islanders' area, and they were shocked that a couple of 'Palagi' (pronounced paalangi and meaning white men) businessmen would be going at it in the street. That was usually their prerogative.

So how did two dodgy Englishmen get into this unseemly street brawl? From a nodding acquaintance, Toofats and I got together in a couple of business ventures. They were good, but nothing spectacular. He was also doing a bit of bookmaking and I had introduced him to the main man in bookmaking in New Zealand, Bert Clapham. Toofats wanted to meet Bert, as he needed a bigger bookmaker he could lay his bets off with, if he was holding too much on a particular horse. I was able to arrange a meeting between them. Bert accepted my word that Toofats was 'solid' and therefore would not welsh on bets and payments. If that situation did ever arise, I would be the one that Bert called on to answer for him.

I suppose that favour had helped my cred with Toofats. Anyway, one thing had led to another and Toofats and I bought a small advertising business that was going broke. We were able to buy it for a song through the machinations of Toofats' slippery lawyer, who had been acting for the company and it owed him some fees. You know how it is with lawyers and fees. It's like corned beef and cabbage; where there's one the other isn't far away. Anyway, I was particularly excited, as one of the company's assets was a fabulous steed, one that I felt entirely befitted an ambitious young man on the way up such as myself. It was without a doubt the best-looking car in Auckland. I could already see myself lording it up and down Queen Street in this, 'looks like you are loaded' car. A sharp lesson was about to be delivered. The car was a gleaming, near new, Silver V8 Daimler, fit for the Mayor of Auckland. In new car-starved Auckland of that time, this was the Stradivarius of cars, and it was mine. Owning it made me a fully paid-up card carrying member of the crowded posers club. I was to learn the truth of that much misquoted Shakespeare saying, 'All that glisters is not gold'.

The car came with the company. We just took over the very low balance outstanding on the hire purchase agreement. The deal between Toofats and me was that the car was mine as I was going to be running the advertising company from my offices in the High Street. The acquisition of the car and what it provoked was the start of a major incident that was to trail me most of my life in Auckland. It would take me further into a world of intrigue, suspicion, violence and jealousy. I suppose the upside was that there was rarely a dull moment. I did learn from it; I learnt the very hard lesson that your past never leaves you.

That however, was only the start of the brawl problem. The whole mess originated through

Toofats' reputation with the police. It turned out that he was under regular surveillance by police intelligence. That meant that the police logged any vehicles that he had an interest in, or was observed travelling in. That information was recorded and crosschecked, including where and when seen and who else was in the vehicles.

At the time I was more or less unknown to the police and had no record. However, my presence in this car and my association with Toofats caused them to have a look at me. In doing this, they contacted and then questioned the car dealers who had originally sold the car to the company. In the course of the detectives talking to the car company employees, they had crossed the line in voicing their opinions of us. Their verbal trashing of us caused the management to panic, and to worry about payment for bills for servicing and repairs.

The young detectives doing the investigation must have seen themselves as a cross between Jack Regan of the *Sweeney* and the cops in *Hill Street Blues*. Their over-the-top approach had really spooked the garage owners. They were the very reputable firm of Coutts in Great North Road, the Jaguar agents.

It so happened that just before the detectives had visited Coutts and alarmed them; I had taken the car in for a ten thousand mile service or something similar. I had previously taken the car in for servicing and some minor work on a couple of occasions. Payment had always been made by cheque as soon as an invoice or statement was received in the post. When I arrived to pick up the car they informed me that I could not take the car without payment. I queried that decision, but they told me that those were the orders from the Boss. I argued the case and said that they should have informed me of this new arrangement prior to my leaving the car with them. I also correctly argued that there was a monthly credit arrangement in force, as was evidenced by the previous invoices statements and payments. In addition, as I was not in the habit of carrying around the company chequebook, I could not pay them then. I asked them what the problem was, but could not get a satisfactory answer. By this time I was getting very annoyed; it was Friday afternoon and I needed the car for the weekend.

I rang Toofats and filled him in on what was happening and within minutes, he arrived there. He was very angry and that was not a pleasant sight. He tried to remonstrate with the supervisor, who now had two burly mechanics to back him up. The situation was developing into a standoff, the supervisor wouldn't back down; he said he was only following orders. He rang his boss who would not come to the phone, let alone come back to the showroom. I could see Toofats was finished with arguing. With guys like him a change comes over them. He walked over to me and from the side of his mouth said, "Have you got that spare key?"

"Yes mate, I have."

"Okay, get in the car, start it up and drive out when I open the door."

I nodded in agreement. Old Toofats just strolled up to the huge sliding doors and pushed them open. One of the mechanics and the supervisor foolishly took their lives in their hands and went forward to block the doors opening. It was a one-sided trial of strength; Toofats just kept pushing until the doors opened and I drove the car out and onto the Great North Road.

We weren't so naive that we thought that would be the end of it, but we also weren't prepared for what did happen. I had a great weekend with the car. Mary and I drove down to Whitianga for a lovely weekend on the beach with the family of a friend who worked with her. Monday morning rolled around and I was breakfasting with my friend, the Aussie pro golfer. He was in New Zealand to play in the Open and as was usual he was staying with us. After the important job of breakfast was finished, I decided to visit Toofats at his premises situated downtown in the Turners and Growers vegetable produce market. It was a combined butcher's shop and market café. This was another of the pies that Toofats has his fingers in. He was a buyer and supplier of produce to many Auckland restaurants, private hospitals and pubs. It was a good business; he never had problems with being paid promptly, and no prizes for guessing why.

It's now about eleven-thirty, I am sitting there with Toofats when the butcher shop manager rushes in saying, "there's a car load of jacks (cops) outside". Well I have never seen such a commotion; all three hundred and twenty pounds of Toofats is moving at speed. The back door to a lane is thrown open. A hatch to the next-door premises is opened, boxes and packages are being jettisoned through the hatch, someone the other side is gathering them up and then the hatch is noisily slammed shut. Toofats sits down and then he looks alarmed, he jumps up, grabs his jacket which is hanging on the back of his chair, gives it to me and says, "bugger off through the back way, and keep this for me."

The back way is a hidden exit installed by Toofats. I do not need telling twice; I am moving as he is speaking. I do not know why I have to move, as far as I knew I did not really have to, but I was caught up in the exhilaration of the moment. I am clutching his jacket as I slip through the back entrance. It feels heavy and something is clanking on my side. I find myself on the fishing boat's berth on the Western Viaduct basin, my old scows' habitat.

I sit down on one of the bench seats by the swing

bridge, making out as if I am a tourist. I am madly curious to see what is in Toofats' jacket pocket. What it was caused me to go cold. I had put my hand in expecting to find a box of jewels, or some such thing. What I actually gripped was a twenty-two calibre revolver, fully loaded! It was about then that I realised that this was not a game of goodies and baddies; this was for real. I remember thinking, as I was sitting there with Toofats' gun: "Christ' how did I get into this?" It seemed only yesterday that I was a carefree, young, innocent seaman, well nearly, wandering the world, wide-eyed and open-mouthed. Now what I was seeing and experiencing was changing me. I felt that I was on an unstoppable descent. I realized how far behind I had left that wide-eyed boy.

I stashed the gun away; there was no way that I was going to be walking around with it. I knew that alone would carry a heavy penalty. I would tell Toofats where it was and let him or one of his runners retrieve it. I made my way to the advertising premises in the High Street. This was my company's office. I had set up facilities there for the new company. It was on the fourth floor. There was a lift, but I always used the stairs. I used to run up them, using it as a keep fit thing.

"Hello," I called out. There were a couple of salesmen labouring on the phones, not easy on a Monday morning. The secretary/receptionist was tapping away sending out accounts.

"Any problems, any calls?" I enquired of Elsa, the secretary, who incidentally was Toofats' wife. As he was big, she was small. A petite, pretty and well-educated woman; she was streets different from Toofats. Although I had some naughty thoughts about her, which she did not show any hint of sharing, I thought that she was best left well alone, as I did not fancy broken legs or a shotgun blast. Well not at that stage anyway; though things did change later when she had left him.

"No, everything is okay," she said breezily. She's had a good weekend I thought to myself.

"Has Mr Smith phoned?"

"No, he hasn't."

"Okay, get him on the phone for me please, but don't say it's me on the line, got that?"

"Yes, I've got it," she said with a knowing look.

My intercom phone buzzed.

"Mr Smith is on the line for you."

"Hi mate," came booming down the line, "can you come round? It's important."

"Okay, I'll be there in ten minutes," I said. I strolled around nice and easy. Toofats always saw the funny side of any situation. I sat down opposite him; he looked at me and started laughing.

"Come on," I said, "give it me, what's going down?"

Toofats was sitting in his especially strengthened chair. He had a smile on his face, as if he were sitting in the Hippodrome listening to Tommy Cooper. Only he was not; the joke was on me.

36

"This is the situation," he managed to say whilst trying to suppress laughter; he was laughing because the axe was falling on me, not him.

"The cops have a warrant for your arrest."

"C'mon Toofats, stop kidding, what's going on?"

He shook his huge head,

"I'm not kidding mate."

"What? What's the charge then, why me, c'mon Toofats, what's the charge?"

"Well," he said very seriously, "you can't go around stealing cars, can you?" He paused for effect.

"It's against the law you know," he said, warming to his subject.

"Stealing a motor vehicle, tsk tsk tsk," he threw in for good measure;

"Yes that's it, a silver, late model Daimler." He gave another chuckle. "Let me think now, er ... yes that was it," he said smiling, "yes that's definitely what they said, you stole a car."

"What a lot of bollocks," I said.

He was enjoying my discomfort and said, "never mind the swearing mate, you're in deep shit. They say you stole it from Coutts Motor Dealers on Great North Road last Friday afternoon."

"Toofats, for Christ's sake mate, c'mon, why me? You were there too; it's you they would want, you're having me over, aren't you?"

"No mate, deadly serious now; it's you they're after."

How can this be? I own the car; how can you steal your own car? It appears the police think you can, particularly if they want you to have done that.

Toofats is using his long experience of dealing with the police. He has organised an appointment for me with Peter Williams, New Zealand's top criminal lawyer and a friend of his. When he told me about the appointment I immediately thought there must be more to it. Peter Williams was a real heavyweight. Him acting on a phoney car theft blag? It was like using Einstein to teach five year olds. This was very strange. Keep your guard up Lenny, there is more to this than meets the eye, flashed through my mind.

Off we go, Toofats and me, to the old Lister Buildings in Wellesley Street. In those days, Peter was still making a name for himself and the offices though central were not plush. However, who wants a plush office law firm, one that wins is the best in my opinion. I had previously met up with Peter; he was trying to find a buyer for a sensational rag type newspaper that he and a colleague of his, another very bright criminal lawyer, Kevin Ryan, had somehow acquired or invested in. They had thought I was a likely buyer, but it was not for me.

At the time I should think Peter was in his late thirties. He was an athletically built person, who kept himself fit playing squash. Looking at Peter, and speaking with him, it shone out like a bright light that here was a man on the way up. We were ushered into Peter's office by his very attractive secretary, whom I had the pleasure of getting to know very well a few months later. Apart from being a beauty, she was a lovely girl; but unfortunately, she shipped herself off to the UK. Something to do with a breakup with a jealous boyfriend, I understand.

Peter was the sort who worked hard and played hard. In those days, he had an intense dislike for most Auckland detectives, if not all. They in turn, could not be said to be in love with him either. This was mainly because of the many bloody noses he gave them in the courtrooms of New Zealand.

"Lenny," he said as soon as we were sitting down. It was a strange thing that, most people I ever knew in New Zealand referred to me as 'Lenny,' not Len, though sometimes they used other derogatory words they could think of and they could think of plenty. He leaned over and shook hands.

"You seem to be top of the hit parade in Cook Street." (This was a reference to the Auckland police station).

"It certainly looks like it Peter, but what's going on, it seems a bit low level for the effort they're putting in."

"Yes," he said. "Trevor," referring to Toofats by his real name, "rang me, so I called the station, to find out the basis of it all. They're not saying much, but I think they're wondering who you are since you've been appearing around town with Trevor, and this is a chance to tag you."

"This is great," I thought. "I've kept my nose clean through quite a few tricky situations these last few years. Then, I do some business with Toofats and immediately the shit hits the fan.

Peter was not only bright, he was a shrewd man, and he read my thoughts. "Look, Lenny, this could actually be a winner if we play it right."

"How can it be a winner? Even if they have to drop the charges, it's not a winner."

"Trevor tells me you had established a credit account with them. Is that correct?"

"That's a stone cold certainty, Peter."

"Right then," he said, "If that's correct, they have a major problem, but first we will need to get it thrown out at the deposition stage in the Magistrates court and the best and quickest way to get what we want is to let them arrest you."

"Oh, is that all? Thanks mate, that's good of you," I said, but it was drowned out by Toofats' laughter. Peter leaning forward said:

"Look, it's like this; we go to court, then when it's thrown out, as it surely will be, we'll have a great civil case against them. We can sue for malicious prosecution, false imprisonment, damage to your reputation especially with you being a clean skin."

This was downunder slang for a person who had not been convicted of a criminal offence.

"It will happen just like that. Are you up for it?"

So that's the reason Peter was involved. It would

need a hammer to crack this walnut.

"Yes, count me in," I said. "Let's get the bastards. But, er ... how much would I, we get?"

He replied with one word: "Plenty."

So that was it, I was now in the open and this was to be round one, of quite a few rounds, with the Auckland police over the next thirty odd years. The other Lenny was emerging. However, though I visited the Magistrates court a few times, and the Auckland Supreme court three times in the following years, I was never to suffer a conviction, or lose a courtroom battle. One wonders what the veritable Mr Dan, the metalwork teacher of my boyhood, would have made of those visits; maybe he would have got an inkling of who the 'thieving little bastard' was after all.

I like to think that positive state of affairs was not entirely due to the top and very expensive legal representation I employed. I felt supported in that contention by the following piece of information that came to me. It came from a Mr Lloyd Brown, an eminent QC and a top class guy, who was a much admired man in Auckland. I came to know Lloyd quite well over the years, leading to his once acting for me in the Auckland Supreme court. After the end of the case, over a few drinks, he described me to a fellow member of the Auckland Bar, as one of the best witnesses he had ever had at his disposal. I hasten to add that although I was most flattered, the compliment was not reflected in dear old Lloyd's fees.

However, we go back to the meeting with Peter, who is now in full flow as he scents another put down for the Cook Street demons, as the detectives were referred to, plus a healthy fee for inflicting it. I agreed to the action only on a 'no win no fee' basis and that was long before that became the norm. Peter, or P.A. as he was known, hummed and hawed as he had to, but agreed on a straight percentage.

"Right," he said, "this is what I propose. I think it essential that they prosecute and take us to the Magistrate's Court for depositions. To encourage this to happen, I want to antagonise them by drawing up a prepared statement, which will not give anything away, which an interview might. They hate prepared statements. I will suggest that you are prepared to be arrested in my offices and then when they attempt to question you, we will hand over the signed, prepared statement, all agreed?"

He looked at Toofats, then to me.

"Yes, all agreed," I said with some trepidation.

As a precaution, I slipped out of Auckland for a couple of days to give Peter the chance to prepare the statement. As agreed, arrangements were made for my arrest in his offices. This was all cloak and dagger stuff and quite new to me at that stage. Peter was correct in his appraisal of the police.

They had some idea I was a fugitive on the run; that maybe I was not who I said I was. That would have been true in earlier days, but it was not now. I had been lucky; the good offices of the Freemans Bay Labour party stalwart, Bob Elsender, had put that to bed. The trouble was that in those days the police could and did act in a much more unfettered way than is possible today.

The day of the arranged arrest duly arrived. I dressed as they might expect an English crook on the run to dress, smart but flashy. I went to Peter's offices early in case they tried to pre-empt the arrangement and arrest me outside, which in fact they tried to do. We were able to watch this manoeuvre from the office window. Eleven o'clock sounded on the large clock in the office and they entered bang on time. There were two demons and they both know Peter very well. The usual meaningless pleasantries exchanged; they then formally arrested me on a charge of theft of a motorcar. They asked me if I had anything to say.

"No, not at this time," I said. Peter then stepped in and advised that he had a prepared statement and that was all the information I would be giving. They showed their obvious displeasure at this turn of events. They then advised that I had to accompany them to the station for fingerprinting and photographing. On Peter's insistence, Eb Leary, Peter's Junior accompanied me. The whole episode moved smoothly along as if it was professionally choreographed, which I suppose it was. In less than two hours, I was back on the street, allowed out on police bail.

We had arranged to meet up in the bar of the old Central Hotel, directly opposite Peter's offices. It was a watering hole for the criminal lawyer fraternity and their clients. This bar was always busy, especially when high profile cases were on in the courthouses just around the corner. At times, it was like a moving backdrop to the headline features in the crime pages of the morning's New Zealand Herald. The old Central Hotel was a hangout for most of Auckland's criminal barristers. Peter and Kevin Ryan were regulars there. These two were the first that assorted villains would call when about to face charges. The extraordinarily successful record achieved by these two very fine advocates was evidenced by the constant queue of desperates sitting in their waiting rooms. They sat there while hope and despondency fought for prominence on their countenances as they mulled over their transgressions and the consequences they could be facing. This montage of faces and the emotions so easily read from their troubled expressions always fascinated me.

In my time of patrolling these corridors of infamy, hope and despair, I was also aware of the fact that these same corridors produced two outstanding New Zealand Prime Ministers from its ranks. I refer to Jim McLay, a National Party PM who worked for, and later was in partnership with, Peter Williams for many years. The other was David Lange, an out-and-out Labour man. I always saw him as the nearest thing to a true socialist in that heady world of politics that he aspired to. He advanced little old New Zealand on the world stage. While Prime Minister he made his mark with a resounding victory in a famous, internationally televised Oxford Union Debate. In it he comprehensively bested his opponent, the redoubtable American right wing fundamentalist and TV evangelist, Jerry Falwell, on the moral question of nuclear armaments.

His great advocacy in that televised debate endeared him not only to the New Zealand public, but also elevated him and the country to a higher standing in international affairs. David was certainly a man of the people with a massive social conscience. He was always there to defend anyone. He didn't cherry pick, he was a genuinely good man. Unfortunately for all, he died quite young and was to my mind a great loss to New Zealand.

I was leaning on one of those high barroom tables waiting for Peter and Toofats to appear. While propped there I chatted to some interesting Auckland characters. Bert Clapham came in with a couple of his henchmen; one was Brickie Malloy, an Aussie armed holdup man. Do not be confused by Brickie's name, he was not called Brickie because in an earlier straight life he had been a bricklayer. He was so nicknamed, because 'brick' was downunder slang for ten, and he had completed a ten-year stretch in an Australian prison.

Bert wandered over to me and said, "what about a game?" He had a couple of punters we knew well, and he needed to relieve them of some money. We set the date and time for the Huapai Golf Club. It was a lovely course, situated about twenty miles north-west of Auckland. One of the attractions of the Huapai Club that amazed visitors was at the start of the back nine. A flock of beautiful peacocks lived there. They just strolled the fairways, strutting their stuff, as we all did I suppose, but causing no problem and adding to the pleasure of the day. The golf club was in the middle of a horse training territory, specializing in trotting and pacing stables.

The game Bert had set us up for was with two well-known pacing horse trainers and gamblers, who it is best not to name. Suffice it to say, they were a couple of notable sporting characters. In those years we both had interests in horses trained by them. Bert's alleged interest could never show or be recorded. This was because of the regulations of the draconian New Zealand Gaming Act and trotting club rules. I was called into the office of the racecourse inspector, Mr Charlie Dudley, as they correctly suspected that Bert and Toofats had hidden interests in the two horses I was racing. I denied it and he reluctantly accepted that, mainly because I was a clean skin and remained one.

Bert had gaming convictions and that coupled with his reputation stood against him; consequently he was barred from legitimately owning racehorses, or even going onto racetracks. This was a very sore point with Bert. The merest mention or reminder of this humiliating state of affairs was an easy way to distract him, or break his concentration. It was enough to send him into spasms of rage. At those times he swore that the world and everybody in it was ganging up on him. He would curse the racecourse inspectors who all carried photos of him. It was a great ploy for his golfing opponents and one we often used in critical moments on the course; it never failed. It was invaluable just before he putted as he was a good money player.

The planned game against the trainers was one that we badly wanted to win; strangely, it was the only time that we played on the same side. We viewed this game as a good way to recoup some of the huge training fees for which they so regularly and unashamedly slugged us. I happily report that we did and very thoroughly so.

There were a few angry barbs thrown in the bar, but they calmed down and we took them on a solid night on the town. We enjoyed the steak with spaghetti special at the Italian restaurant, Eido's in

Upper Queen Street that we used to patronise. Then more wine and women filled the bill nicely (all with their money) at a friend's club.

I am pleased to say our association with them paid off in a number of ways. One of them had developed some valuable contacts with some shady characters involved in horse racing in America. He had travelled and raced over there; he swore they were Mafia linked. They were a group of owners and trainers based around the famous Yonkers track just on the outer edge of New York City. The deal was that he would buy well performing young horses for on sale to his contacts in New York.

Pacing horses, like flat racing, had a rating system. The horses were rated according to the number of wins or places they achieved. The more a horse won or was placed caused it to be rated up a class or division. This was pretty much an international standard. In those days, pacing and trotting horse racing were not as stringently controlled as their counterpart in flat racing. In horse races it is very difficult to fix or guarantee the winner. People talk about making them go faster with various stimulants, but that was an unreliable and difficult way to do it. Conversely, it was a lot easier not to win or to run a place. This was a lot easier to achieve with young, not so well known horses. Skilful sulky drivers could do this and evade a steward's suspicions.

The obvious racket was to purchase promising young horses, race them, but keep them on the bit and not let them perform as well as they could. Arrange a couple of races so that they didn't run well, in fact, they ran dead. It could be easily done with co-operation from just two other drivers, and hey presto it was just enough that they did not reach the rating class they actually should have. That gave them a tremendous advantage when they eventually raced freely.

The trainer's friendship was mutually beneficial. The open house and facilities of the Pacific Sauna available to him and some of his owners, especially the Americans when they came over, served him well. In return we sometimes got the nod, not on winners, but on the ones that could not win. If two or more horses in a race were not trying it altered the makeup of the race completely. Therefore, while you still could not guarantee the winner, an astute better had the odds in his favour. This was just one of the perks we enjoyed in the exchange of favours between us.

This flamboyant character was great company and loved a drink. He liked nothing better than to sauna at the Pacific; then he would undo all the good weight loss by having drinks in our upstairs free bar. Every time he came in, either with company or alone, it developed into a party. Our free bar enjoyed a great reputation. It attracted all the great and the good, sportsman, politicians, crooks, cops, plus wannabees of every vocation.

TALKING ABOUT THE INFAMOUS
PACIFIC SAUNA, LET'S TAKE A LOOK

The Pacific Sauna became a hugely successful enterprise, one that I jointly owned with Ray Miller, an old Woolwich boy and a former shipmate on the Dominion Monarch. A part of Ray's career before joining me as a partner was as a substantial bookmaker. Unfortunately, for his sins, poor old Ray got himself caught; unfairly he always maintained. He paid the price; one months loss of liberty in Mt. Eden Prison.

This had ongoing consequences. A feud developed between Ray and a certain vice squad detective who had arrested him. This feud carried on into our Pacific Sauna activities. The infamous Pacific became a Mecca; it attracted punters right across the spectrum. Ray and I just grew with it and our friend Jimmy was never far away, which had an unspoken benefit for us which will become apparent later. The stories and happenings around the Pacific are legendary and I will relay them further along in this tale. For the time being, I think it fair to say that the Pacific in its heyday had an equivalent level of local recognition to the Follies in Paris, or Raymond's Revue in London. That was easily evidenced by the many international tourists who came to us having heard of it in their travels. Anyway, it's back to the matter at hand; the debriefing at the Central Hotel.

I was still chatting to Bert. The word was already out about my arrest. After a few minutes in strolled Peter. They shook hands like the old friends they were. Then Toofats came in which led to more shaking of hands, but an air of tension had crept in. Bert, realising there was a problem, rightly made to go, taking Brickie with him, which was a wise move. The goodbyes and the backslapping were concluded, but it was a little prickly. It transpired that there was bad feeling between Toofats and Brickie over some long ago slight, probably in prison. Whatever it was and neither of them ever said, I had a distinct feeling that it would not go away. One day it would have to be settled if Brickie remained in Auckland.

After they left, the atmosphere lightened. We trooped off to the dining room for lunch. The expected debrief took the entire time from entree to dessert. Peter thought everything was going to plan and it was just a matter of time. That sounded a trifle too easy to me. But, there again, thinking about it, how could they have a case? It had to have been malicious. After all, we did have established credit, I did own the car through the company and I was the sole director. The popular belief was that Coutts could not claim a Workers Lien as they were operating a credit account with my company. Give Peter his due, it all happened just as he foretold.

I appeared in the Magistrate's court for what was known as the depositions; a legal term covering the checking of all statements and evidence prior to moving on to a higher court, if the evidence produced justified it. It is a hearing mechanism to avoid wasting a Court's time. I do not want to make too light of it, but the Magistrate hearing the depositions came down solidly for me. To the extent that he observed that 'he would have thought I would be receiving advice to take the matter further'. The charge was deemed unsupportable and I was free to go. We celebrated long into the night, starting in Peter's office and then continuing across the road in the Central Hotel. The scope of the celebration widened as Eb Leary, who was a party animal of renown, joined the growing gathering with some very attractive totty. They were posh friends of his girlfriend, wanting to meet up with the much-publicised characters of Eb's employment. Life on the edge does have its rewards. My last recollection of the night was at a flat in Parnell, Eb and I with a bevy of females and bottles of wine scattered around like confetti. We still had a long way to go to finish the planned court case manoeuvre; but it was a given that we competently finished the required 'manoeuvres' in the Parnell flat.

WE TAKE THE FIGHT TO
THE ESTABLISHMENT

To Peter's credit he really got things moving very quickly. He filed the relevant papers and then succeeded in getting a special date for the hearing in the Auckland Supreme court. It seemed no time at all before we were back in a courtroom. This time it was the big one. The case was given to a very tough senior judge to hear; we suspected that was no accident; it was Mr Justice Speight.

The preparation and the supporters lining up on either side, reminded me of the preliminary machinations of a world championship heavyweight contest. There was much more at stake than my winning and securing a healthy damages payment from the police. Malicious prosecution cases were very rare and there was a lot depending on the outcome. There was interest from the very highest echelons of the Justice Department. Quite amazing really as it had been created by a relatively minor charge, an alleged car theft, but it was more than that to them, it was a precedent.

All of a sudden, the big day was upon us. I met Peter in the grand foyer of the impressive old Supreme Courthouse. Those old structures with their grandeur and their long history of great civil and criminal trials seem to send out a message of importance and solemnity that impresses itself upon even the most experienced litigants and their representatives. It certainly always had a sobering effect on me in the three times I appeared there.

The interest in the trial was evidenced by the knot of reporters in the foyer, which was quite amazing, as Auckland at that time only had two newspapers and one television news channel plus a couple of radio stations.

As I recollect it the case went on for three days and obviously I was one of the witnesses. The main point Peter questioned me on concerned whether I did have established credit with Coutts, which I confirmed. He had pre-warned me to just answer the questions and not to give my own opinions, which I did, but not without difficulty.

I think the cruncher however, was that he had also subpoenaed Coutts' accountant, who could do no other than confirm that a monthly credit account had been in place, although they did belatedly send a letter cancelling it but that was done after the incident. The letter of cancellation in fact confirmed our contention, which was that the credit arrangement was in place. If it was not, why was there a need to cancel it? There were many red herrings brought in to damage my credibility. Senior detectives, who were well known, were there in force and just being there was their method of sending a message to the jury. They included Superintendent 'Black Jack' Stevenson who, at the time, was based in Wellington and was well known to many New Zealanders. His presence there was notable, as he had not been involved in the case.

The case also turned on the fact that the detectives had overstepped the mark in their dealings with Coutts. Peter laid great emphasis on the furore they had caused and the recklessness of bringing the unwarranted charges against me. In the end the action of the Police was found to be malicious. It was a landmark case and accordingly was recorded in the New Zealand Law Reports.

The judge found for me, and entered judgment against the Police for a significant sum in damages. Peter was beaming; it was not just the money; he really had an innate dislike of injustice and was prepared to fight it wherever he found it. After the conclusion of the case, we became quite good friends. I often went out cruising with him on his yacht. On one memorable occasion, we cruised up to Mansion House, the original house of Governor-General Sir George Grey on Kawau Island. He brought it and upgraded it in 1862 as his holiday home. In more recent times, it became a yachtie's hide-away. Many a lost weekend of carousing was enjoyed there. If the ghost of Governor Grey, which was reputed to appear there, could talk, I fancy the Auckland divorce rate may well have escalated.

Interestingly, given the cavorting that often went on aboard yachts moored there, the island itself is named after the Maori word for the bird, the shag. Our so-called quiet break somehow turned into an uproarious couple of days. I always appreciated Peter's efforts on my behalf and his friendship in those exciting days. Even after all these years have passed, I think very fondly of Peter, Eb and the Ryans, Kevan and Gerald. Auckland characters and boundary pushers, each and every one of them.

THE CAUSE OF THE BRAWL WITH TOOFATS

Before I launch into the reasons for the brawl with Toofats, I have to set the record straight about it. It could well appear that I am pushing myself as a fighter and 'blowing my own bags' as that is termed downunder. The truth is quite the opposite. I am, and was always known, more as a ladies' man possibly, but definitely a chancer and a dresser. I lay honest claim to all those virtues, if they qualify as that. I was not in any physical way a fighter. In the incident with Toofats I was scared shitless, as the saying goes, but there was no other way. Had there been one, I would have gratefully taken it.

Anyway, let's get on with the story. Two weeks after the judgment in our favour I got a phone call from Peter to the effect that the eagle had laid the golden egg and it was pay out time. I called around to his office that afternoon. He presented me with his bill, which equated to about the agreed percentage. I agreed that he could deduct it from the monies due to me. With that agreed he gave me a cheque for the balance, which I carefully put away in my wallet.

I was realistic enough to know that though I had won the case, I had not won the war. This might well be just the first round. I suppose the amount that I had retained was equivalent to the value of a cheapish house at the prices of the time. I said my goodbyes to Peter and thanked him once again for his efforts. My next port of call had to be Toofats. He would be looking for a share of the spoils and I knew we would have different ideas on that. What was that song that kept going through my head? "There may be trouble ahead". I could not help singing it to myself, on the way to his lair in the markets.

I felt like this was not going to be a good meeting. I entered the café; it was a real greasy spoon affair.
"Hi mate," I said to Toofats, sitting in his special chair.
"Well mate, today is the day," he boomed out, "let's do the carve-up now."

After showing him Peter's statement, we discussed the balance, if you could call it discussing. As soon as he realised I was not going to share it down the middle, he just hit the roof. Toofats Smith wanted half of the proceeds after Peter was paid, and he was looking very determined about it. I was equally determined that fifteen per cent was the maximum I was prepared to pay. The way I saw it was this: the whole case had centred on me and it had only really worked because I was a clean skin. I would have to take the promised repercussions. Auckland detectives were very angry over this; they felt they had been made fools of. They had made it obvious with snide remarks when I passed them in the court foyer and believe me they were not joking. Toofats wasn't having it; he made threats that he was quite capable of carrying out. Anyway I stuck to my guns (unfortunate phrase that). The result was that we agreed to meet again the following morning at his house, when hopefully, he would have calmed down; no such luck.

I went to his house the next morning as arranged. I knocked on the door and waited keeping as calm as I could. Elsa came to the door, she silently mouthed, 'be careful'. I went into the kitchen where he was sitting. He was eating a huge breakfast off one of those big roast dinner plates.
"Well?" he grunted, without even looking up.
"Sorry mate, I haven't changed my mind."
I hadn't finished what I had planned to say, but he went berserk.   It was not just the money, now it was a control thing; he had to be the boss. He saw himself as the 'Silverback'; this was a challenge he had to fight and fight he was going to.

We were exchanging heated words in his kitchen, when he suddenly turned around glaring at me and charged me with a long butcher's carving knife in his right hand. He was making slashing and stabbing motions; this was very dangerous. I darted back through the kitchen door, skipping backwards up the long hallway to the front door. I could not turn my back and take my eyes off him. I had to retreat going backwards. When we reached the open front door I felt safer and knew I had a chance. I could not jump in the car and do a runner much as I wanted to. Had I tried to he would have reached me in the moments spent opening the car door and getting in.

This was like the Billy Parslow thing from Book One all over again. Funnily enough, even while this attack was taking place that thought was in my mind. This however was much more deadly. I recognised my best chance was in space.   I had not let him corner me in the house, and now I was outside I didn't want to run. If I had done he would have wrecked the car and me, when and if he got his hands on me.

Even though the action had been going for less than a minute, I saw that he was gasping for breath. I didn't know if it was through lack of fitness, or anger, but I sensed a real chance. I looked around for a weapon and there was the perfect one. It was one of those old fashioned, metal, milk bottle crates. I could use that to block the knife, and bash him with it, which I did. Luckily, for me, I was much fitter than he was. I capitalised on Toofats' lack of condition and took the fight to him while taunting him as to his tiredness. I really worked him over verbally. His arms were dropping; he was breathing in great gulps, but still trying to stab me. He would have, had he been fitter. I am convinced he would have killed me if he could have. The knife clattered on the crate a couple of times, but he was a spent force. He dropped the knife, so I dropped the crate, he lumbered forwards, but it was no contest now. I just kept out of his grasping reach, and peppered him with good shots. This was taking place in broad daylight, in the middle of Richmond Road, on a Saturday morning.

The Pacific Island neighbours were out on their verandas enjoying the show. Someone had wisely called the police, which was shouted to us. I just turned and got into my car, he was leaning on his. He gasped: "this is not over", but I thought, yes, it is; however, I had to leave him something.

Monday morning rolled around and I go to our bank, the A.N.Z in Victoria Street West. There had been a few cheques in the post office box that morning that were burning a hole in my pocket. They were payments for ads in one of the Bowling Club cards that we were publishing.

The cheques in my pocket had me thinking about how the business was prospering. It caused me to have a thought of how I might be able to fix the bad situation that I was now in with Toofats. It had to be fixed, and the answer came to me, it was like a bolt out of the blue. It had to be a face-saver for both of us really and it was. It was also a fantastic opportunity for me to rid myself of Toofats and take the business forward on my own.

I had walked into the bank and into a surprise. There stood Toofats in the queue. He had a couple of small bruises on his forehead and cheek. I hesitated, expecting a charge, or at least a verbal attack. To my surprise all I got was a friendly, "hi mate, did you have a good weekend."

"Er ... yes, yes I did."

"Okay then come down to the office later for a chat."

I nodded, but I thought that might not be wise, with all those knives and his back up. I could well end up in the big fridge hanging on a hook. I would not have been the first.

I went back to my office. I sat there for a while and did a few sums. Then I rang Toofats.

"Hi mate. Look I want to have a talk, but I don't want to come there."

"Don't trust me I suppose," he said with a chuckle.

"Yeah mate something like that."

"Fair enough, where then?"

"The grandstand in Victoria Park",

"Okay, when?"

"Now," I said. That wouldn't give him any time to lay a trap, or to get a team around there.

He chuckled again and said, "Okay, I'm coming now."

I got round there in minutes, I sat to the back and in the middle so I could see what was going on and had plenty of exit room. After a few more minutes, he arrived on his own. He came to the stand, I knew he would not want to walk up the steps to where I was, but we could easily communicate across the rows of seats. From there he could not have got me with a knife and I didn't think he would risk a gun in the open and more to the point, not until he got paid. He was not stupid.

"Okay Lothario," he said, "What do we do now?"

"Trevor, I have a proposition. I think it's fair and I think it can fix things."

"Okay, fire away," he said.

I put it to him that I was running the business and there was no input from him. He agreed.

"Look I said, that can't carry on forever can it?"

Slowly he agreed.

"Well this is my plan. I will give you half of the money I got from Peter, less twenty per cent, as I will be copping all the shit from the demons now. However, in return, you give me your share in the business. It won't be any good for both of us now; too much has happened. What you say to that?"

He argued over the twenty per cent as I knew he would, but it was a way out for both of us. We eventually settled on ten per cent. With that agreed, he said he would sign over all his shares to me. I stood up walked down to him and stuck out my hand; he took it and held it.

He said: "I could kill you, or batter you now."

He was right, he could have; he was immensely powerful.

"But you won't get the money then," I said, a little

65

nervously.

"Right on, but I'm happy with that deal. Go and get the money and the paperwork and I'll sign and that's that."

"No repercussions; it's over?"

It was like the Billy Parslow thing again, pride had to be protected; it was the way of things.

"Yes, my word on it."

I accepted it, and knew I was safe. What a life, I thought. Anyway, that was the story of the brawl. While I won the case and the dispute with Toofats, the long-term price was too high. I had to move on.

I PUSH MY WAY INTO THE
RACKET END OF PUBLISHING

I had been taking it easy, but it was time to get back on the horse, or do some exploring. A few years previously, I had started in the publishing business. It had progressed quietly, but due to circumstances and other shareholder involvement, I had not exploited it to its full potential. At that stage we were busy scamming with the old bowling club rort. We were printing their scorecards free of charge but lashing them up with local advertisers. I took that scam the length and breadth of New Zealand, literally Kaitaia to The Bluff. It was a good earner, but like them all it had to dry up. The next thing I did was to manoeuvre it, so I owned the business on my own without Toofats. I had decided to get serious about it. I'd become aware of a vein of gold developing in the lower echelons of the publishing industry.

Some years previously in Sydney a bright Aussie advertising hustler had an idea about how to increase sales. He realized that he would get a better hearing if he tied his pitch to a charity or community cause. He soon spread this concept to all manner of publications. He used the charity pitch to sell the adverts as being on behalf of deserving organisations, not for a dodgy publishing house that kept the revenue. The carrot for the charity or community organisations was simple. They would get their regular newsletters or quarterly or yearly magazines produced free of charge. This represented a considerable saving for them; they didn't really have the resources needed to take on that job. It usually fell to well meaning, but amateurish committee members. The savings the charity made were miniscule when measured against the receipts that the publisher received. The enterprising Aussie who kicked this scam off was called Percy Outridge. He started what became an Australasian-wide operation. He had commenced business using a hotel foyer for an office and a public coin operated telephone to make his sales. He did well and I believe he deserved every penny of the fortune he made.

An Aussie friend of mine fuelled my growing interest in this endeavour. He was a young professional golfer who used to come to New Zealand to play the burgeoning golfing tour. He, like many young sportsmen, sometimes supplemented his earnings by moonlighting in various jobs. My friend had gravitated to the dubious calling of telephone selling, or 'blowing' to use the vernacular. This had taken place in his hometown of Sydney. My golfing friend was a typical Aussie, always looking to make a few bob on the side. He used to stay with Mary and me whenever he came to play the New Zealand golf circuit. He was a very good player and had represented Australia. He shall remain nameless, as his life is very different now.

At that time, this rort was well cornered by Australian interests. The thing that powered it was the unique type of salesmen, the blowers, like Roger from Book One, who had done so well for me on the fire extinguisher project. Blowers tended to be failed Aussie conmen. They were generally on the run in New Zealand from the Aussie authorities for a variety of offences.

My golfer friend and I spent a lot of time on the golf course. Sometimes it was just practice for him. Other times it was for money matches, often against Bert Clapham and whichever dubious partner he brought along. Bert was also a very successful, illegal bookmaker. Because of his calling, it was inevitable that he was a cohort of leading New Zealand criminals. He was always up for a bet on the golf course, the nature of the beast one might say.

Coincidently and it was such a break for me, at this time, the Aussie outfit my golfer friend had worked for in Sydney had opened an office in Auckland. He excitedly told me all about it. He knew it was right up my alley and he knew I would be interested in getting into this Aussie-dominated racket. He arranged for me to have a work trial as a blower; they were always looking for good prospects. Nobody in the office knew me, or the real reason behind my visit. I went in one evening with my friend who introduced me as his pal looking for a job. They were all Aussies to a man. My friend and I had practiced the spiel at home. He had been giving me a crash course in the high-pressure phone selling techniques that made this such a profitable business.

I started on the phones that very evening. We were cold calling plumbers, electricians, small builders and the like. They were probably at home relaxing when we called. We were asking them to support an appeal for injured sportsmen. The support was by way of by buying an advert in a magazine that would deal with safety techniques, concentrating on local sports organisations.

In the sales pitch we exaggerated the circulation. We pushed it as mostly being local. It was an ego stroke, letting their friends and neighbours know that they as local businesspeople were doing their bit for local sports clubs and services. I think it made them feel good to see their names out there. I made three sales after a bumbling start that had everybody in stitches. I just rushed my spiel down the phone. I must have startled those first plums I spoke to; or they may have thought an injured sportsman was on the other end of the phone.

I went in again the next morning and met up with the crew again. They were typical blowers, all with a story to tell. There were some real characters amongst them. One of them was nicknamed 'The Tree', short for the fabled tree of knowledge. The reason being that whatever subject came up for discussion he would present himself as an expert on it and bore all present to tears. Then there was 'Silent Eddy', so named because he would sit staring at his phone for an hour or more psyching himself up. He would then burst into action, applying himself only to the job in hand. It was as if a personality change took place. He then worked feverishly for two hours in an attempt to make the money he needed for the weekend and invariably he succeeded.

They were a strange lot, but talented at what they did. Blowing was an occupation that was not as easy as it sounds. It can get hard to keep on picking up that phone after a few knockbacks. To keep on doing it day in and day out while on a bad run can be a soul-destroying experience. That was probably the cause of Silent Eddy's vigil. A bad run would find him fixated; staring at the phone. However, this calling enabled a lot of freedom and allowed for a lot of drinking time.

Good blowers were in very short supply, so there was not a lot of room to discipline, or organise them. It was really a case of cajoling good results and attendances from them.

After the week spent learning the ropes, I was ready to start 'plucking'. I commenced in opposition to the Aussie firm. I had bribed the Aussie blowers to join me and it was onwards and upwards. What a ride that was, read on and 'read all about it', the old paper sellers call covers it nicely. I discovered the secret to employing these unusual types. It was always to have another good publication up your sleeve. When working on the new publications they could make good money. They were strange beings, but they were generally survivors. I found them interesting and humorous, also I must add, very profitable. One of the ways I used to keep them happy and preferring to work for me was a simple little ruse. Like most other members of Auckland's growing criminal fraternity the blowers used to congregate in a very busy Auckland pub, the Albion Hotel, on a Friday night. It was almost like a roll call of desperadoes. I stood for their drinks for two hours. It wasn't cheap, but it was a good investment, a very good one.

No discussion of blowers would be complete without mention of Charlie Ring. A kind fate sent this outstanding blower to work for me in the early days on my own in this business. I had quickly become major opposition and an irritant to the Aussies. Charlie had crossed the Tasman for undisclosed reasons. He was outstanding in three disciplines: one was blowing; the second was an unerring talent for seducing older women and the third was the fact that in his younger days he had been an Australian champion ballroom dancer, which greatly assisted him in the second discipline. He had skill in a fourth talent, this however, was an area where competition in New Zealand was fierce and so he barely stood out; he was an alcoholic.

At that time there was a very popular TV show on Sunday afternoons. It was *Come Dancing* and I think it went out live. The show was a favourite of my wife Mary and we often spent Sunday afternoons watching it (if it was raining and I couldn't play golf).

One Sunday as we sat and enjoyed the show I was telling Mary about Charlie Ring, the great ballroom dancer who was now working for me, when, as if by magic, Charlie glided across the screen. His face had that fixed smile common to all ballroom dancers, the mask that they seem to maintain in any situation. The scene was magnificent. The beautifully attired dancers floated, swirled, twirled and were as one with the music. It was a demonstration of dignity and grace that captivated the audience and viewers. The floor was full of dancing couples. It was a competition waltz. One had to admire Charlie's twirls and turns that avoided any collisions. The scene was graceful, magical, and professional, but there was something amiss.

As the flock of dancers pirouetted, leaning far

backwards, they danced with total concentration. Then suddenly, but gracefully, appeared good old Charlie. He was twirling with the best of them, only he was very drunk and dancing on his own. He danced the whole dance as if he had a partner in hold. The whole episode was captured live on television. Poor old Charlie; in his drunken stupor he had lost it completely. The organisers later issued a statement apologising for the incident, but they had felt it would have been incorrect to stop the waltz. They announced the winner and the other placings. Charlie was unplaced and worse still, he was banned from attending all further events.

I found myself attracted to this non-conforming bunch of blowers. It was a large part of the reason I enjoyed the publishing venture. I found that I could mix with and understand these people, who were different, but talented, in their own ways. I was able to exploit their take on life. They seemed to sense in me someone who on some levels knew them well. However, more importantly, I could provide the vehicle that was their lifeline.

IT WAS NOT WHAT I KNEW,
IT WAS WHO I KNEW

I still had my office downtown in the High Street. I reached a deal with my old friend Jimmy Hewitt. Jimmy was now a senior member of the Waterfront Union and had given me the go ahead to produce the Waterside Workers publications.

I had also capitalised on my old Freemans Bay contacts. One was my brother-in-law Rocky McGlynn who along with Garry Duffty controlled the Auckland City Council dustmen co-op. Their word was law in that outfit. Selling adverts allegedly approved by them had tremendous pulling power. The old dusties were a popular group in Auckland. They were out there in shorts and singlets in all weather. They worked on a 'job and finish' arrangement that meant as soon as they completed their round they went home. They didn't walk, they ran. It was common to see a current All Black, or a Rugby League Kiwi, running and working with them. For them it was more training. It was for the extra fitness it gave them. In any event, it all added to their popularity.

Another very important contact was Bill Anderson. Bill was an old Freemans Bay boy and ex-merchant seaman. He had fought his way up from a truck driver. He was now the influential secretary of the Northern Drivers Union and seeking a nomination to the Federation of Labour. These were both very powerful institutions in New Zealand. In those years of unfettered union strike power Bill and the drivers were a formidable organisation. He was a card-carrying member of the New Zealand Communist Party. I came to know him well and he was an honest, true believer. He was for many years an uncompromising thorn in the side of the employers.

Jimmy and Bill were well known and respected. When you had a phone call from them, or someone working on their behalf, you listened. It was a mighty trump card.

In the fifties, sixties and seventies trade unions were a very powerful part of the tapestry of life downunder. They were equally as powerful in New Zealand as they were in Australia. This situation was a magnet for the criminal fraternity. It applied particularly to waterfront unions, the Melbourne waterfront being by far the best-known example of this. The infamous Melbourne Painters and Dockers Union had a long history of criminal control. Members of the highest echelons of the union were routinely involved in bank robberies, bookmaker robberies, gangland disputes, hits and extortion of ship-owners. Criminals with connections to the union were regularly supplied with alibis covering their whereabouts. These events are all a matter of record. Many books and reports have been written on the subject. Many investigations and commissions have been set up to investigate their activities, usually unsuccessfully. The great American film, 'On the Waterfront', featuring Marlon Brando, was based on that same subject. It portrayed similar union activities and control on the New York waterfront. The storyline for that film might well have been taken from what was taking place in Melbourne through those years. There have been many hits and shootings in the battle for control of the Painters and Dockers union, usually in the run up to union elections. Although the Melbourne waterfront led the way, other major ports, to a greater or lesser degree, shared that philosophy, but not the level of violence, not in New Zealand anyway, but that was the only major difference.

I figured now was the time to capitalise on my trade union contacts. Though little old Auckland was not New York or Melbourne with all their graft, waterfronts down under abided by the same rules. Look after your own first. Who you knew and how you were trusted played a significant part in whether you progressed or not. Seamen, ex-seamen and dockers all looked after one another. Any benefits, sidelines, or rackets that were available, were always kept in-house as it were. I was there with a headfull of ideas to exploit the situation. I was an ex-seaman. I had good contacts.

I was established and had the ability to put projects into practice, and above all, I was trusted.

Jimmy Hewitt, who became a very close friend of mine, was an ex seaman. He had been involved in the fracas (covered in Book One) in the bar of the Britomart Hotel when Birdie, the police officer whose job it was to catch ship jumpers, tried to arrest our friend Georgie Porter. Jimmy, an ex-amateur boxer, was a real staunch knockabout bloke. On leaving the sea, he had joined the Waterfront Workers Union at first as a run-of-the-mill wharfie. In no time at all, Jimmy, who was very bright and had great negotiating skills, was 'elected' to the executive of the union. That and the other contacts gave me a real leg up, but I was the right guy to exploit the opportunities, for them as well as me.

UNDERWAY, IN A BIG WAY

Jimmy had consolidated his position and power base in the Watersiders Union and union politics generally. He was a very valuable friend with lots of contacts and power. Through him, I was able to add further publications on behalf of other unions to my portfolio. New angles were constantly required to keep the blowers occupied and on their toes. Through Jimmy Hewett and his contacts, I was able to provide that.

I suggested new ways of funding and ways of free production of their in-house union publications. I also organised the fundraising for the annual Picnic and Golf days for both unions. This came to them free of charge, the drinks, food, prizes etc. courtesy of kind industry sponsors, all arranged by me.

Like all deals, it was only good if it was good for all parties. My blowers had a field day, as they were able to call on behalf of new publications and sell the support adverts to firms associated with the industry. They were very comfortable, passing themselves off as belonging to the unions, which in a veiled way they were.

The publishing provided a good lifestyle and good money, but there is only so often you can go to the well. They all dry up. It was the same old story; after a couple of years I was getting itchy feet again and looking for a change. Unfortunately, it was never in my nature to stay put and wring the life out of a business or situation. Life was always best for me when I had new challenges; new horizons always made me feel alive. I was compelled to live life on the edge. No matter how well my business and affairs may have been running; I always saw other opportunities, which excited me. It was a condition that I was never able to control. I understood and considered the entirely practical, common sense arguments put to me by Mary and by other close friends. No doubt, they were correct. I was in a good place; I should have kept building on what I had. Had I done so, I would definitely have accumulated more in the way of material wealth. However, I was headstrong and driven by another unidentified, shadowy factor. Maybe my restlessness was a hangover from my very insecure younger life; who knows? I only know I was driven. I had to move on; it was strange, I only found satisfaction and a temporary haven or security in new ventures. I'm inclined to think that subconsciously I thought I could not rely on any current situation. It was always too good to be true. I was scared it would change and let me down. So I was doomed to move on. I was always trying to find that tantalising state of reliability that I craved, but which mentally stayed just out of reach for me.

COME INTO THE OFFICE AND
HEAR A TOP BLOWER AT WORK

Ted the Tree of Knowledge was probably the best blower of all. He wandered into the office at about ten thirty.

"What's on and what's hot?" he enquired of me, while grabbing a coffee from the dispenser. The Tree was an interesting bloke. He had a history in Aussie, which he rarely spoke about. However, there had been a couple of occasions where he started to open up after a few drinks. His expression on those occasions was that of a man reliving a bad dream. He would then retreat into himself and drink. He had a hard face; it reflected a life of surviving and continual struggle. I think he had been a man who had tried many avenues in life, but had not found salvation, success or fruition in any of them. I think he had eaten from that bitter table of the 'might-have-beens'. I think that most of the blowers had sat at that table in their time. It was probably an important ingredient in what was required to keep picking up that phone and winning the battle against self-negativity. That ingredient was the necessary driver in projecting a positive personality down that phone.

"Hi Tree, my old mate, you look like you over revved up that motor of yours last night!"
Tree, looking sardonically at me.

"Yeah, it was a big one; that Kitty's a goer and can she drink? I'm really suffering."

"Mmm ... well that's a pity mate, I've got a real hot one for you; it's a forty-eight page publication for the wharfies' sports club. It's new, it's hot and it's yours, if you're up to it. I can give it to Love Oil otherwise."

"Fuck off, Len, you promised me this one last week. Mate I think it is you who's over revving. It's affecting you in the memory department. Just let me finish this coffee, and I'll get stuck in; I need a good earner, what with that Kitty costing me a fortune. Anyway fuck old Love Oil, he had that good Dustman's picnic job. You gave that one to him last week and he made an effin fortune. He never stopped rubbing it in down the pub. I felt like decking him."

He took his coat off, rolled up his sleeves, and sat down at his desk.

"Right what's the rort? Can I call on behalf of Jimmy, and lay it on a bit?"

"Yeah, that's the go, but best to be a bit careful. Hit the freight and truck companies first, then the shipping companies and the stevedoring outfits. There's the plum list to work off. All the yes men's names are on it, first, surnames and phone numbers, it's a doddle. Go to it Tree, make some money."

Ted the Tree phones a major trucking company heavily involved in delivering and clearing goods and cargo from the wharves.   He would have checked the name of the MD, or the man who could give the green light; we called them the 'yes men'. Anyway, have a listen to a real pro, a star in the business at work.

Tree checks the list and dials a number. "Good morning," he says to the receptionist, "Mr Abbott, please."
"I'll just check Sir; who's calling?"
"It's Ted Birch, Waterside Workers Union."
Within a minute, the receptionist is back.
"I'm putting you through to Mr Abbott now, Sir."
"Morning Mr Abbott it's Ted Birch here, Watersiders Sports Committee. I'm giving you a quick call on behalf of Jimmy, you know, Jimmy Hewitt. He said to make sure I gave you an early call on this."
Mr Abbott is good at his job and regularly deals with the Union, so he knows who Jimmy is.
"Morning Ted and what can I do for you?"
"Well it's like this Mr Abbot, we're putting out our quarterly publication, 'The Watersiders'. It's due out next month and we need a bit of assistance from the outfits we work with to support it with an advertisement; you know, spend a bit of your advertising budget with us. Jimmy passed you to me to deal with as he's tied up on that dispute down on Jellicoe Wharf."
"Is everything okay down there?"
"Yep, all fixed up. You know how good Jimmy is at

sorting out these problem areas."

"Glad to hear that; he's a good bloke, Jimmy."

"Yes he is Mr Abbott. He's well respected, fair to all and he keeps everything calm."

"We can all follow that lead, Ted."

"We sure can, Mr Abbott. We need to stick together and work together, don't you agree?"

"I certainly do, Ted, yes, I certainly do; you boys are doing a great job down there."

Tree is confident now.

"How about it then, Mr Abbott, can we count on you for support? The boys will appreciate seeing your company feature in the magazine. We feel it promotes goodwill. We all need a bit of that. How about it then, can I put you down for a page? We were thinking of the inside cover for you, it's a prestige position and by the way, the magazine also has a feature on safe working procedures."

"Yes, we're happy to work with you lads on this, put us down for the full page."

"Thanks, Mr Abbott. I'll send the confirmation and details directly to you and maybe you can send back the copy. Otherwise we're quite happy to draft something up for you."

Tree then adds for good measure and thinking long term, "thank you for your support, Mr Abbott. Right then, I gotta go now and do some real work down on Kings Wharf. By the way, I'll give you a call next time round. The boys will certainly appreciate your support, thanks again."

Job done!

The letter of confirmation was also an invoice. Payment often came back straight away. The blower would probably make the equivalent of two day's pay, if not a bit more. The charge out price for the advertisement was about three hundred dollars and we would sell about thirty pages. A nice little earner, you might say.

It's a bit strange, but in looking back on those balmy days, it seems the weather was always fine and the traffic lights always green. Most days I was on one golf course or another; if not playing, then meeting someone or other in the clubhouse. The golf course constantly beckoned. Who was I to argue? Things were running smoothly. I should have been content, but I was not. It seems unbelievable, but I was apprehensive.

PUBLISHING WHEEZES, THE OLD 'BILL 'EM AND BOLT' ROUTINE

Publishing provided many wheezes. As well as union and professional magazines there were also the trade registers. They were excellent earners for me in those days. You may recall my brief foray into Sydney, with the Asian Restaurant Register. They were all much of a muchness; the only change being the trade or profession targeted. The trick was simple; all I did was design very official looking invoices and billed the recipient for their listing in the official sounding register. A certain percentage of them always slipped through the payment system. My method of operation was simple. I didn't use my regular office for the registers. I thought it more circumspect to rent another small office, usually tucked away from the main stream and always furnished. The next job was to get stationery printed that gave the project its identity. That was a very important aspect of the deal. The heading on the top of that invoice could make or break the scam.

I would purchase the window envelopes in commercial quantities. I had a franking machine; it was cutting edge stuff this. I also, very fortunately, had a post office contact (another golfer) who saved me a huge amount of time and money. The envelopes were put in bundles of a hundred letters;

the bundles were then placed into canvas bags. For some reason the number of bundles were never counted. Oh well, these things happen.

I had a superb accomplice on hand in Dawn. She was attractive and friendly; she exuded an aura of credibility and dependability. She often worked with me on publishing projects that sailed close to the wind. Dawn was reliable and staunch. She was an expert at dealing with dismayed punters and register clients, who had somehow managed to track us down; ten points for determination, no easy job that.

"Yes, I quite understand your disappointment, Sir," she says as she shuffles papers and leans forward in low cut blouse.
"But I am sure there will be a logical explanation. Unfortunately, Mr Gilchrist (me) is overseas on an inspection trip at the moment, but he will certainly be in contact with you on his return."
The irate punter mumbles something about cheques.
"I beg your pardon sir, oh no, I don't sign cheques."
Once again, she leans forward, refocusing the punter's attention. She was a well-made girl and knew how to use her advantages.

With all the prep done, Dawn would get in a couple of casuals and set about preparing lists and start addressing envelopes and sending them out. I would have selected a target, say dentists. I can honestly report that the dentists enjoyed a very high rating in the gullibility stakes. Probably all that mercury they inhaled over the years doing fillings, or maybe it was the nitrous oxide, a quick sniff of that could make the world look rosy.

In reality, it was the old numbers game. I relied on gullibility and poor administration for the invoices to slip through the payment system. In its heyday around 10% of them did. I promoted and printed these grandiose sounding registers for all and sundry. I was an equal opportunity purveyor to the gullible and didn't give one group preference over another.

Unfortunately, once again all good things do end, but I squeezed this scam pretty hard before it did. I managed to stay just in front of the Cook Street police, who were searching for ways, including harassment, to put an end to this good earner. Sometimes I was just lucky, but I was careful to make it as hard for them as possible. In that regard, I must have been good. Through those years, although I made Supreme and Magistrates Court appearances, the fact was, I never lost a case brought against me, and consequently I never lost my liberty.

A SAD DAY WAS ON US. THE DEMISE OF THE OLD 'BILL 'EM AND BOLT' ROUTINE

The unfortunate demise, of this low overhead and particularly well paying wheeze came about largely through the blandishments of a friend. Since he was one of the instigators of it, I could hardly complain. He was a good friend of mine who shall remain nameless. He, with two friends, had enjoyed a great deal of success with this wheeze in London. He had since become very respectable and successful in other fields. One day he called me and asked me to join him for dinner, as he wanted to discuss a situation with me. Knowing him as I did, I guessed he wanted a favour. I joined him at the Dynasty, in Fort Street, a very good Chinese restaurant in Auckland's downtown area.

We had a couple of drinks and it did not take long until he spilled out a very funny tale to me. The upshot was he challenged me to put out one of my registers for New Zealand lawyers. This request apparently resulted from a conversation he'd had with his lawyer. It had centred on his nefarious activities in London. Those activities had included the birth of the bill 'em and bolt routine, more properly known as the outlawed Pro Forma Invoice scam.

The well-known and senior lawyer was emphatic

that it could not happen to his profession.

"No, no, he had said, not here, not to us, we are far more professional, it couldn't be done." He was adamant about it. He should have realised he was talking to a very competitive man. My friend, being well known for having an outrageous sense of humour, and unable to resist a challenge, prevailed upon me to test the abilities of that noble profession.

As it happened, I had recently suffered at the hands of one of their brethren, so I was easily persuaded to target them. I had previously considered it and decided against it. I knew there was a growing call to outlaw this method of billing and was wary of awakening a sleeping giant.

I think it fair to say that at that time lawyers were enjoying a revered position in society, which has since been lost. It was a privileged and well-paid occupation. However, it was the late sixties and the times they were a changing; people were starting to wake up.

I first checked out different law journals and periodicals. I noted their titles and dates of publication. Dawn and I did some research. We came up with a name similar to, but not the same as, the publications that were circulating and subscribed to by the profession. I think I titled it 'The New Zealand Legal Register'. It sounded grand

and the sort of thing a respected law firm would be subscribing to.

"Okay Dawn, let her roll; send out the invoices." My friend was obsessed by the scheme, and impatient for results. We didn't have to wait long. As was my normal practice, I gave it ten days or so prior to checking on the returns. I confess I was very nervous about putting my hand into the post office box. I had rented it under a pseudonym. I had been plagued by visions of a large detective waiting to grab my hand on the other side of the box. However, that pleasure was denied me. In fact the bloody box was full with a notice for me to go round to the back, for further mail that the box wasn't big enough to hold.

I was very wary. Could this be a trap? Was the imagined detective waiting for me on the inside? I am pleased to report the answer was no, he was not. I put the mail into two carrier bags that I scrounged around for and found. I was amazed at the amount of replies that were waiting for me. Who would have known that lawyers were so generous? I certainly did not.

The law firm that had been the incentive for this caper was one of the early responders, much to my friend's delight. Remember this all took place over forty years ago, so my memory may not be quite correct, but I am reasonably sure that I gave that particular lawyers' cheque to my friend, to assist him in the bragging rights. However, I did not hand over the cheque straight away, not until I was sure that all the replies we were going to get were in.

As it happened, my instincts were correct. There was a huge clamour led by baying lawyers. As a consequence of their getting stung stronger legislation to stamp out that particular bit of soft villainy was rapidly introduced. Sadly, it was very tough legislation involving jail terms and massive fines. No sense of humour some professions.

Amid all this, my marriage was still going well at this stage. Mary was happy; she loved our life. She had a nice car and friends with whom she spent her time. Everything in her life was rosy, with the possible exception of me. I was a handful, but her disposition was up to it. I played golf most Sundays with Jimmy Hewitt and a group of watersiders; we had a club within a club. Unfortunately, the social side of things just exploded. A couple of marriages broke up and another couple were threatened. Sometimes our Sunday round, which started at seven o'clock in the morning, didn't finish until midnight. The card tables were always busy; the music didn't stop; the company was great. There was one memorable occasion; four of us didn't get home for two days. Even good things come to an end.

ALL WAS NOT LOST, NATURAL JUSTICE ARISES

Life never ceased to amaze me. While the Legal Register scam was in progress I had the good fortune to become intimately acquainted with a striking looking, mysterious lady that for the sake of confidentiality, we shall call Fanny. She was hugely intelligent and probably the brightest lady that I ever serviced. We were both in our mid-thirties and available.

At the time I was enjoying the high life. I was living on the golden mile that was Takapuna Beach. Ask anybody who ever lived there, or knows of it and he or she will tell you it was nookie trap number one. In those days, I was a dedicated morning runner. With the beach as part of my garden, it was a pleasure not a drag. Fanny was also a dedicated runner so being of the hunter persuasion, I made sure that our paths would cross and there would be an early morning encounter. I made sure that she saw me exiting or going into my beachside townhouse. The next step in the courtship was engineering a chat. I did this by the simple expediency of stumbling as we were about to pass each other on the run. We stopped and chatted; Fanny insisted on helping me to my place and up the steep concrete stairs to the terrace door.

I invited her around for a drink that evening which she accepted. I left the door open with a note pinned on it for her to come on in. As Fanny entered and walked down the long hall, I had the sound system sending out the good old Pavarotti leg opener, Nessum Dorme. The timing was perfect, after a bottle of good white wine and a further dose of Pavarotti, the seduction scene was set.

I had congratulated myself on the smooth execution of my honey trap. In my conceit I thought that I alone had set the seduction snare. Not quite so, I was amazed and staggered by her willing and exploratory approach to sex. We were soon into the most advanced of sexual practice, usually reached only after a reasonable time into an affair. Her appetite for deep penetration was unrivalled in my experience.

We were lying back exhausted, well I was. I had persuaded her it was great to just lie still and listen to the water lapping on the beach. I thought that was a good line to buy some time before her next assault, which I just knew was coming. Listen to the beauty of the lapping water had worked for me in the past, but on far less intelligent conquests. I knew the respite was only temporary on this occasion. While we were lying there and in an effort to buy some more time, I enquired about her day job, the night one seemed well taken care of. This is where the mystery started.

She was casually secretive. "Oh it's nothing that you'd be interested in." She was guarded and cleverly steered us away from that subject.

"C'mon darling, tell me that naughty story again, you naughty man." Round one to her. Over the next two or three weeks it was the same. Whenever I broached the subject she cutely sidestepped it. I began to think she might have been a police plant, as she was quite inquisitive about me and my friends, but gave nothing away about herself. The thought that she may have been a cop had benefits. It was an added thrill for me. Maybe I am strange, but the thought certainly had aphrodisiac effects. We enjoyed a wide array of sexual fantasies. I have wondered many times since; is there a link between a robust exploratory sexual inclination and high intelligence? That is one for Mr Freud, not Mr Russell.

The affair was about two months in. I had been enjoying the wonderful returns of the legal and other registers, when the lawyers' pressure made the registers scam untenable. One could say they screwed me good and proper. It hurt and I was bitter.

Fate however is a strange animal. There was a mini golden dawn around the corner. I tackled Fanny about her occupation and yes, it transpired that she was an accomplished lawyer employed in a leading practice in Auckland City. So there it is, it may be that the moral of the story is that though they screwed me, I had the benefit and pleasure of royally screwing one of theirs.

THE AMAZING BRAILLE TELEPHONE DIRECTORY CAPER

About a month earlier I'd thought up an opportunity, but I'd held back on it until I'd managed to part company with Toofats. I had hit on the idea of publishing a Braille telephone directory for the blind. As far as I could ascertain it was a world first. The Directory had an innocuous start in life. My schemes often did, but rarely finished that way. This one came to life, by way of a drunken man called Tony Harris in the Albion pub in Auckland. The Albion at the time was a popular meeting place for various crooks and fly-by-nighters. It was also a sly grog den. For those not familiar with the term, it means that it operated outside of its permitted licensed hours. It was a situation that the police often turned a blind eye to in this type of pub, as it made it easier for them to find who they might be looking for.

The Aussie blowers were amongst its regular, shady clientele. Tony, who was not an Aussie as it happens, was a nice bloke sober, but he was an absolute pest in drink. I had walked into the Albion looking for a minor 'Aussie sport' who fancied playing golf for money. I was hoping to lure him into a game with me and one or two of our pals. I should make it clear that in those days it was hard to find guys who thought they played well enough and were able and willing to heavily back themselves. Consequently, we were always on the scout for new punters. Bert had heard about this guy and the fact that he drank in the Albion. So, we had arranged to meet there and do the business with him.

Well, what I actually walked into was poor old smashed Tony. Not that that was a surprise. He was mumbling to himself while trying to look up a number in an old telephone directory. He wasn't able to manage it on account of his inebriated state. "I'm blind effin drunk and can't read this crap," he kept shouting, while attempting to balance his huge rump on a rotating bar stool. Tony had short fat legs, so was unable to reach the floor to steady the moving stool and he had the large directory in his hands. He was trying to keep hold of it in one hand, balance himself and pick up and drink his large vodka and coke all at the same time.

All this was to everybody's amusement. Laughter and cat calling was drowning everything. Tony, in his stupor, made as if to drink his vodka while attempting to turn and place the directory on the shelf above the phone. The extra movement caused the stool to turn, unfortunately the other way from Tony. He looked confused, lost his balance and belly flopped onto the floor pulling the phone off the wall in the process. His huge beer belly saved him from serious injury; anyway, drunks rarely hurt themselves in a fall. However, the key thing for me was the following plaintive outburst from Tony.

"For Christ sake if I was effin blind it wouldn't have been this hard to read an effin phone book. Pick me up Stewart," he said to his blower mate from his home town of Dunedin. I do not know why, but his drunken words triggered something in my brain. I suppose it was because I was always alert to possible money making schemes and rarely ruled anything out before giving it Leonard's Plimsoll Line Test.   That was when I saw it clearly, a Braille telephone book for the blind.

I could see its potential and sensed a winner unfolding. The charity sympathy angle would be huge. As it happened, I was looking for new publishing opportunities. I was thinking ahead; I was concerned with how I would tempt the Royal New Zealand Foundation of the Blind to sanction what I was planning. It would require a bit of theatre to get them onside.   Looking back, I think a fair bit of acting came into play and was probably required for success in most of my activities. As Shakespeare wrote, 'All the world's a stage and all the men and women merely players.'

The events of that Albion evening were dominating my thoughts. As per standard procedure, I consulted the 'entrepreneur's bible', the reliable telephone yellow pages. I found the Blind Foundation address. It was in a very nice part of town at the top of Parnell Rise on the road leading into Newmarket. I had passed it nearly every day, never realising what an impact it would one day have on my life.

I rang them.

"Good morning, can I help you?"

"Could you connect me to the director or the most senior manager available please?"

"Yes sir that would be Mr... can I tell him who is calling and the nature of your business?"

"Yes, you may. My name is Len Russell and it's a matter of fund raising."

"Thank you, Sir, I will connect you now."

With that she transferred me to the appropriate manager, who after a brief conversation agreed to meet me the following week. I had been very conservative in how much I told him about what the project entailed. I said that I felt it was better that we be face-to-face when going into detail. It was very fortunate that I said, 'face-to-face' rather than, 'eye-to-eye' which I could so easily have done. A warning bell had rung in my head, that old antenna of mine had detected danger again and possibly saved me from a catastrophe, for when I eventually turned up for the appointment with him I discovered that in fact he was blind.

The next few days were a blur of activity for me. I swatted up on the organisations supporting the blind and partially sighted members of the community. I discovered that their main funding came from local charity drives. In addition, they had a national collection day annually. I also discovered that, as is the case in most organisations, it was rife with jealousy, politics, back stabbing and the usual jockeying for positions. Funnily though, this situation and knowledge of it, proved invaluable to me in combating the treacherous actions that later were attempted against me. A group that was unhappy with the ruling clique in the Foundation, tried to use the arrangement entered into with me as a means to derail the existing power structure in a takeover bid.

With the help of an artistic friend I put together a storyboard showing my vision of the project. It depicted the marketing points that I felt would be employed. It was jam packed with visuals illustrating them. It made clear assumptions on income and the likely marketing costs. Within the proposal, I called for the directory to be printed in-house, by the unsighted Braille machinists, giving extra and needed work opportunities within the Braille Training School. I had discovered this gem in my research and was placing great faith in it being a good sprat to catch a mackerel. Though I was successful in my pitch, unfortunately the visuals did not carry much weight in my negotiations; they were not much use in dealing with a blind man, no matter how good they were, or how cooperative he was. 'You Idiot, Len' was the thought tripping through my head.

However, fortune always seemed to favour me. A popular local entertainer and friend of mine, Tommy Adderly, another pommie seaman and ship jumper, also from the Dominion Monarch, who featured in Book One, was instrumental in introducing me to a very valuable ally, a blind saxophonist named Claude Papisch. He was not only a great soloist sax man, but was one of life's rebels and was really close to Tommy. Claude often appeared in Tommy's shows and as I was a regular at Tommy's gigs, I knew of him very well. I realised he could assess and guide the project from a blind person's point of view and provide a necessary credibility.

He readily agreed to act as a consultant for me and to allow the use of his name to further the project. I confided my plans to him and he was very impressed and supportive, but immediately warned me of the minefield I would be walking into. When at a later date things turned decidedly dirty, his support and contacts in that community turned out to be invaluable and probably saved me from another court appearance.

The presentation had gone well and generous terms were agreed. The big thing from my point of view was the fact that the Foundation would be producing the Braille Directory. This was such a strong marketing weapon for me. Imagine the credibility it gave the sales spiel. It meant that the punters' generosity in buying a Braille advert, also gave work to the unsighted. Add to that the fact that the first page of the directory would feature all the usual emergency numbers, but in Braille, a service previously denied them. Unfortunately using those tactics to sell the project somehow seemed below the belt to some people. However, from my viewpoint the end justified the means.

The first job, as always, was to organise a new Post Office box for that anticipated golden flow of cheques. The second important job was to rent some office space, as near as possible to the Foundation. The old address credibility swerve again. Then I got hold of my mate Geoff, who worked in the Post Office. He was always able to get around waiting lists and get those so important phones installed quickly; for a fee of course! Then some study time developing the sales spiel.

With those jobs all done it was time to pull in a couple of top blowers to kick the show off. The first blower I went after was Roger, the smart, sophisticated Aussie (a contradiction in terms?) from the fire extinguisher days. The timing was good and I was pleased to have him back. For his sins, Roger had taken on a new, very high maintenance lady; consequently he was in urgent need of funds to keep the relationship going. I had to give him a good advance, but he paid off. I worked hard at keeping that lady in Roger's life going as the more money he needed the more sales he would make.

The other blower I went after and got was an old friend and accomplice from other endeavours, Ted Lambert; this was 'Love Oil Lambert', so known because of his first foray into the world where you don't clock on in the morning. His nickname was born in the public bar of what was then the Auckland Hotel in Queen Street in the mid-Sixties. This hostelry was a meeting place for pommie ex-merchant navy guys. At this time, Ted Lambert was working as a rigger/painter on the docks and he used to appear in the bar in his dirty paint covered work clothes. I think the fact that we would be there clean and groomed in casual clothes and obviously not involved in physical work rather frustrated Ted. One day Ted burst into the bar and exclaimed that he had burnt his work clothes and was joining us, even though he wasn't sure what we did. As a joke, it was suggested to Ted that he go into the 'aphrodisiac businesses.'

"What's that? Africa? Africa? I can't go to Africa." Gales of laughter rang out, but Ted had a good nature, he took it well. It was graphically explained, but in the simplest possible terms. The sex aid business was in its early days in Auckland. Thinking about it, that is probably an exaggeration; I don't think it existed at all. Anyway, the suggestion was planted in Ted's mind and after that none of us gave the matter much more thought.

There was a famous weekly scandal newspaper called the New Zealand Truth. The 'Truth', as it was commonly known had always been outrageous and bizarre. Its modus operandi was to carry news and stories that the normal papers were too uptight to touch. The Truth carried this liberal policy into its advertising department as well. Our budding entrepreneur resolved to exploit this.

Ted's move into the world of commerce was startling in its simplicity and was successful enough to release him from daily toil and earn him a few bob. His plan was to launch his new product, a sex aid that he named 'Stayhard Love Oil'. He offered his unique, guaranteed to stimulate, wonder potion for sale in the classified products advertising section of the Truth.

Ted's advertisement made extraordinary claims as to its benefits when applied to one's penis prior to use. Its claims covered longevity, firmness and causing certain madness in one's partner. The purchaser, via the instruction sheet, was told that to achieve the best result, his partner should apply the potion slowly to his penis. Well I ask you, if that did not guarantee a successful outcome one wonders what would. The real masterstroke (pardon the pun) was in the manufacture of the Love Oil. In those days there was a gents' hair oil sold in cute little ladies waist type bottles. Ted's simple production method was to purchase stocks of these bottles of hair oil. He would then empty the clear oil, into a big powered mixing bowl; add generous amounts of chili powder, pepper and a little eucalyptus, to spice it up. Unfortunately, there were occasions when old Love Oil Lambert, whilst suffering the heady effects of success fortified by large alcohol consumption, was too generous with the eucalyptus. The final touch was giving the whole concoction, a good five minutes or so in the power-whisking bowl.

He regaled us with stories of the perils of production. We joked about it and suggested he should wear a white coat whilst in his kitchen that aspired to laboratory status. He would wash the labels off the bottles, attach his own printed labels which bore the most extraordinary claims, then refill the bottles with a generous helping of the magic potion. His great joy was to send them off to his clamouring customers. I know this story takes some believing, but this really happened just as I've outlined. Health and safety issues and false advertising rules etc. did not have any application in those days. I often smiled at the thought of a zealous customer receiving a bottle with too much eucalyptus and having it spread or slipped to an intimate body part. The results would be excruciating. Wonder of wonders, it happened.

Ted came rushing in one day with a letter from an irate punter. The letter referred to exactly the aforementioned situation. The punter went on to describe his shock and the unbearable pain it caused. He described in minute detail the body part which was burnt, and worse the difficulty of access to soothe the offended part. His description of himself when the overflow first touched on the intimate spot was hilarious. He described his antics as similar to a demented dervish dancer. His relief only came when he managed to get enough water into the bath to cover the body part. His description of himself trying to fill the bath whilst undressing and gyrating was too much for us and brought no sympathy, only gales of laughter. The strange thing was that in compensation he demanded not his money back, but six bottles of the potion free of charge. He had gone on to explain that notwithstanding the accident, he and his wife very much enjoyed the beneficial results of the potion.

There was a further twist to the tale; Ted was so proud of his success, particularly in our eyes, that he took to bringing in his customer replies for us to read. It was staggering to read the household names that sent for Stayhard Love Oil. Remember this was innovative stuff at the time. New Zealand being such a small place comparatively, it was inevitable that a variety of people we knew showed up in the purchase replies. Ted had about six months before his account with the Truth was finally closed down. It was mainly the result of complaints from the wowser population who were zealous in their role as guardians of public morality. Although Ted's potion had to be withdrawn from public usage, he forever remained 'Love Oil Lambert' in our company.

Love Oil gravitated to blowing and became an accomplished and confident at it. In fact later on I sold my publishing business to him and a partner of his, as I was moving into another field. Love Oil and I agreed on a price for the purchase. I was happy to do the deal, but mystified as to where this large amount of money was coming from, as I knew that Love Oil did not have it. My curiosity was soon satisfied; Love Oil walked in with his new partner, whom I knew. He was the brother of New Zealand's most notorious safebreaker, Pat McSweeny and I guess he was looking for a legitimate home for some of that hard burned cash of his brother's. Love Oil handed me a bulging brown A3 envelope. I opened it and large bundles of notes protruded. I took them out to count the money. I should not have been surprised that most of the notes showed signs of being singed and a little damp. I showed no concern and just carried on counting. It was all there, we shook hands and that was that.

However, that was in the future, and for now Love Oil was happy to join the Braille Directory team as a top-earning blower. He and Roger did very nicely. Roger kept his girl and Love Oil lived his Champagne Charlie life style. That pleased me greatly, as the more, they earned, the better I was doing. We then went to work in earnest. Our story was a full out sympathy support push. We made our calls with heavy reference to the Blind Foundation. We requested that the company used a part of their advertising budget to support this publication which assisted the blind and partially sighted. We stressed that the blind were consumers too and that they were a part of the fabric of Auckland. We were good at what we did, possibly too good. We started making many sales. I had hired my trusted accomplice from previous publishing endeavours, Dawn, as office administrator. She attended to sending out sales confirmations come invoices. Her speciality was in taking all incoming calls.

"Hello, you have reached the Braille Directory offices, Parnell, can I help you?" She was superb. As we progressed, I started to tweak the operation to add credibility and speed up cash flow. I organized Braille strip proofs of the punters listings to attach to their invoice. It was a cute touch and produced even better results. I think it gave the punters a real comfort and feel-good factor. It certainly did me.

I was really keeping the pressure on Love Oil and Roger on those phones and driving myself very hard. I really led from the front. I didn't want to put any more blowers on; there were not many who were good enough and who could keep their mouths shut, particularly when drinking. I had figured it was best to keep this project under wraps for as long as possible and not invite media speculation. After about ten weeks of amazing progress the first dark clouds started to appear. It began with a call summoning me to a meeting with my contact at the Foundation's offices in Parnell, almost next door. I arrived at the appointed time; my trusty antenna was telling me that there was a problem waiting for me, and it was a big one. I was kept waiting for about thirty minutes, so I made my way back to the receptionist. I advised her that I could not wait any longer and suggested that they call me to arrange another time. She immediately rang through to somebody in authority. She then requested that I wait there for a minute and the meeting would take place. I was ushered into the same office I had previously attended. I was expecting to see the same person and soothe any ruffled feathers. This sort of panic often occurred in the early stages of publications.

Sitting in the chair was a new face. It transpired that my man had been supplanted or sacked and I was facing a new broom; one full of hostility. He opened up with the bald statement that the foundation no longer wished to be involved in the project, as it feared for its image. He laboured the point that no official written contract existed between us; however, as I pointed out to him, there had never been a request for a written one by either party. We had proceeded on the word of his predecessor. That had then been supported by the letter of intent I had sent him covering the proposal, which outlined the terms and which had never been denied or questioned by the recipient. Our position was strengthened by the meetings and discussions that had taken place and were all documented. These meetings had been amicable production meetings where I had been shown through the Braille work rooms and shown the early production work on the directories. They had concluded without any hint of rejection of the project.

I confess that I had deliberately kept the contract part of it low key; I had realised the manager I was dealing with wasn't very experienced, therefore my best chance of achieving permission had been to stay under the radar. Instinctively I had known that it would be better for me not to push the decision further up the management scale. I also knew a contract did not have to be in writing and could be inferred from people's actions, so I stuck to my guns. My adversary was as determined as I was to prevail. I knew there was no possibility of negotiating a new deal at that stage. I sat there in my chair and tried to figure out possible outcomes. The worst result could have been a fraud charge with all the sympathy on the side of the Institute. In saying that, there was no guarantee that it would succeed. However, I knew the men in Cook Street would relish this opportunity. I knew that I had an arguable case so the best thing was to stay on my feet and go on the attack. My opponent made the mistake of playing his trump cards too early.

His first and obvious barb was the old, we have had legal advice and we do not acknowledge any contract between us, and therefore ask you to desist with this project. Please note our solicitors will be writing to you to that effect. His second thrust was to advise me with a smirk on his face that as there was no contract between us, they would not now be producing the Braille Telephone Directory in their workshops, so he advised that I should return all the advertiser payments. If you think about it, that statement alone indicates that they were expecting to produce it and saw themselves as a party to it. He then triumphantly advised me they were considering laying a complaint with the Auckland fraud squad. Phew, these things can be a little bit like boxing; sometimes it is better to let your opponent punch himself out. I did not argue, I did not concur; I just said you will be hearing from me and left.

Back in the office, I considered my options; I talked it through with Love Oil and he was of the same opinion as me, that in the short term we should go for it and drag in as many more sales as we could. The main reason for that was we both felt it important to hold our stance and show them that we considered our position correct and defensible. I then contacted Claude the musician and set up a meeting with him. I had a plan starting to formulate which would spike their guns to a certain extent. The main problem we faced was excessive bad publicity, which would affect past and future sales. The Directory was proving extremely profitable so I had to fight to keep it going as long as I possibly could. A niggle in my mind would not go away and it was slowly dawning on me that they had not pushed that issue of bad publicity. I was starting to see a chink in their amour, but at that moment I could not quite understand what seemed to look like reluctance on their part to expose the situation. I decided that it would be a good thing to find out if they had a skeleton in the cupboard concerning this. If my assumption and instincts were right it would be a good start to levelling up the playing field. Perhaps the meeting with Claude would help. I felt I was moving in the right direction and starting to take the fight back to them.

At this point I think I should clarify that Claude was helping me, not just to be bloody minded about the Foundation, but more because he felt they didn't do anywhere near enough for the rank and file of the blind who they were tasked to support. I met Claude and explained very honestly the situation that had developed and the difficulty I was facing and how bad it could get. He asked what he could do to help. I told him there were three things that would assist me; the first priority was to find some Braille typists so I could produce the Directory without the Foundation's involvement. Claude immediately said he thought he could sort that out with a couple of people. They would have to work in secret as they would be crossing the line. This was a great start. The next issue I quizzed Claude on was my feeling the Foundation was wary of bad publicity. Unfortunately, Claude could shed no light on that one, but I was quietly confident that there was something they were worried about and didn't want disclosed. The third request was for him to ask around and find the underlying cause of their reversal of attitude. Maybe what was happening was just the result of a new broom scenario, or was it something more sinister? He said he would try to find out and get back to me, but he would not be putting anybody into a risk situation. A couple of weeks slipped by and I got the expected lawyers letter. We carried on selling as hard as we could. I was sitting in the office about to call another punter when it was as if a light went on in my head. I remembered about a comment my original Foundation contact made in the early negotiations. I remembered asking him how many directories we would need to produce. He smiled and seemed a little evasive. He said something like: "let's not worry about that now. It won't be your problem; we will be making and distributing them." I was not about to rock any boats so I left it at that. Perhaps there were far fewer blind or partially sighted people than was the public's perception. If that was the case, then maybe it was embarrassing for them and they were concerned that that knowledge might move into the public arena. It could then have an effect on their fundraising from the public and Government sources. If that was so, I readily understood their disquiet. I began to realise they were also worried about the success, or otherwise, of their major collection day. This was really an overreaction because no matter how successful we might be, our receipts would be miniscule compared to their National Blind Day collections. I suspected there had become some concerns amongst their hierarchy that our sales would interfere with their regular donors, especially once our success became obvious.

That was it, apart from the internal power struggle, I had found the underlying cause of their backtracking; our own success had frightened them off! I was convinced I had cracked the case. At least now I had something solid to fight back, or negotiate, with. I might even be able to convince them that the Directory was giving them good exposure; that it might actually assist their collection day and that their unfortunate internal squabbling would be the major cause of more problems.

The Auckland grapevine was always a reliable barometer of what was going on, a good source of information and a way of transmitting messages. Every community operates one. I heard that the Foundation management had been told by their own legal advisor to tread lightly with me. I sensed that though they were not backing down, they were definitely not rushing things. If the grapevine was correct, all I can say is they were well advised.

A few days after my meeting with Claude he rang me and said I would be hearing from a couple of ladies who would undertake the Braille production work for me. That was great news, but there was one more problem; I had to import two Braille printers. I managed to do that and now I was fully independent of the Foundation. Unfortunately, we had to tone down our pitch. We could not now pass ourselves off as directly working for them. I had anticipated that. I had fermented a plan to cover that hiatus and give us the required clout in our opening pitch.

Things were improving, but we were not out of the woods yet, although we were still selling very successfully. There remained the danger of the men from the Cook Street fraud squad should they get a sniff of the falling out with the Foundation. I thought the time had come to have a final sort out meeting with the Foundation. I arranged it to be unofficial and through an intermediary, it took place in a Chinese restaurant on Newmarket's Broadway. I took Love Oil Lambert along with me. The meeting got underway quickly; there was no time wasted on any niceties. The Foundation representatives just restated their position, saying again that there was no contract and that we should desist with the project straight away. They believed we were operating under false pretences and they were going to make a complaint if we didn't cease our activities, mainly because they believed we could no longer produce the directory, which they said with a smirk and that we were presenting ourselves as representing the Blind Foundation.

Love Oil, who, like me, had been sitting quietly, spoke up, "Look here, don't you think this has all got out of hand? Don't you think it's hurting everybody unnecessarily? If the whole thing had gone as planned, both parties would have profited and the Foundation's profile would have been lifted. Surely you can see that?"

All that elicited was negative mumbling. Love Oil and I had planned that little speech, to see if their thinking could be advanced prior to us letting fly with our guns. They would not change their position.

"Okay then, we may be wasting our time here talking to you, but we haven't been wasting it for the last couple of weeks. I need to inform you that we will be producing the directory and we will not be stopping selling yet. The situation that you have forced us into is slightly different. We now have the capability to produce the Directory ourselves. We have Braille printers and we have Braille machinists. They are working right now, right as we speak. So gentlemen, there it is, you can't hold that threat over us. If you attempt to interfere with our new production facility I will sue the Foundation and you gentlemen personally for damages and defamation."

I paused to let that sink in.

"Secondly, we do represent a group of short sighted and blind sufferers, who have organised themselves into a Co-operative Association called The National Co-operative for the Blind. That is how we are presenting ourselves to our advertisers. Once again should a complaint, which would be unsuccessful, come about by your actions, I repeat, I will be suing you two personally." I stopped and let that lot hit home. Some of it was bluff and as regards the 'Co-operative', I was still working to bring that about, but they had no way of knowing that. They looked a bit shocked, but still stayed negative, mumbling that the bad publicity they could bring on us would stop everything. It was time for the big guns now.

"I would advise you to rethink that. It has come to my knowledge that the total number of Braille readers and blind and partially blind sufferers you cater for is actually very, very small. In fact it's so small that you don't publish accurate figures as to their numbers and if that got out into the public

domain, it might dispose your supporters to be less generous with your charities and collections."
I paused.
"Look, I genuinely don't want us to go down that road." (I didn't and in fact, wouldn't have.)
"I don't think anybody's interests will be served by that coming out, as it surely would in any court case that might arise. I think that is the major reason you got cold feet and have pulled out of our deal, compounded by the in-house politics involved." They each reacted with body shifts, but said nothing. I give them credit; they were tough nuts.
"Okay, then, you don't need to admit that, but you would be wise to consider it. I suggest that before you take any pre-emptive actions you go and talk to your solicitor and come back to us. We will always talk." I stood up. "Let's go," I said to Love Oil, but he was already on his feet; he knew the value of timing. I paid the bill and we walked straight out of there.

They came back a few days later with a compromise. We could finish this first Directory and they would not stand in our way, but they would not assist us. In addition, they would not be making any complaint, but they felt it in everybody's interest that we did not do it again in the following years. I was happy with that, as I did not want a public fight on such an emotive issue. I genuinely did not want it to impact on the blind community.

We researched the opinion of the blind community and Braille readers as to the merits of the Directory. They felt that it was a good thing and fulfilled a need. In fact, their need was greater than that of sighted people. I did receive a visit from Cook Street, I think it was D.S. Gerry Hugglestone and D.S. Charlie Sturt. I knew them both and they were sensible guys; they could not believe anybody would advertise in the Directory in the first place and made some disparaging comments about it. They could not see grounds for any charges and did not want to promote any bad publicity. I think they had been spoken to from the top floor. I did not know that for sure, but anyway, all's well that ends well.

Interestingly enough, Charles Sturt was very ambitious. He took advantage of a police support scheme to successfully study for a law degree. Once in practice, he became acknowledged as New Zealand's top authority on 'white collar' fraud. As a result of his expertise, he was later appointed Director of the Serious Fraud Office. He may not remember me, I however remember him when he was cutting his teeth. His success was never in doubt, well done Charles.

To conclude this bit of legalised larceny, I think the following deserves saying. The Braille Directory was born in a storm, as many good things are. While you may revile or not appreciate the methods used to sell it, the lasting gain is that a similar product is now available to the unsighted to assist them. In particular, the ability to get access to the emergency services numbers is now considered invaluable. I think the venture, even with all its problems, was meant to be. Sometimes in life, I think we are just tools. That may be a bit too philosophical, but it is certainly a possibility.

DODGY FRANCHISE SELLING TRICKS DEVELOPED THE SKILLS I NEEDED FOR THE BIG ONE 'FENCECO'

As the Braille directory and other scams illustrated, I had developed a knack of spotting a gap in a market for a needed product. I had also developed the skills to make them work. It was a matter of conceiving a suitable product, then using my tried and tested plot lines to take it to the market place. I would develop a prototype of the product and then form a company with a solid sounding name and a good address, with dummy shareholders whose names closely resembled those of senior and well-known businesspeople to give the company credibility. I came to understand that people believe what they want to believe and I let them. Following the completion of those details, I was in a position to set about marketing whatever that particular product was. I would then push it using various innovative marketing ploys that generated consumer interest. That put me in the position of building it up as a life-changing product about to be launched on the waiting market. 'About to be', that was the safety valve for me. It was always about to be launched.

The next step in the scheme was to promote it as an excellent opportunity; the old 'get in on the ground floor' routine. My modus operandi was then to sell on the exclusive sales rights of the product in designated areas. In this way, I appointed many budding entrepreneurs in provincial towns and cities. There were three or four occasions when the same budding entrepreneurs applied again for the rights to different products that were about to change the world. It's hard to believe, but we sold different deals to two of them twice. I would not dare say what towns those two came from in case it reflects badly on the rest of their population.

It was then my habit to move on from city to city in New Zealand repeating the formula. I think I was attracted to the itinerant and luxurious lifestyle it allowed me. It must have been the bargee gypsy coming out in me, though that hardly explained the luxurious element. I really enjoyed lording it up in top class hotels, entertaining potential investors and their wives to slap up dinners. Many deals were consummated over the last bottle of Champagne, with declarations of lifelong friendships tipsily sworn to. In the boring provincial towns of those days a little bit of glamour went a long way; it wasn't too hard to impress.

I had generally sorted out my next move, or next opportunity, prior to the previous project finishing. On the other side of the ledger, I had a nice wife and family. My wife, continually and correctly as it turns out, harangued me to keep hold of the businesses. Mary was particularly vociferous in the case of a business called Fenceco, a straight and very successful wooden fencing business. Nevertheless, it blossomed using the dubious selling skills I had developed. I started it on Auckland's North Shore and then successfully took it to four other New Zealand cities. Fenceco, for my readers who did not read the first book, became a very successful nationwide business; it was born from very humble beginnings. We were back living in Beachaven. Time had flown past, the clothing business, the fire extinguisher scam, some of the publishing ventures were all well behind me. We had to move back to the house on account of our growing family. Our life in the glamorous city flat was curtailed as domesticity demanded more bedrooms, more space and a garden for the kids to play in. Our home was a nice little three-bedroom house in an outlying suburb on the North Shore, however, I had other plans about housing.

In New Zealand in the sixties, the government was running a scheme to assist people; particularly young married couples, or those with limited financial resources, to house themselves. It was a scheme whereby you were encouraged and assisted to buy your own home. The success of the scheme was made possible by the availability of very cheap mortgages supplied by the State Advances Corporation. The going rate of interest charged by them at that time was below three per cent per annum.

This hugely popular scheme linked together various builders, landowners, insurance companies and the mortgage suppliers. The builders would develop large tracts of suburban land, putting in roads and subdividing the land into quarter-of-an-acre building plots. To promote the house sales the builders would then build a few show homes of varying designs. They were all attractively furnished and decorated to a very high standard. Then with lots of promotion, flags flying, competitions, barbecues, and sometimes bands, they would have open days. They would then offer purchasers a choice of the available building plots, coupled with a choice of the various house designs and colour schemes.

With those details and choices settled and the state advances mortgage approved, which it usually was provided the applicant had a job; building of the dream home would get underway. It was a good and very successful scheme. It had that essential ingredient for success, the important core value, it made everybody happy. The New Zealand housing shortage was solved, it seemed, almost overnight. Group housing estates sprung up everywhere, in every city, town and hamlet. There were great money making opportunities. Everybody seemed to be buying his or her own home. Everybody seemed to be happy. The only cloud on the horizon was that we were all broke. This was the normal situation of people moving into their new and first house. Can you remember what that was like? I think we have all been there, first house, loads of expenses, furniture, legal expenses, concrete paths, fences.

Fences, fences, something was stirring in me. Fences, they were not only a major expense, but at that time there was very little choice available. And they were not included in the house package. There was just the unsightly Number 8 wire type, or build something yourself. That way was not cheap, after sourcing the materials and then hiring the special tools needed to do the job. There I was one day, sitting in my house, thinking about how I could get a nice new fence. I wanted to fence the house off, but I really wanted to make it look better and get some privacy and thereby increase its value. As you do when buying or extending a house, I had bought some house and home type magazines to look at various internal colour schemes. I was flipping through an American one and it just jumped off the page at me. There it was, a beautiful American style home, surrounded by an amazing looking ranch style fence as they termed it. That may not sound much of a big deal now, but believe me it was then. They were virtually unknown and certainly not readily available. Bingo; what an opportunity I thought. My mind had gone straight past my own fencing requirements; instead, I could see a wonderful business opportunity. I immediately set about planning how to turn this into a business. As you can imagine I had resources, but would need more to float this idea. That however was never enough to deter me from a project.

"Ron, how are you?"

"Okay, who is that?"

"C'mon Ron you know it's me. C'mon, Ron don't be a plank, you know it's me, this is important." Ron was a difficult person but a brilliant carpenter. He was just the bloke I needed to help get this deal underway.

"Ron mate, don't fuck around, it's Len, and this is important."

"Okay, okay, what do you want?"

"Ron, I have a project underway that needs a carpenter. It'll suit you mate. It's a good one Ron and you will make a good quid or two from it."

That galvanized him.

"C'mon Ron, rattle your dags and get down to the Poenamo pub as soon as you can."

"I can be there in a half an hour; see you in the House Bar."

I had an ice-cold lager and one waiting for Ron, which he knocked back in three gulps. As soon as Ron put down his glass, I filled him in about what I was so excited about and what I wanted from him. Ron was not the entrepreneurial type and was grudging in what he thought of its prospects. That really suited me as I didn't want to breed my own competition. Brave words, but later I did just that. The copycat brigade would be in action soon enough after I blazed the trail.

Ron took my rough drawings and the magazine home with him. I asked him to draw me up some proper plans around the styles I was suggesting. Most importantly, I wanted him to design the styles so that one-size planks were able to fit any of the designs. I then asked him to measure and give me the quantity of the materials and timber required to make a six-foot panel with one fencepost. I was then able to know what my cost would be and to add on a healthy profit per linear foot of fencing. It made the whole deal so easy. Quoting individual jobs became just a matter of measuring the length to be fenced and then multiplying the total footage by the basic footage cost.

While all this was happening, I had arranged to lease a small factory showroom in Sunnybrae Road, Takapuna as the home base for the enterprise. I then turned my mind to a very important part of the jigsaw. This was financing the sales of fences. A very good friend of mine was a minor car dealer. He had told me of a contact of his in a lawyer's office that supplied the finance for his car deals. I had kept this information in my head because I knew that one day it would be useful. I got myself an appointment with that person. As it happened, he was a household name in Auckland, whom I knew from another matter. I was able to sell the lender on the idea of making hire purchase available to these homeowners who wanted to buy the fences and improve their properties. I persuaded the lender that the purchasers must be a good risk as they had all recently had mortgages granted and they were all in steady employment. He went for it. Whoopee, I knew I had a winner now. The purchaser only needed a ten per cent deposit and bingo; his fence would be up in two weeks, or less. Moreover, my first part of profit was paid up front from the ten per cent deposit. The balance came to me from the finance company on completion of the finance agreement. It was a great deal for everybody and those are the ones that work the best.

I had managed to talk a big timber supplier, Graham Thurston, from down Rotorua way into supplying me with the required timber. I had persuaded the supplier to give me an initial two months' credit. That, as you can well imagine, really helped me get started. One more largish problem was looming. I needed some special pieces of equipment. Ron advised that I needed a particular and expensive type of bench saw. It had to be capable of handling and cutting the standard lengths of plank timber. It also had to be capable of cutting the four-by-four, tanalised fence posts that I hoped we would be using lots and lots of. Lenny boy had to get his thinking cap on. Though I had always made good money, I was just as good, if not better, at spending it (a habit I passed on to my daughter). A large dose of lateral thinking was required.

Once again the problem was enough money. Thinking my way around such problems was starting to come naturally. I placed a phone call to a tool supply company where an American gambler and horse owner I knew, Harry Steinberg, had a connection. Harry was a golfer, but not a very good one. He was a bit of a character and he owned one of Australasia's finest horses of that time called Broker's Tip. The name tells you something about Harry. Broker's Tip had won many classic races downunder and had made a lot of money for him. Harry had come to New Zealand to open up a branch of Global Publishing. They were one of those American companies who peddled sets of encyclopaedias door-to-door to gullible families. The sales representatives all worked on commission. They were all highly trained in American high-pressure sales techniques, which were new to New Zealand. His Auckland manager, Richard Linklater, was well known to me. Richard was an ex-London bobby, but had rather changed his allegiances since coming to New Zealand. For a while he was part of that English safe cracking gang with my friend Keith Morgan. I had seen old Harry struggling around a couple of times on a course I often played. I had noticed that the chap he played with was a main man in that a tool company. I had developed a nodding acquaintanceship with him and Harry. Perhaps subconsciously I knew he was a future connection. I contacted Harry and told him I had a deal I would like to discuss with him.

I offered to take him out for a round of golf to discuss the proposal as we played. The course that I suggested was quite hard to get a game on if you weren't a member and it was very expensive. However, as it happened, I had contacts there. I knew that he would want to play there and he jumped at it. I had arranged for a couple of golfing friends of mine to join us. We had a great day. The game had been a very tight one, contested right to the eighteenth green for a result. Harry and I had won and he was ecstatic. He had enjoyed the company and surroundings and insisted he would be buying the first round of drinks out of the substantial winnings.

Harry's offer of drinks, as was usual, had been met by much banter, and calls from the opposition of, 'too bloody right you will Harry and your bloody bandit mate Len can buy the next one.' Everyone was smiling as we went to the cars to put our golf gear away. We washed up and made our way into the palatial lounge. True to his word, Harry hit the bar first. We sat there in great comfortable chairs, enjoying a couple of foaming cold lagers each, while dissecting the game.

Later Harry and I were in the bar on our own. It was now or never, I thought, but Harry, maybe reading my mind, beat me to it.

"Len that was a great day, now what is it you wanted to discuss?"

It was a beautiful warm summer day. The course was spectacular. The colourful hibiscuses dotted around were in full bloom. It was an altogether very pleasant afternoon. There is something magical about a winning round of golf. I could not have a better setting or atmosphere to make my pitch.

"Okay Harry, it's like this," and I proceeded to tell him what I was planning including my longer-term intention of taking the project nationwide. Fortunately, Harry liked and quickly understood what I was doing. He was well aware of the building boom going on at the time. He understood the subsequent opportunities it was throwing up. I figured the time was right so I told him, I needed about fifteen grand's worth of equipment and tools to get underway and I was short of funds. I informed him that his friend, who I had seen him golfing with, stocked the equipment I needed. In those days bank money or credit and the like was not as available as it became later. Well as it turns out, I had approached the right guy.

Harry lent me the fifteen grand privately at a friendly rate, to purchase what I needed from his friend's company. It was on the proviso that as I expanded, I bought all equipment through him and reduced the loan by a quarter every six months. He charged me seven per cent interest on the loan. This was a great deal for me, as it was for him. He ended up doing very well from it. Crafty old Harry had negotiated a very healthy commission from the tool company on that purchase and all the others that followed on from it.

Over the years we often laughed about it and how it happened. His one question though was always, "Len, did we really beat those two guys?" One was an ex-professional and the other played a good game, particularly for money. I will leave it to you to decide. The last time I saw Harry was in Double Bay, Sydney, where he had moved to, taking Broker's Tip with him and winning more races. He had still not decided, but he still chuckled over it.

Fenceco took off like a rocket. Within six months, I had bought the freehold of the factory that the business occupied. I had rented out the little group house on the shore again. With my vastly improved situation I bought a lovely two-storied, five bedroom 'des res' as the agents called them, in one of Auckland's best suburbs, leafy, tree-lined Epsom. Next, I upgraded the wife's car and let her loose on furniture shopping for the new home. I knew that I would be going out of Auckland a lot, so I thought I would make things as comfortable at home as possible.

I then set about spreading the business. As the business flourished in Auckland an amazing thing happened. There was a chap and his brother who ran a service station three doors up the road from what was now the Fenceco factory and show room. One of them approached me with an offer to buy the business and rent the factory from me. The deal he offered was a good one, so with my future expansion plans in mind, I agreed to sell subject to him operating in Auckland only, plus paying a royalty on his gross sales for the next three years. That being on top of the very healthy purchase price we had agreed. Another bonus was the very healthy lease payments on the factory. This enabled it to be valued up to twice the purchase price. Eventually on the advice of their accountants, they even bought me out of the royalty payments with a lump sum. Remember, to open, establish, and sell, was my original plan. And the great thing was that this was a real deal, not a scam. I had created something of real value. The deal also set me up to expand to other centres, which I did, very successfully. I should point out at this point that I had a philosophy about businesses and the selling of them. Quite simply it was this; always try to sell on what we termed, 'the up'; in other words when it was doing well and make capital gains, at that time untaxed in New Zealand.

I opened and sold off three more branches of

Fenceco in the next eighteen months or so, which was a good result. I sold each of them to very keen buyers. They all paid a healthy purchase price plus an on-going royalty on sales. It sounds too good to be true. So why should I sell them? The answer was that I knew there was a problem looming. I was expecting it. I suppose this is also my answer to my wife Mary's criticism that I should have kept Fenceco and its branches. Every man and his dog with a shed and a saw, started to get on the bandwagon and copy me. They worked in their backyards. They cut prices to the bone. What had been an exceptionally profitable business became a marginal living. These copiers included my wife's cousin. Against my better judgement, I had given him a sales representative's job. He stayed a few weeks. In that time, he learnt enough to start on his own with a funding partner. Though I was annoyed at the time, I realised that that was exactly the sort of thing I did. I may be many things, but I do not think I ever qualified as a hypocrite. The guy that coined the old saying, 'keep your friends close, and your enemies closer' really knew what he was talking about.

I was pretty well set up by now. I had used the profits from Fenceco to reduce the hefty mortgage on the house in Epsom. We still owned the little house in Beachaven, also with a very small mortgage. I could have paid it off but the State Advances Corporation interest rate was so kind, that it would have been unwise to do so. Mary had a smart little near-new car and she and the kids were happy. I was driving a late model Jaguar. It was previously the chauffeur driven car of the M.D. of Shell Oil Company. It was the largest model they ever made. I think it gloried in some title like the XK or Mark Ten. I suppose it reflected my ego. Large cars seemed to be the required badge of successful entrepreneurs. I had foolishly started to think I was clever. I also realised that I could not sit back on my laurels for too long. It was not just a case of money running out. I needed constant stimulus. Every new project was an adrenalin rush. I just loved the whirl of establishing a new enterprise. I took my mandatory month or so off and spent most of my days playing golf. Then I used to meet with my mate Scotty in the evenings in the Pool Bar of the White Heron Lodge in Parnell. We used these pleasant evenings to plan our next move.

THE DRAUGHT BEER DISPENSERS, A GREAT EARNER AND GREAT FUN SELLING THEM

For some reason or other, enterprises and products always seemed to jump in my lap; mind you, I was always on the lookout for them. With any new product that came along, I would apply Len's Plimsoll line test. If the result was good and the product appeared capable of being successful in the hungry new opportunities market I would develop it, or store it away for future use. I had a simple system to follow. The first and major expense was always in acquiring or manufacturing a sample of the amazing new creation. At that point, I had to put the seed money up to develop the project. Therefore, I had to have belief in two things; one, could I sell it as a business to investors and two, did it appear to fill a consumer demand on some level? If it did, I had a proven system to manipulate it. I would hot-sell a few of the products and then withdraw it from sale pending a National fully advertised release. I knew how to fabricate some initial demand. With that in place, I could create some early promising market research figures. God forbid that I was wrong on those two issues, if that happened then yours truly was the bunny. After satisfying myself on those two questions, I could then start on all the affiliated chores that had to be completed. These were the practical things such as premises, phones, stationery and an office girl in place. I then had the major task of creating the sales presentation kits. These were so important to the success or failure of selling the deal. Remember that in those days there were no computer systems and no spreadsheets that I knew of that would make the task easier. Once again, lady luck was with me and I think my lack of education worked for me. I was able to put things forward in simple terms, which were easily understood by the type of applicants my for sale advertisement attracted. This often resulted in the deal being agreed, contracts signed and payment made by bank cheque at the first meeting. All of this conveniently completed without the bothersome interference of solicitors and accountants. Those professions could not fault the deal, but often pontificated in order to justify their fees. With investors it was of the utmost importance to have that first investor on board and happy. This set the ball rolling and made the job of attracting other prospective investors so much easier. There were times that I 'invented' the first investor. I could always find a willing volunteer to fill that role. My job probably looked simple on the surface. In reality however, the skill required in holding and interesting the applicants was a rare commodity. Then knowing when to close the deal was another skill, not easy to teach or learn. No matter what the 'in demand product' that had been dreamed up was, the same principles existed to capitalise on it.

Here's the advert that preceded one of my best projects:

This in demand product is guaranteed to return the fortunate purchaser a magnificent return on his investment, plus an enjoyable lifestyle. This outstanding product is associated with the brewery industry and comes with their support. This opportunity is suitable to run from home with a wife or a partner. Though diligence and commitment are required, an easy personality is a special advantage. A general knowledge of local sport is also an advantage. The limited number of work hours needed adds greatly to the successful applicant's lifestyle. Please direct your interest in writing to:

The Group Accountant
Wholesale Liquor Supplies
Draught Beer Dispenser Dept.
Corbans House
Hobson St,
P.O Box 480, Auckland

My adverts were so compelling and promising that I was tempted to apply to myself for one of these prestige opportunities. I had leased offices in the Corbans building in Hobson Street. Corbans were nationally known beer and liquor wholesalers and wine merchants. The address gave enormous credibility to any interested party. I believe it was instrumental in significantly increasing the number of applications we received and it strengthened our hand in the ongoing negotiations.

The Draught Beer Dispensers were hugely successful and attracted many applicants. To the punters there was a fatal attraction in this beer driven opportunity. To invest in a business that had beer as its main ingredient was tempting. We were actually selling the exclusive rights to sell the dispenser machines not the beer. The punters however, felt the lure of being in the beer business; a feeling we did not discourage. This feeling was further encouraged by the copious amounts of drink that we fed them during the presentation.

However, for a moment I need to digress and acquaint you with my boxing activities, as they were a huge benefit in this escapade. While I was working on this and similar schemes, my boxing interests were developing a life of their own. I was managing a very promising young, light welterweight boxer, Joey Santos. He went on to win New Zealand and Australasian titles and eventually challenged for the Commonwealth Championship, which in those days meant something. Had he won that championship he would have been in line for a shot at a world title. Unfortunately, he ran into a grizzled old pro by the name of Joe Tettah who had fought top men all over the world. The thinking in our camp was that

Joey was up to the job, as at that stage of his career, he was unbeaten. We were also encouraged by the fact that Joey's elder brother, Manuel Santos, a top world-class lightweight, had recently beaten Joe Tettah in a main event in Melbourne. Manuel believed that Joey was good enough to beat Tettah. Joey Santos was a great lad and a famous name in New Zealand boxing circles. Managing him was what helped to propel me into full-blooded boxing promotion.

My involvement in boxing and the publicity it gave me hugely assisted the success of marketing these other opportunities. The punters generally knew of me and that gave them a good comfort level. That and later my well publicised role in rugby league illustrated a firm and public connection to sport. Looking back it was a priceless asset. Fortunately, at that time all the publicity I received was positive. The fact was that whatever we sold, whatever the product, what we really sold were dreams. We all dream of a life of successes and conquests. In many cases, we did provide the vehicle, which sometimes gave the purchasers hope of achieving such a dream.

I met one of our beer machine purchasers some years later. This was Jack, a real backcountry Kiwi bloke. We collided at a social occasion. As soon as I spotted him, I recognised him. I thought this could be embarrassing. Our man made a beeline for me. I was blessed with a fantastic memory (in my line of business it was a required asset). As he approached, I stuck out my hand with a big smile and said: "Hey, it's Jack, how are you old mate?"

"Len, mate, it's great to see you, how the bloody hell are you, you old bastard?" When he said that I knew all was well. Strangely, in New Zealand 'old bastard' was a term of endearment. It turned out that Jack, who was single when he took on the beer dispenser agency, had suffered a life changing experience. In his words, it went something like this. "Fuck me, Len, what a turn up for the books. Christ Len you would not believe how things turned out. What a fucking laugh, I got stuck into flogging the draught beer dispensers and it was great. I sold about half of that pile you stitched me up with." (I remembered I had persuaded him to double his order at a discount rate). "The trouble was I was getting pissed all the time I was presenting them. All me mates in the sports clubs thought they were just 'Jake' for the job. The trouble was they never bought them on the first presentation. They always took three or four visits to be convinced and they would have half the pissheads on the club committee there to check on them. Of course, I had to drink with them, just as you said I would have to, Len!"
"Well Jack, that doesn't sound so bad; what was the problem?"

"Mate, there was no problem apart from the fact that I was permanently pissed."

"Well, that wasn't too bad was it? What happened next?"

"Didn't you know Len? The next thing was your mate Scotty came down to help me out. Jesus Christ he fucking helped me out all right. When we weren't demoing the dispensers and getting pissed, we were out at the races. It cost me another three grand betting on his certainties. It was funny though; he made all the bets with a bookie mate of his in Wellington on the phone. Anyway, I had to give the money to Scotty to square him up."

"Did you really, mate? That sounds a bit naughty," I said. (I was ready to blame Scotty for everything if things got nasty.) Anyway, it sounded like Scotty had fiddled himself a good bonus with the old, 'my mates a bookie' con.

"Well no mate," said Jack, "everything turned out Bonza," he said grinning a toothy grin.

"Scotty introduced me to this great Sheila and I'm a married man now, I only got her through the beer business."

"Really mate, how's that?" I asked, intrigued by where the story was going.

"Well fuck me, Len, I thought you knew her. Anyway, her old man died and left her two boozers up around Ekatahuna way and one near Masterton. Hang on a minute while I grab her, you can say hello. She thinks you and Scotty are great jokers."

"Really, she does? Well that's great," I said with

some mental relief as he disappeared.

"Len, Len," said Jack excitedly pulling on my shirt sleeve, "this is Pearl, me missus, ain't she a beauty?"

I turned and there in front of me was a smiling, Maori woman of large proportions. She had a happy open face that bore the look of a lifetime of social drinking.

"Lenny, Lenny," said Pearl, who had obviously had more than a few drinks. She pulled me into her with those great arms, and we rubbed noses in a 'hongi', a Maori kiss.

"Oh Lenny," she said, "if it hadn't been for you tucking my Jack up with those beer dispensers, I would never have met him."

"That's right, yeah mate, that is fuckin' right," interrupted her darling Jack looking deliriously happy over her great shoulder.

"Otherwise I would have been stuck back at the freezing works with the rest of the boys."

Pearl eventually let me go; I could not have fought my way free if I'd tried.

"Lenny, if you're ever down Ekatahuna way, come and stays with us. The boys in the boozer would just love to meet you and old Scotty again."

"Yeah, and if you get another deal like the dispensers come and see us, they worked for me," added Jack.

It turned out that Pearl knew her business. She

had set up a nice little business hiring out the dispensers for private functions fully loaded with nine-gallon kegs of cold draught beer. So there you have it, once again, all's well that ends well. More importantly, sometimes the deals worked.

New Zealand at the time suffered under draconian licensing laws. Though the infamous, 'six o'clock swill' had been defeated, pubs and clubs were still restricted as to the hours they were allowed to operate. The Sunday trade in particular was a no-no under the laws as they stood. Not many of the rugby, soccer, cricket, golf clubs, and there were thousands of them, were big enough or official enough to have a licence to sell alcoholic drinks. More to the point, they were not financial enough to have a cool room and thus the ability to store and sell draught beer in their clubhouses. Kiwis love their draught beer, but were forced as often as not to drink warm bottled beer, sold illegally, under a trumped up locker system. Under this system, the beer you drank was supposed to be your own that you had previously purchased and stored; which it obviously was not. Furthermore, because of the amounts they needed to stock, it was always warm, which rather pissed off your average Kiwi bloke. The system was archaic and suited nobody, including the police, who did not like enforcing this unpopular law on regular Kiwis wanting to have a drink in their sports clubs. The only people supporting it were the wowsers, who still held a certain sway in New Zealand politics.

So there you have it, a shambolic system crying out for a bit of help from a couple of lateral thinking opportunists. Scotty and I sat down to discuss the possibilities of soothing the drinking problems of the sporting masses and making a dollar at the same time. We immediately recognized the sales potential, but we needed to find out if the machine was suitable and did work reliably. We knew they were for sale in Australia and tracked down the Aussie promoter by the simple ploy of finding one of his advertisements in the business for sale-classified section of the Sydney Morning Herald. There it was,

----

Seeking investor/distributors for this wonderful, groundbreaking new product, blah, blah, blah.

I telephoned the Sydney number and a very efficient secretary replied. I sought some details on the product, but she advised that information could only be acquired by visiting the head office in Sydney and having an interview with the sales director, a Mr Paul Rodda.

Apparently, he was very busy at the time interviewing applicants from out of State, but she would be pleased to make an appointment for me.

It could only be in two days' time, as they were inundated with applicants; yes of course they were.

Well done girl, I thought. She knew her stuff. It turned out that she was Paul Rodda's girlfriend and that always makes them more committed. I explained I was calling from New Zealand and confirmed arrangements to phone back or have the sales director phone me for a discussion that might be to our mutual benefit. Scotty and I sat chatting about the exciting possibilities, willing the phone to ring. It did, less than twenty minutes later.

Paul Rodda and I hit it off immediately; we each recognized a kindred spirit. We decided the best way forward was for Paul to come over to New Zealand at our expense, bringing a machine with him. Once he was here, we would cut a suitable deal with him. It transpired in the conversation, that Paul, like Scotty and me, was a rugby league fan. Coincidently the Aussie league team, the Kangaroos, were touring New Zealand at the time. I think this all helped in persuading him to come over as quickly as possible. Particularly when I held out the blandishment of tickets to the sold out rugby league games against Auckland on the Tuesday and the coming Saturday Test match, against New Zealand. He could not get on the plane quick enough.

We booked our quarry into the newly opened,

Intercontinental Hotel. Scotty went out to the airport to pick Paul up and I met up with them later. Paul was pretty much what I had expected; a friendly, but very shrewd, Aussie; not one to take lightly. He was a big fella who had the look of the streets about him. In the conversations that followed, it became obvious that Paul's philosophy was the same as ours. It was simple, find a product then advertise it and its unique selling appeal. Sell the sales rights for an exclusive territorial area. In this case with a stock of ten machines every time a sale was made. He made all the usual promises of sales budgets and marketing support, plus vague promises of extensive TV advertising. When we did our interviews, we always had copies of the TV schedules conveniently displayed. Then we blathered on about the constant flow of referrals that head office would pass on, that sort of thing. These were all very powerful psychological selling tools that we used to grease the wheels of the sale. Our approach and expectations were so similar; it was easy as falling off a log to make a deal. In less than an hour, we had an agreement. Paul would assign the exclusive rights to the product to a company we would form to market it. With us having the exclusive rights, we had a great comforter for our purchasers; particularly should they want to involve their solicitors in the transaction. We would manufacture the dispensers in New Zealand; I had already been in contact with a small refrigerator and cold systems manufacturer I knew. I had shown him the product images Paul had used in his adverts. It was delightfully simple.

All it was really was a standard refrigerator with a compressed air system and without a freezer unit or shelves. The cabinet had an access point positioned in the top panel through which the chrome stem of a hand held dispenser passed. It then entered into the barrel of now cool draught beer. The pump system was powered by a little high-pressure gas bottle, which pumped the cold draught beer up through the dispenser and hey presto; you had cold, draught beer always available.

We designed our ads and decided that the city of Napier would be our first target. We had read that many redundancies were taking place down there. We ran an advertisement and it produced seven replies. We hired a temp girl to come in and serve as a secretary and we schooled her in making intro phone calls. We then sussed out the applicants to decide whether they were worth interviewing or not. It is amazing how much you can glean over the telephone with a bit of experience. From the seven replies, we made four appointments, kept two in reserve and discarded one. The day of the big test rolled around. Scotty and I were in high spirits as we went off to Napier, a beautiful Art Deco city in sunny Hawkes Bay. Whenever we travelled on such missions we enjoyed an ego-fuelled adrenalin rush. I readily admit this sounds corny, but we felt like we were old time invaders, about to ransack the town. We had previously streamlined the trailer made for transporting the prized dispenser. It gaudily advertised the product, its association with beer and its benefits. On arrival at our destination we carefully and strategically parked where our potential investors had to pass on the way in to see us. It conservatively featured the message that we were the sole and exclusive New Zealand distributors of this fine product. It also featured a line drawing of a happy sporting type quaffing a foaming cold draught beer with great and obvious relish. It is true; a picture can be worth a thousand words.

The first applicant arrived. There was a light nervous knock on the door. We had the glittering dispenser set up in the middle of the room with a monogrammed smock covering it. There was some very quiet music playing. I was on the telephone and Scotty was ushering our first applicant into the room. I smiled at the applicant, and frowned a little at Scotty. Then while still looking busy on the phone, I said "Yes, yes, I'll look into it, however I am sorry, but that area has been allocated. We have taken the deposit. Maybe you could think about Palmerstone North. After all, it's not far from you. Anyway, I have to go, call me back on my Auckland number. I then turned to Scotty and with a manufactured scowl:
"You could have been a bit hasty about Rotorua;

we'll have to talk about that later."

Scotty, looking pained and a bit sheepish, introduces me.

"Jeremy, this is Len."

"Hi Jeremy, thanks for coming in."

We shake hands; I smile.

"What a lovely city, it must be a pleasure to live here Jeremy. I always enjoy coming here; it's usually to play golf though. The wife loves it here, she wants me to sell up and come and live here," I add as a joke, "with her of course."

We all laugh. A jokey laugh amongst the boys is always a good start.

"Jeremy, sit down and tell me about you." I look at and flick through the notes Scotty has handed me.

"Well, Len, I've just been made redundant from a stevedoring company. I'd worked for them for twenty years."

"Have you? That's rough."

"Well it's not too bad, I was going to look for something a bit easier anyway."

I doubt that, I thought.

"Yes of course, there comes a time in life when you want to do it for yourself," I said supportively.

"Yes, that's it. I don't want to make a fortune, just an easier living. I have a good side-line," he said, with a shadow of a smile. I ignored it.

"Okay, Jeremy, how are your people skills, are you all right meeting new people?"

He can hardly say no.

"Yes I do. I love meeting people, always have," he said with great conviction.

I made an obvious gesture of putting a tick in his file.

"Jeremy, this is most important. What are your sporting interests; in fact, are you interested in sport? It's a big factor in what we do."

That question to a Kiwi is like asking 'do you go to bed at night?' we are seriously in Pope and Catholic territory here.

"Len, I love my sport, I'm a season ticket holder for rugby; a member of the squash club; I've been a committee man on and off over the years. Oh yes I'm with you on that one," he said with gusto.

I look studiously at Scotty who has been making notes.

"I think we had better show Jeremy what our product is."

Scotty looks back at me, hesitates and then strides over to the dispenser and with a flourish, pulls off the smock.

I explain the benefits of the product for sporting clubs etc. I touch on the archaic licensing laws and Jeremy emphatically agrees. I point out the extra profits for clubs by having the ability to sell draught beer. Jeremy butts in, "I agree Len, the members will like that better as well, shit what a great machine. I don't know why the breweries didn't come up with this. Christ, our club will have a couple."

"I'm glad you appreciate it, Jeremy. Now I'm sure you understand why I must have sporting people involved."

"Of course, Len, it'll be great in the clubs."

"Len, I think we should show Jeremy how it works," suggests Scotty.

"Okay you had better pour some. Nothing as good as trying is there? It's so simple, just like serving behind the bar." With that Scotty filled a glass.

"Do you want to try that, just to check it is cool," Scotty says to Jeremy.

He has obvious interest now. It's like that hoary old joke, about marrying a pretty woman who owns a pub. This is right up his street.

"Er, yes, pass it over here, I'd better try it," he says with a wide grin. "Struth that's bloody good, why don't you guys try one?"

"I can't, I have to see more people yet, but Scotty you have one with Jeremy."

"Look can I leave you two? I have to see the manager; he wants to get one for his ski club, would you believe that?" I say. "Even in the ski fields they want one."

"What time is the next appointment?" I ask Scotty.

"We have three more enquiries for Napier and that other bloke is coming over from Hastings at five o'clock."

"Okay I won't be long. Excuse me Jeremy, this is important."

Jeremy is on his second drink by now.

"No worries mate, I'm okay here."

I leave them alone for about forty-five minutes; then I go back. By now at least three or four more drinks have gone down, and Jeremy and Scotty are great mates.

"It looks like we may have to leave this machine here, he wants it for the function room, they can't serve draught there," I say to Scotty.

"Remember I told you the other day that lots of hotels and motels are like that," says Scotty to me in a scolding manner.

"Yes, yes, you were right, good on you," I say impatiently.

"Well Jeremy, what do you think of the product?"

"She's a bloody beauty, just what's needed."

"Well I have to see more people, but I'll explain the deal to you."

Jeremy is slightly pissed by now.

"No need cobber, your old mate here, Scotty, a fucking good bloke, explained it all, and I want to be in it."

Scotty smiles the smile of a pro.

"Scotty, have you explained everything, how many machines and the exclusive area fee, the whole deal?"

"Yes, Len, and I don't think you should bother with anyone else. Jeremy here is a good bloke, a real sport. And he played a lot of sport; he still plays league and squash."

Jeremy is happily nodding away and still drinking.

"Oh that's good" I say, "In that case Jeremy could

be just the right chap for us."

I'm talking like Jeremy isn't in the room.

"But I still have to see the other people."

"Why? You have a perfectly suitable bloke here and I like him. Why disappoint the others? That's all you'll do. What they don't know won't hurt them."

Jeremy nods his head again.

C'mon Len, Scotty is right here and he wants me to be in, don't you mate?"

"I don't know, if that's the right thing to do," I say.

Jeremy is getting really agitated and is half pissed by now.

"C'mon Len, I like you blokes, old Scotty here is a Bonza bloke," he says taking another swig and emptying his glass.

"I've got the dough, no problems there. C'mon mate it couldn't be better. Scotty will come down and give me a hand to get started, Len, I want in."

"Okay then, but you will have to sign the contract and pay the fee and fifty per cent deposit for the dispensers now. If I trust you and sign you up and turn the other applicants away, you must realise, that is a big thing for me to do. I could be in deep shit in Australia."

I turn to Scotty and say, "And you will have to cancel those other appointments; not the Hastings one though."

Scotty and Jeremy look at each other.

"What is going on, what are you two up to?"

"Len, I told Jeremy he should take the Hastings area as well; he can run them both and I'll give him a hand with it."

I tried to look frustrated.

"Christ mate, what have you done that for?"

"What's the problem Len, why not let him have the whole territory?" Bob said rather irritably.

"I'll tell you why not; he probably can't afford it for a start and I have budgeted for ten dispensers there as well. I can't muck around with the budget and production schedules just like that. If I do let him have it, you know what the Aussies are like; it's got to be a proper deal and can he afford it?"

"Look, Len calm down and lets all have a drink and talk this through."

Scotty is firmly on Jeremy's side now and Jeremy is nodding away in agreement.

"Okay, I could do with one now."

Scotty fills three glasses, hands them around, then turns to Jeremy and says, "I'll have to tell Len about the money, okay?"

"Okay, Scotty, up to you, it should help," Jeremy says tipsily and a bit arrogantly. We have him now.

"I've got the dosh, Len, don't worry about that," he adds.

Scotty looks around the room in a theatrical manner and dropping his voice says,

"Len it's like this; Jeremy here has told me he's an SP bookie."

This refers to a starting price illegal bookie.

"He controls the bets in two pubs down here. He has for years. The money is no problem. He wants a straight business and to pay as much as we can let

him in cash. I said that would be okay for some of it to be in cash. What do you think?"
I maintain a serious face. I finish my drink and signal them to do the same, which they do with no trouble. Scotty refills all round.

"Look, it is like this, I want to do the deal with you Jeremy, but I must be sure you can operate both areas."
I make as if that is the problem. Scotty right on cue comes in with:
"Len, don't worry, I'll be down here a lot."
I know he will be. Scotty is a real racing and gambling man. Now he will have a tame bookie he can 'help'.
"Okay then, I'll give it a go, but if I take the chance, you'll have to sign up now. You can pay the exclusive fee in cash. I will write the deal as one thousand, not five thousand for each of the areas. Is that okay with you?"
Jeremy smiles and nods his head vigorously.
"You will have to give us four thousand in cash, and give us a cheque for the other thousand and the fifty per cent deposit on the twenty dispensers. Are you sure you can manage that?"
Jeremy was swaying and smiling happily.
"It's not a problem, Len."
He had a wide tipsy grin on his face, as he wrote the cheque and we signed the agreement.
"Len, if Scotty runs me to my bank I can get the cash from my strong box now, then it's all done and

dusted. No questions asked."

I thought to myself, what a lovely old New Zealand saying that is.

"Okay then, Scotty will look after you," which he most certainly did; and as only a mother could.

We worked on the dispenser deal for about six months; we made excellent money, and had a great time appointing happy agents all through New Zealand. I remember one very successful week when we sold three deals without returning to Auckland. The last was another very welcome cash deal from a guy who owned a garage. We should have had a photo of our celebration in the car as we drove out of town. It happened just as we were about to drive out of the motel in a small lower North Island town. The whole deal was signed, sealed and delivered in just three hours. That was from arriving and parking in the motel, to packing the dispenser onto the trailer and leaving. This memory has stayed with me ever since. We were just leaving the forecourt of the motel and our happy client was leaving as well. As we were about to pull out of the forecourt, he waved us down and hurried over to us. Our hearts sank, we thought he had buyer's remorse and that trouble was looming. Far from it, he leaned in the window and said, having just passed us something like three thousand dollars in cash and two thousand in a cheque:

"Hey you jokers, what were your names again?"

What a relief, anyway, as we left the town limits I

threw the cash in the air. It fluttered around in the car like confetti at a windy Wellington wedding. Oh yes, the good times were good, so very good. I think those moments; in a less responsible way of life, was what side tracked me away from the more normal, but definitely more secure future I could have carved out, by staying put, particularly in the 'Fenceco' and the still to come, 'Sharpies Golf Barns'; both very successful enterprises. Well as the world says, 'you win some and you lose some.'

I used to have visions of crowds of club members smiling, quaffing away on their beloved cold draught beer. It was not a hard vision to sell on, as all of the agents saw it and shared it. It was strange, but in all of these deals you reach a stage when you want to get out and feel you have done well enough out of it. Usually however, it was that the inevitable problems had started to arise and it was imperative that you got out. The applicants were slowing down, it was time to say goodbye to the beer business. At about that time, I had renewed an acquaintance with an old buddy, Nick Treacy. He had stumbled onto a good little earner that needed the old, Len Russell expansion touch. It was sitting waiting for me, I realised its potential, 'Trailer Business', here I come!

TRAILER FOR SALE OR RENT
THE NATIONWIDE, 'MOVE YOURSELF'
TRAILERS DEAL

This new opportunity reminded me of the famous Roger Miller song, *King of the Road* with its line about 'Trailers for sale or rent'. I found myself humming it whenever we discussed, or I thought about, this new get rich scheme. This little earner involved the marketing of move yourself trailers and dumpy trailers. In this project, we were involved with another larrikin, an Auckland character named Nick Treacy; an ambitious Irishman who always aspired to better things. In fact in his regular life he was a skilled sommelier at the superb Top of the Town restaurant in the Intercontinental Hotel. Nick was one of the early guys to push against the restrictive drink licensing laws. He suffered quite a few convictions in his endeavours of opening clubs and selling booze out of licensing hours and worse, in unlicensed premises. He was a frustrated Al Capone.

The trailer deals followed the usual format. We advertised up and down the country for agents to operate these specialized trailers for hire businesses. We granted/sold sole and exclusive rights to operate in designated areas. The successful purchasers were required to buy an initial stock of six trailers plus an exclusive rights fee of two

thousand five hundred dollars. The method of operation was simple, not costly and it worked. However, good as a deal might be, or sound, the investor deals did not sell themselves; they still required selling and that is where method, experience, confidence and bullshit came to the fore. Nick Treacy had started this business with two trailers in Auckland. The trailers, which were only horseboxes, were made by a small, two-man engineering company in Glenn Innes. The key to this being a profitable business lay in three things. One was the trailer itself; it was a fantastic static or mobile advert for itself. Picture one of them, a box trailer with an all-round background colour of white. Proudly displayed on them was this message, painted in bold red letters, it read,
'Move Yourself Trailer for hire, $10 per day.'

Then there was the phone number and address of the operator. It was simple and it worked, it was a great side-line business to run from home, which was Nick's plan till I got a hold of him and filled his head with ideas of expansion into a New Zealand-wide network. Which in retrospect absolutely proved one thing; which was that even a good conman could be conned, for Nick was certainly one of those.

The second feature that made them successful was the fact that the trailers were all road-registered, so they could legally be parked on busy roads for maximum exposure. It meant that an operating yard was not required. So apart from the street parking being a successful way of promoting the business, it was also a convenient method of storing them. As a safety precaution, they were fitted with a state of the art locking device. The operator only needed to keep one at home or base to service the demand. The third reason for success was the very high cost of using moving companies. Then there was the advantage of the many people out there who did not require a big truck to move, think students and singles. It added up to a really good sales pitch.

After some brain storming in Nick's illegal speakeasy, just down from the Albion pub, we hit on an idea that needed testing. We decided to repaint a trailer with the additional message, 'Local Agent needed for simple business, suitable to run from home. For details phone ... etc.' We would tow the van to a target town and park it in a high visibility place. After a day or two, a few tentative enquiries would trickle in. We always figured that if we got replies we would make sales. Our strike rate was about three replies required to make one sale.

Even though the trailers were a viable proposition we still needed a story to back up the sales pitch. We needed that final inducement; that little bit of magic that persuaded the target agent to sign the contract and write the cheque. What we needed was what we used to call a 'comforter'. The best one was usually another agent who was happy.

U Haul, a massive American enterprise geared to hiring out trailers and trucks for self-moving was a feature story in a magazine I stumbled on. Reading it gave me the idea for the much-needed comforter. I realised that to make this miniature version of U Haul work, we should re-gear it and promote it on the same business plan that they had succeeded with in America. It was the old get in on the ground floor opportunity - look how successful it was in America mantra. The key element in the U Haul method was the ability to hire and move, then drop your trailer off with the resident local agent. This was only possible with a nation-wide range of agents. I was excited about this tremendous add on. I was convinced that this was the comforter we were looking for and which we would surely need.

We now had a real story to tell. It was so convincing we used large blow up copies of the U Haul success story on the vans and in the high-powered applicant interviews. This new angle that allowed hirers to move intercity without having to return the trailer to home base was such a good story. It not only cut the cost and travel inconvenience for the hirer, but more importantly, it gave us an inflated story of great potential. We now planned to have the drop off agent receive a part of the hire fee, in the form of a drop off charge we built into the hire contract. The potential agent now saw himself as part of a nationwide enterprise. The nervousness that goes with stepping out in business, possibly for the first time, was extinguished. We all like the comfort of belonging. This whole proposition now moved from a good idea that was tempting, to a ground floor opportunity, an opportunity not to be missed. With this new weapon in our armoury what we did was persuade the agents to sign on now and just work the trailers locally. This was just until we could introduce the national network, which would greatly increase the agent's earnings and more importantly, the worth of their investment in the exclusive rights for their area. Subtle hints concerning a potential future buy out by a mysterious figure were stage whispered. It was someone with whom Len had been having discussions. Scotty explained that I was not able, because of a confidentiality agreement that I had to sign, to disclose any information. To further thicken the plot, Scotty became their best friend once more, and in his private conversations with the agents he drove them to a state of excitement and greed with his valuable inside knowledge.

Scotty could be anybody's best friend very quickly if there was a payoff looming. He would bitterly complain that Len's long involved discussions left his mind elsewhere, leaving him, Scotty, to do all the work. It was a sure way to get their confidence and belief in him, which helped set them up for the next pull and the easy exit.

Over a period of six months we sold nine agencies, which left quite a few areas still available. This was a deliberate ploy to assist our exit plan and get another pay off. Scotty and I figured now was the time to leave. We knew the great plan of the National Grid could not eventuate due to cost and probable low usage, but it had been the best of comforters. Nick Treacy was still a believer in the National Grid and the buyout possibilities. Scotty and I had not kept him in the reality loop. He was as smitten as the agents were. I suggested to Scotty that he best friend Nick and suggest to him that they could buy me out of the deal completely. They could then sell the idea to the agents, whose further investment money could fund it. Those two would then be in a great position to make a cartload of money when the project went national. In addition, there were plenty more areas to sell. Then there was the real benefit, they got rid of that know-it-all prick Len. What a bonus.

Hook line and sinker was how much he fell for it. Scotty was a great man in the middle. He made a huge show of negotiating with me, appearing to twist and turn and almost fall out with me. His efforts on behalf of the consortium were untiring. To whet their appetites the story we concocted was that U Haul were planning to come to Australia and

New Zealand and their strategy was to invest in existing companies. They would then use their experience and resources to expand. He let it slip that he thought U Haul were looking for a fifty per cent interest in our main company. I had taken the precaution of writing to U Haul and made some phone calls on different pretexts. I figured it could be valuable cover should I need it at a later, difficult date.

After a great deal of heart-wrenching dialogue, I eventually settled for a healthy pay off, leaving Nick and two agents as the main men owning the project. Scotty protested that he only wanted to help the agents and was pleased to act as the sales manager and consultant for them, for which they considered him a fine bloke. I slid off into the sunset and a glorious golfing holiday in Hawaii. Then really spoiling myself I carried on to Surfers Paradise in Queensland for more golf and meeting up with a few compatriots.

Scotty disentangled himself later, leaving Nick and his newfound friends to carry on empire building. Nick would have done okay, he would have prised more funds out of them for his oyster farm investments; his fall back scam. To this day, you can still spot the odd trailer parked in some provincial towns. The project trundled on for a few years filling some local demand, but never reached the expected dizzy heights of the kind that are usually only reached in dreams.

THE SOUTH PACIFIC MARKET
THE DEMENTED SCHOOL TEACHER AND
ANOTHER VISIT TO THE SUPREME COURT

A few more months had passed. I had been busy forming and organising promotions for the South Pacific Boxing Association. Scotty was back ready for duty looking for a new deal and it didn't take long to present itself. We launched into the Great North Road property deal and the South Pacific Market. Not only was this a quite unique and legitimate scheme, but it would also be performing a public service; yes that's what I said, a public service; but despite that trouble lay just around the corner again.

This really was a perfectly legitimate property deal; at least it started out like that. However, it landed us once again in the now familiar surroundings of the Supreme Court. Scotty and I were charged with fraud. It was the result of another hasty prosecution brought on by the bitter and long memories of the Auckland police officers.

The success of the beer machine and hire trailer businesses had put us in good stead with our bank manager. In addition the boxing promotions were starting to attract a large following and media publicity largely centred on me. The first one at the Intercontinental Hotel had been very successful. I'd had the foresight to gift a couple of tickets on a good table to Jim the bank manager, with whom we were developing a good relationship. We had taken him out with us a couple of times for lunch, drinks, and things. He was a nice guy, but a bit of a lonely man who had found himself stuck in a small branch of the bank and wasn't going any higher. From his conversations, we gathered he was pretty much brow beaten by a domineering wife at home.

Not much in business beats a bit of goodwill. Consequently one summer morning found Scotty and me in a meeting with Jim. He had phoned and asked us to see him about a matter which could be to our benefit. A bank manager's phone call does not usually have that connotation, in fact, quite the opposite. We got the formalities out of the way, which included my dropping another couple of tickets on his desk for the next boxing show.

"Look chaps, I have a bit of a problem I think you could help me with and make a quid yourselves."

"Jim, we would be only too glad to if we can; what's the problem?"

"Well it's like this; a client of mine has got in the crap. I had lent him some money and things haven't worked out and it won't look good for me with the bloody area manager. He's a prick and doesn't like me anyway."

"Shit Jim we can't let that happen. Lay it out for us."

"This bugger I lent to will go under soon and I won't

get the bank's money back, but there is a way out. The guy bought that single story building next to the Irish Centre on Great North Road; do you know it?"

"Yes I know it. I wondered what was going to happen with it. Funnily enough, I looked at it the other day when I was going past."

"Well, if you boys want that building I can work it for you. I have power of attorney over it as part of the bank's security. I can give you a mortgage so you guys get the title and the bank gets a dollop of its money back; that helps me, can it help you?"

"Jim, this all sounds okay. How about Scotty and I go and take a look at it and then meet you for lunch at Tony's in the High Street, say at one o'clock. I'll have a table sorted, is that okay with you?"

"That's fine Len. Here are the keys. See you at one."

Scotty and I waited till we got out the door before we allowed ourselves to celebrate. We knew instantly the value of the prize that had dropped into our laps. The Auckland property market was just taking off then and this was a good piece of real estate. It stood on a major road leading in or out of the city. It was well positioned and surrounded by inner city suburbs. There had to be something a couple of eager entrepreneurs could find to do with it and thereby increase its value. We jumped in Scotty's Ford Falcon station wagon, and made our way to Grey Lynn just a few yards past the Ponsonby Road and Great North Road junction. It was in the middle of where a lot of the Pacific Island immigrants had settled. Our prize was on the main road, slap bang in the middle of them. Many buyers or developers may have been put off by that. Not me though; I had a special connection in the area through three valuable assets. One, I was an old Freemans Bay boy, myself; secondly, by then I had forged strong links with the Ponsonby Rugby League Club. Thirdly and very importantly, I was deeply involved with and known in, the Pacific Island community via my boxing activities, as most of my fighters were Island boys. I generally made a habit of dealing with them through their community leaders such as the Reverend Sio. Through those connections I held a lot of sway there, as would become apparent when the trouble started.

Scotty pulled up right outside the premises; I jumped out and unlocked the big folding double doors that spread almost right across the entrance. Scotty drove the Falcon in and we surveyed the shell of our next project, whatever that was going to be. The building was one of those long single story high stud types, built for light industry. It looked as though at some point in its history it had been an engineering workshop of some kind or another. We strolled around tossing out ideas for its use and then discarding them. I was looking for premises for a gymnasium for the boxing, but that was something I wanted for myself and my plans for that didn't include Scotty. As this property was offered to us jointly its use and how we exploited it was something we had to agree together. We sat in his car and brainstormed. Then we hit on it; we would develop it as a Pacific Island market. Our quickly formulated plan was to divide it up into separate stalls; retail areas that we would lease out to individuals to own and operate their own little businesses, selling whatever product or services they chose. We knew the emphasis and demand would be on Island crafts, foods, clothing, souvenirs, etc. In fact we also got enquiries from bargain shoe dealers, plastic kitchenware sellers, fabric dealers, cheap carpet dealers; all sorts of opportunists saw it as a venue for their schemes. We figured after some quick measurements that we could put in up to twenty good-sized stalls. We knew that we could charge premium rent rates per foot. We also knew we would create a strong demand for these sites. Auckland was full of people wanting to start their own little businesses. We were also confident in our ability to talk this project up, creating demand and therefore the ability to charge key money from the sub-leaseholders.

That was all very promising and good, but really we knew that our main profit centre would be in the sale price we could achieve when we sold the building on, fully tenanted. The sale price would be determined by the annual rent return we could deliver. In Auckland at that time, a leased property generally could sell to an investor if it showed a ten per cent gross return. As an example, a building that was returning ten thousand dollars a year in rent would be calculated to be worth one hundred thousand dollars, all things being equal. Considering we were going to get this building, at mate's rates, we were looking at making a killing.

We had about an hour before the lunch appointment with Jim. My friend Tony, of Tony's Restaurant, didn't take bookings as he was always so busy. I got the use of a phone from a shop along the road and persuaded Tony to hold a three-seater for us as a favour. I had to promise him two tickets for the next boxing night. With that important detail covered we did some quick sums to assess what we referred to as, 'the earn.' In other words, what we could make on the deal. We also calculated the possible key monies we could pull off the punters.

Everything was looking Bonza. We calculated twenty lots of key money at fifteen hundred a time plus twenty rents, all with a couple of months in advance. Scotty was salivating; this was going to be a great deal. Even so, I knew it would still need an angle to get the stallholders excited and keen to buy in. No matter how good the deal, it would still need a story to ginger it up, all deals did.

We knew accurately what our costs would be. What we had to do now was fix a price with Jim, that kept him covered, while keeping the purchase price as low as could be for us. We calculated roughly what it was going to cost us to clean and tart up the building inside and out, including the building work and materials needed to build the separate stalls. I seem to remember that we needed about six grand to cover those things comfortably. Remember this was somewhere around 1971 and six grand did a lot in those days. Now we were going to work on Jim to provide that improvement fund, as well as the purchase mortgage plus a low, low, price. Here we go again.

We walked into Tony's and the owner met us at the door. He had obviously been waiting.

"Len, this joker on your table has brought someone else with him. They arrived at a quarter-past-twelve. I figured it was important for you, so I sat them down early in the little lounge room. They're on their second bottle of Penfold's Wolf Blass black label, at ten bucks a time. I just thought you would like to know," he said with a wry smile. Tony was another very smart Aussie. Tony with his brother and John Banks, a genuine boundary pusher and an interesting character who eventually became the Minister for Police and Mayor of Auckland, opened a chain of those restaurants. They were extremely successful and very good.

Some years later, in John's election campaign, he astounded us all with his tactics, but very clever ones as it turned out. It transpired that John's dad was an old crim. He had been a top of the range safe man and burglar in his day. As it happened, that little morsel of what could have been a scandal caused John no harm at all. I think in a way he used it to show that he was a 'good ol' boy', a Kiwi through and through, which he was. In any event it worked.   Such is the egalitarianism found in New Zealand. But the apples never really fall far from the tree. John was recently removed from parliament as an MP because of electoral fraud.

Tony took us through to our table; he then brought Jim and his friend from the lounge to join us. What a shock. They were both half pissed, but that wasn't the shock.   The shock was his friend. She was a quite attractive woman. Jim drunkenly introduced us to her as his 'very good mates.'
"This is Tricia, my girlfriend; I bet that surprised you boys didn't it. C'mon didn't it?"   He repeated himself rather tipsily.
"That surprised you didn't it? "He said again.
"You didn't think boring old Jim would have a girlfriend, now c'mon did you?"
"Well yes, Jim it sure is a surprise, especially one as attractive as Tricia. Have another drink," I said. I knew then everything was sweet and we were in a 'gotcha' situation.

We all enjoyed a great lunch; Jim, Tricia, and Scotty really gave the Wolf Blass a spanking. I persuaded Jim we had to talk the deal through there and then. He agreed with a huge tipsy grin. I noticed his hand suspiciously up Tricia's skirt, he was lucky he didn't touch Scotty up on the other side. I thought it prudent to tell him of our plans for the premises, while he was, shall we say, otherwise engaged. Also, while he had this other more important skirt task on his mind, he just nodded.

"Yes, yes, Len." He beamed, and asked us to get the stall-holders to open trading accounts with him. Apparently the area manager had been lambasting him on that score as well and was urging him to get some new accounts rolling.

The upshot was that we got the property at a very good price. It was even sweeter as the bank mortgage covered all the costs. The icing on the cake was that he also generously agreed an overdraft of ten grand for the alterations, which coincidently, left some 'change' for Scotty and me. The plus for Jim was that he was able to recover the other client's unsecured loan through the deal.

The next step was to get the key money secured and for that we would need a very impressive floor plan to beguile the punters with. Ours featured hordes of customers all crowding and jostling for bargains; all with happy faces; all clutching parcels and packages of recently purchased items. Whoever coined the phrase, 'one picture says more than a thousand words' knew what they were talking about. This plan was a minor masterpiece; it showed the finished market from three different angles. The stalls were cleverly illustrated; crammed full and absolutely decked out with colourful stock. It really sold the dream. The building quickly became a hive of activity. We had the entire interior cleaned and painted. We upgraded the front of the building. We had a magnificent 'South Pacific Market' sign painted and fitted prominently outside. It featured that seductive image of the Central Mall in a South Seas Island background. We installed a sound system playing Island and Maori music which drifted out through the open doors. We then had another sign mounted on a huge frame inviting interested parties wishing to be a part of this exciting scheme to come in and register with us. Then stealing a trick used by the group house builders, we built one stall as a demo. We ran a couple of large baited hook ads and waited for replies to come in; and they surely did. We signed and took deposits from four applicants on the very first day of interviews. We concentrated on the marketing and quickly sold most of the stalls. Everything seemed rosy.

At that time in New Zealand, 'weekend trading' was not permissible. A late Friday night system operated instead. Things were still pretty much locked down by the unions and the church in relation to Sunday trading. Big changes were coming, but they had not broken through yet. In our verbal sales pitch, we 'alluded' to these coming changes. At the time, this issue was under constant public debate. There was the usual correspondence to newspapers and radios talk shows etc. We took it upon ourselves to join the debate and kept a continuous avalanche of letters flowing to newspapers columns, under nom-de-plumes. We then had associates phoning in to the talk shows. We used that to push a positive note about the outcome of this very public issue. We hinted to the punters that we knew quite a bit about changes to the law that were in the pipeline.

A couple of prominent councillor's names had been surreptitiously mentioned as supporting the concept of the market, which they did. Somehow or other that support had been stretched to changing the trading hours. I cannot think how that could be! When that happened, a licence would be available to trade on weekends. In anticipation of problems in this area we made sure that there was a massive grey area between what was said and possibly assumed and what was written and signed for in the agreements.

THE OLD 'GET OUT' MANOUVRE

Scotty had a particular talent for buddying up with the punters. It always worked. He, called it his 'old mating' method, whereby he made friends and confidantes of the agents. Supposedly this was all very much behind my back. From this position, he would persuade them of the good long-term prospects of the project and that it would be a good deal to buy me out, then control their own destiny.

They invariably and unwittingly, gleefully embraced the idea of doing to someone else, what had been done to them. Their very astute and now best friend Scotty naturally was entitled to, and took, a fee for his strenuous efforts on their behalf. It was a virtually foolproof method of bailing out of dodgy situations. Which in all honesty is what most, if not all, of our projects generally finished up as.

In anticipation of likely unrest and troubles ahead with the stallholders we thought we should have the exit strategy in place early. Once again it involved Scotty assuming the role of best friend. He was so good at it that sometimes I wondered if it was assumed. He could convince anybody he was a lifelong, loyal buddy. He was so accomplished and vigorous in the role that I think he sometimes confused himself. The first step was to form the stallholders into an association with a committee. If Kiwis had one weakness in their makeup it was an overzealous attitude to micro-democracy. They loved committees; they saw them as the panacea for all administrative ills. If three or more Kiwis got together for a common purpose, were planning an outing, or had a grievance, they formed a committee. For our purposes, it was the perfect vehicle to offload a potentially big problem. They jumped into the association idea; Scotty had been doing some gentle stirring on the inside. It was along the lines of how much better they would be than me at running the market, especially if they controlled it themselves. This was particularly so because I always had other projects and boxing on my mind which distracted me from the market. We recognised that it was very important to have them in charge prior to opening and the problems of weekend trading coming home to roost. As expected, although I feigned surprise, I was approached by a committee of three stallholders who had elected themselves as spokespersons for the newly formed, grandiose and soon to be constituted, South Pacific Market Traders Association. The intrepid delegation, were led by a bolshie failed schoolteacher who now had dreams of being a successful businessman. Scotty had picked his target well and in secret drinking sessions had fired him up with dreams beyond his wildest imagining. I don't suppose there is any need to add that his teaching career was flagging. This was his chance to be a king of industry, if only he could unseat me. He could then take over the reins of the market for which he and his new and only friend Scotty had very confidential plans to take nationwide. He saw his little stall, which he had entrusted to his wife to run, and the winning of this commercial joust with me as his way up that great commercial ladder. That ladder could take him to the success that had so far eluded him in his life. Now he had a newfound great friend who really seemed to understand him and recognise his talents and who also liked him as a man. That was something those other bastard teachers and headmasters he had known in his life had never done. The world was now his to conquer, but he had to get rid of Len first. He saw his wife and acquaintances viewing him in a new light, almost heroic, as he made his mark and plundered the commercial world with this great opportunity that had come his way.

Robert the schoolteacher led off. He was, he said, acting for all when he spoke. I acknowledged that as his elected right. His brief was that the 'association' felt that I was not able to address myself enough to opening and promoting the market. While all agreed that the market was a great concept, it now needed a single-minded person to drive it to its full potential. He was, as politely as possible, asking me to step down and leave the running and development from here on in to him and his committee, but really to him. While he was going through his well-rehearsed routine the other two shuffled nervously, but indicated they concurred with their leader.

I affected a surprised and hurt attitude, while protesting that I was doing my best with the stallholders' interest at heart. I pointed out that I could not stand down, as I had responsibilities to ensure success for the market and that if I stood aside I would still be responsible, but with no input or control it would be a bad commercial decision for me. The discussion dragged on and it broke up with us agreeing to meet again in two days' time, when we had all had time to think of some options. Over the next two days Scotty and the teacher carried on with their clandestine meetings. They kept most of the others in the loop, thereby committing them all. They loved Scotty, so by now I was a complete bastard who had to be got rid of. Scotty convinced them that a fortune was waiting. He knew what I was planning and that was to develop similar markets throughout New Zealand and I was not including him. What a prick, after all he had done for me. (It was the old we're going national trick again.) Scotty convinced them the best way was to buy me out and make me sign an agreement not to compete with them. That would leave the way clear for the conspirators to share in the profits from a national chain run by the teacher, with Scotty as their guiding light.

They came back to me with a proposal. Scotty

declared himself with them as he said he had found out I was planning to do the dirty on him and expand the markets without him. He made a great song and dance about how let down he felt and it was best that we now went our separate ways. I had to suffer a quick public lecture from him on loyalty etc. I asked for more time to think about things and suggested we meet the following day. They agreed, now feeling confident and bolshie. They were going to raise the money between them. Twenty thousand was the figure they would go to on Scotty's urging. However, there was one more clause I needed in the agreement before I would sign and clear the way for them. I made a great show of battling the restrictive non-competition clause, but in the end agreed to it. While that detail was roundly thrashed out, I slipped in my clause saying that I would not accept any responsibility for the on-going business. All responsibility passed to them and I was released from all obligations. I had the foresight to have all leaseholders sign this release document. In their eagerness to have me right out of it they signed the agreement with the release clause. The teacher gave me a cheque drawn on his personal account and the others paid him. I was on the golf course, early the next morning.

The consortium battled bravely on for a few months. After a while it became apparent that a weekend trading licence was not about to materialise. The now very pissed off members of the association had all turned on the schoolteacher, blaming him for this turn of events. The dreams they had built up on his promises were shattered and old stuffy schoolteacher was to blame. It was him who had talked them into pushing me out and now they were on a sinking ship.

Robert the schoolteacher had got completely carried away and hastily thrown in his teaching job, telling the Head and colleagues in no uncertain manner where to get off, demonstrating the newfound confidence of a man on the way up. He had persuaded the Association members to all contribute to his salary; now they had had enough and they saw him as the architect of all their problems. The honeymoon period was well and truly over.

Unfortunately, certain gentlemen in the fraud squad got involved when the school teacher, 'Robert the Burnt' as he was nicknamed, realised that he had been well and truly played and lodged a complaint with the Police. The schoolteacher had become demented. The loss of the money must have hurt; throwing in his job must have compounded it, realising what had happened to him drove him right over the top. He kept calling the Association members to meetings in his efforts to pursue us. He set himself up as co-ordinator of the action group, though we were reliably informed that many of them thought he was in cahoots with us, an idea that we encouraged. It had all become somewhat confusing. He harangued the stall holders and dominated the meetings in his crusade. Speaker after speaker repeated the same sad story. Most of them would then turn on him arguing that all was well until his interference in what could have been a happy outcome for them. They did not know what or who to believe anymore and consequently they harboured deep suspicions concerning him. Apparently, the meetings were a shambles. On one occasion, he was accompanied by his suburban lawyer, who did not really want to be there. The lawyer would forlornly attempt to restore order as everyone loudly vented their anger at the teacher. It was well beyond him. All he had ever done before was some suburban conveyancing. On that occasion Robert the Burnt lost it completely. One of the stallholders had been heckling him. On top of these problems it turned out that that particular stallholder had been bonking the school teacher's missus. Apparently he yelled like a coyote at the moon. He leapt forward and grasped the offender around the neck in his demented rage. Robert the Burnt was a big old country boy and it took all those present to drag him off.

The crap really hit the fan when the lawyer suggested a plan to recoup the investments. All was well until he appealed for a fighting fund to action it.   The stallholders were unusually sensitive to being stung again and reacted very badly.   The request caused a noticeable change in the atmosphere.   For his efforts he was roundly booed and rudely directed to the schoolteacher for money; in their opinion, the person who bore the great responsibility for their predicament.   This new situation and the accusations were obviously causing more grief for the demented one.

The schoolteacher later joined the local branch of the Labour Party, where he became an absolute nuisance. He raved on about the evils of capitalism to whoever would listen.   When given the opportunity to speak his subject never changed. He spouted forth on unbridled corruption, and it being the duty of the Labour Party to clear the country of carpetbaggers and rogues.

He had developed a pathological dislike of Scotty; his former confidante and very close friend who had lead him up the garden path. He conveniently overlooked his own part in conspiring with Scotty against me. The detectives couldn't keep a straight face whenever that part of the investigation was touched on. I learnt later that the fraud squad probably would not have pursued the complaint without pressure from the powers above who were still smarting from the Toofats incident. The case against us was not cut-and-dried and intent would have to be clearly demonstrated.   Intent is the deciding factor in cases of fraud. Our legal team thought that it would be extraordinarily hard to prove; however, we were not that surprised when the Crown Solicitor's office decided to prosecute us.

We appeared once again in the Auckland Supreme Court. The schoolteacher was there with a packet of sandwiches and a flask of tea. There were other stallholders there, but they were avoiding the schoolteacher almost as much as us. His once tidy hairstyle was now unkempt and he had the wild stare in his eyes of an obsessed man. The case went on for four days. The police brought their heavy artillery to bear and the court seemed flooded with senior officers. We thought this was a surreptitious effort to show the jury that they knew us.

The case proved hard for both sides; it had so many twists and turns in it. The judge and jury seemed mystified by many aspects of it. Their perplexed expressions showed that on the evidence provided they were amazed at the gullibility of the stall purchasers. The prosecution were intent on trying to prove that we had set the whole thing up as a con. They had to prove that if they were to succeed. They called a procession of the stallholders as witnesses, each swearing that we had stated that we would definitely have a weekend trading licence. They all stated that they only invested in the stalls on that basis. Whether that claim was right or wrong, it was suspiciously the only point that they collectively professed to have a clear memory on. Even if true, it was so obviously rehearsed. They also suggested that my plan to go nationwide with the project was just a false inducement to encourage them to buy me out. So there you have it, two days of attack and accusations of broken promises. Old school teacher was positively salivating, was this his big moment? He was very confident. He was beaming and constantly button-holing reporters and anybody who would listen to him in the foyer.

In regards to the project going national, I had indeed made plans along those lines. I had instructed real estate agents to locate premises for me to inspect in Hamilton, Wellington and Christchurch a few weeks prior to selling out to them. This revelation and supporting evidence of it threw some doubt on their assertions that it was only a concocted story to part them from their money. Then of course, there was my release clause, which they had all joyously signed, witnessed and agreed to. I don't think they did themselves any favours bringing that up.

Our lawyers did a very good job. They produced evidence of the national discussions and the select committee hearings looking into the changing of shopping hours. They asked both Scotty and me if we honestly believed that changes were imminent in those regulations. Our answer was a firm yes, supported by letters we had sent to various councillors and MPs in support of it. We contended that we honestly believed that the changes were imminent. In fact, trading hours did change some time after the case finished. The issue was so topical it had to favour our argument that we definitely thought the breakthrough was nigh. It helped us whatever way you looked at the situation. Doubt was a priceless commodity and we had mined some. The upshot was that the jury very fortunately thought there was plenty of doubt; too much in this case to convict us of fraud. We also produced the signed stall purchase agreements and not one of them referred to seven days trading, only the fact that we would apply for a licence. Astonishing as it was for some, particularly old schoolteacher, the court found us not guilty on all charges. We were discharged without a blemish on our characters; well the boys at Cook Street probably would not necessarily have agreed with that.

TAKING THE STORY BACK A COUPLE OF YEARS, THE BIRTH OF THE SOUTH PACIFIC BOXING ASSOCIATION

At the start of my venture into the world of professional boxing and management I had attempted to work with the Auckland Boxing Association (the ABA) in a joint promotion venture, but this soon became an impossible task. Decisions were so hard to get; the committee members of that era mostly seemed more interested in protecting their own positions and getting free tickets than in making anything happen. I quickly resolved to push on without them. To do this I needed an umbrella organization as the legal promoting body approved and licensed by the Department of Trade and Industry.

I had studied the legal requirements relating to promoting boxing at the time. I prepared a presentation package and made my pitch to the relevant government Department. I was very pleased that in the face of bitter opposition from the NZBC and the ABA good sense prevailed and much to the establishment's displeasure, a licence to promote boxing was granted to the SPBA, in effect me.

I believe this may have been the first time a licence to promote boxing had ever been granted outside of the existing national controlling body. Thus came about the mightily successful South Pacific Boxing Association of which I was the President and promoter and which revitalized boxing in New Zealand and the Pacific islands in the early seventies.

My first promotion was a huge success; anybody who was anybody was there; every seat and every table quickly sold. It was a glamorous night out that Aucklanders absolutely loved. The press were very generous in their reporting of it. I was still a little naive about them. I learnt later how fickle they could be. Sports-mad and boxing-starved Aucklanders just loved this concept of promoting; which the press likened to a combination of sport, fashion and a 'champagne Charlie' show. The reporters were generous, they lauded it in their columns and we were here to stay. The celebration party went on into the early hours of the morning. Every one of the table holders came to me and re-booked their tables for future events. My telephone went mad. The hotel office was fielding calls from the public seeking to book a table, or get their name on a cancellation list. Many of the callers claimed to know me well. I did not know I had as many old mates. I confess to revelling in it. Could you blame me? It wasn't a bad result for a Ricky boy who'd arrived in the country with the princely sum of eight pence in his pocket.

Like many ventures, it developed a life of its own. It was to take me on a helter-skelter journey, loaded with excitement, notoriety, jealousy and danger. I found myself rubbing shoulders with Australasia's and America's heaviest gangsters and crooks. This has always has been a part of the professional boxing scene worldwide. This was not quite what I had been anticipating when launching the upmarket black tie boxing nights.

Newspaper proprietors sell their papers on scandals, gossip and confrontation. All of these topics are usually connected to politics, religion, sport and show business. They are the usual ingredients foremost in an editor's demands of his reporters. Papers may carry interesting news, international or otherwise, but it is scandal, preferably local, that governs the circulation figures. I soon realized that you had to give journalists just that if you wanted their attention. They thrived on controversy, so I made sure that I gave them plenty of that. By this time I had developed connections to newspaper and television journalists. Surprise, surprise, they particularly enjoyed conducting their interviews in the plush surroundings of Auckland's leading men's club and massage parlour, the infamous Pacific Sauna Parlour. By this time Ray Miller had joined me as a partner in my new venture. Ray was a good man to have with you when there was trouble brewing and in that business trouble was never far away.

There was always plenty of free alcohol on hand served by the ladies of the house. I have never yet met a journo who was not an active supporter of the brewing industry. Funny, but that seemed to slant a lot of the resulting publicity in our favour.

I was regularly invited and happy (posing again) to be a guest on talk back radio shows. I was generally answering questions from disillusioned callers about the Auckland boxing scene and the problematic ABA. The newspapers were following the feud between the two associations and wanting more and more interviews, so we started receiving a lot of airtime.

We gained a lot of credibility when the well-known Bob Jones resigned from the Wellington boxing association, and joined the SPBA. It was a decisive action, which was big news, particularly in boxing and sport circles. In line with the very articulate speaker that he was, there was even greater demand for interviews. Bob could command an audience if he was discussing the mating habits of the long billed Eskimo ant, so his contribution was enormous. His encyclopaedic knowledge of boxing, combined with his political expertise made him a formidable ally in this dispute. There was so much interest generated that we were asked to do a joint interview for the New Zealand Broadcasting News channel. The dispute was now elevated; it was no longer a provincial sports body spat, it was national news. When I was invited on to the talkback Radio shows I confess to planting irate callers who would ring up the show berating the ABA and lauding the efforts and promotions of the SPBA. As it happened the plants were not needed as the topic was hot and plenty of genuine calls came in. After the show, we would have debriefing meetings with the planted callers in the bar of the Pacific. There were always free drinks, humour and female entertainment.

Bob Jones with Ghana's Joe Tetteh who was in New Zealand to fight Joey Santos in a World title elimination bout.

The pressure eventually got too much and the Auckland Boxing Association rolled over. They then limited themselves to promoting and developing amateur boxing for a couple of years. That had been their original brief and to be fair, it was one which they were quite good at. We were then unchallenged in the professional field in Auckland. I had contracted all the key fighters to me personally by this time. We held record numbers of promotions, including National and South Pacific titles and elimination bouts featuring international class boxers. Our shows were invariably sell-outs. I had happily become the lucrative main supplier of Kiwi and Pacific island boxers to the insatiable Australian television networks, who were locked in their own battle. It was a ratings war for their weekly TV ringside boxing shows. I was to find out that the fight game was not only hard in the ring; the really tough encounters took place outside of it. Professional boxing is a very hard place to make money and a harder place still to keep friends.

As an example, take the managers and trainers. I swear they all had personality changes if their charge showed the slightest improvement in form, or managed to sneak a win on an undercard bout. Their mind-set seemed to change. All of a sudden they had a world champion in the making. A reasonable example could be as follows. Think a young prelim boxer who had just scratched a points win in an undercard six rounder. Overnight he becomes a prospect right up there with a Muhammad Ali including his shuffle. In the minds of his manager and family a star and a meal ticket had been born. They then become impossible to deal with. This is as likely as Forest Gump going to bed at night and waking up the next morning as Einstein. You wouldn't bet on it.

As this tale takes shape, there will be more references to boxing. Therefore, I think it incumbent on me to advise readers of some very important facts. As I have said, boxing was as tough outside the ring as it was in it. You may also think that we were quite cruel in some of the methods we used to dominate and control professional boxing. In many spheres of life and often for the overall good, radical methods are required. In support of our actions against the continued opposition and interference of the ABA I would like to quote an extract from the New Zealand Boxing Yearbook 1972, published by Robert Jones Holdings. In specific regard to the Auckland Boxing Association, it reads as follows,

"This body has averaged a mere nine contests annually over the last four years - an appalling record of apathy in the country's largest population centre, with the advantage of its massive boxing loving Polynesian population and the availability of most of the country's boxers actually on tap. Theirs is a consistent record, but is consistently bad and shows in an unfavourable light to the 39 bouts they promoted in 1966 and 1967.

The game has been kept alive in New Zealand despite the above failures due to the efforts of the

following..."

It then goes on to mention Messrs Russell and Scott of Auckland who have, *"put a spark into the sport"* and says that, *"their zeal and energy will undoubtedly see them figure prominently in the sport in New Zealand in the coming years and sparks should fly."*

And indeed we did. We promoted or were involved in co-promoting something in excess of forty professional bouts a year during our first two years alone. That resulted in lots of opportunities, and exposure for the boxers; some achieving high Commonwealth and world rankings. A few achieved international recognition, in spite of interference from a certain Mr R. Clarke, the then secretary of the British Boxing Board of Control, encouraged by the jealous ABA. These men should have supported, not hindered, New Zealand boxing. However real results were achieved and the major upside of all this was that the New Zealand boxing scene was once again taken seriously in the international boxing world.

MORE BOXING, BLACK TIES AND A CHANCE TO POSE IN MY WHITE TUXEDO

Me (left) and Scotty (far right), at first 'Black Tie' promotion in the Intercontinental Ballroom, Auckland. Scotty features in many of the stories. He was a very funny man.

I had become aware of an organization in London called, I think, the Victorian sporting club. I think I saw its boxing activities on television. The VSC was an umbrella organization formed to promote boxing in a uniquely attractive manner. They departed from the usual well-worn, run down, often tacky arenas. They completely changed the concept, and instead took their evenings to top London hotels. The promotions were spectacular, black tie dinner events. I firmly believed that the Auckland public was ready for something new entertainment wise. I had no doubt that they would support something upmarket like this; after all, we had our fair share of resident posers. I couldn't wait to get my white DJ on and join them. I am embarrassed to admit that for those nights I became one of them. I liked myself in the heady role of glad-handing and hosting the punters, sipping champagne and generally showing off. What a stage this was for me to prance on.

Timing is everything and on this occasion my timing was right. I realized that to make this happen there were two major ingredients required. One was a suitable venue and the other a good supply of boxers. Fortunately the Intercontinental hotel, Auckland's first major international chain hotel, had just opened. The hotel was built to capitalise on an expected influx of international visitors to Auckland, as at about this time New Zealand and Auckland with its redeveloped airport were making serious efforts to become major players in the international tourist business. The Big I (as it was known) featured a large, plush ballroom that the hotel management was having great difficulty exploiting. The design of the room could not have been more suited to my purposes; it was as if it been designed for boxing. A deal was promptly agreed. The hotel management at that time was very progressive and did very well out of the deal. The exposure for them was priceless. I promoted there for twelve months attracting television coverage and bundles of supporting newspaper publicity; so they were very happy. The second ingredient needed to ensure success was a supply of skilful, colourful boxers. I was fortunate once again; New Zealand and the Pacific Islands had these in abundance. All they needed was the opportunity and a platform to perform on. It seemed like overnight we turned the top performers into in demand stars.

Joey Santos K.O.'s Rex Redden for New Zealand title in the Intercontinental Ballroom. I managed and promoted Joey to a World title elimination bout versus Joe Tettah, which he lost.

C'MON AND MEET THIS REAL CHARACTER AND BOXING AFICIONADO

"Let's go Len, let's go," Bob called out as he walked determinedly out of the automatic doors of the South Pacific hotel in down town Auckland. He did not have his happy face on, which was quite normal for Bob in the mornings. It was hard to believe that this person, still in his thirties, was a property wizard and self-made millionaire many times over. He dressed conservatively. He did not have a happy countenance, but that was Bob. In reality he possessed a great sense of humour; he was well able to laugh at himself, but that was generally later in the day. He threw his bag onto the back seat and jumped into the front with me. 'C'mon, Len, c'mon, I don't have all day," as if it were me holding him up. I had been there at the agreed time fifteen minutes ago, but I knew there was no point in bringing that up. It must have been in the very early seventies. I was experiencing one of my life's 'ups' and things were going well. I had fallen into the poser trap as can easily happen. I was driving a Roller; Christ I had become one of them, I was king of the posers. I had become friendly with this man, who was on his way to becoming a very prominent citizen. We were both in our mid-thirties at the time. He went on to achieve great success in business on an international scale. He became a force in New Zealand politics. He achieved all this while becoming a best-selling author. Some years later, the New Zealand government deservedly knighted him for his efforts in business and politics.

I had become involved with him through my move into professional boxing. I had heard of and read of him and when I met him he certainly lived up to his reputation. I had been very busy getting my boxing interests off the ground, so it was a certainty that we would collide, collude, or conspire, when we met. It had to happen due to the progressive natures we shared and our mutual desire to take boxing forward. Though our interests were the same, our reasons for doing what we did were not. For him boxing was more than a hobby, it occupied something greater than that, it certainly was not money or fame; he had both of those rascals in bundles. He had been a boxing blue in his student days at Wellington University and had become a boxing aficionado. I think some of the main indulgences in his life were his travels around the globe to attend major bouts from prestige ringside seats. My reasons, on the other hand, were mainly mercenary; I could see an opportunity and was keen to exploit it. I have to confess that at that stage of my life I found the notoriety that went with it fascinating. However, good publicity and popularity can be short lived; there is no such thing as a loyal press.

At that time Bob was serving on the committee of

the Wellington Boxing Association and was about to be elected to the New Zealand Boxing Council. He was rather frustrated at its lack of activity and wanted to apply himself to improving it. Meanwhile, he had been closely watching the SPBA progress and was impressed by it. He had long been a champion of professional promoters taking the lead and thereby returning New Zealand boxing to the status it had previously enjoyed.

My promotions were progressing well. We had hit gold immediately, running our multi-bout promotions and really getting things moving. This was more to his nature and liking; he really did have a love affair with boxing. However the resulting outcome of all this was a pleasant surprise for me, but not so for all of the boxing fraternity. Our prominent New Zealander surprised everybody and resigned his position on the Wellington Boxing Association. He then joined me on my South Pacific Association as the Chairman. Because of this coup, we spent quite a lot of time together through those defining years. Together we became very influential in the New Zealand and South Pacific boxing scene. He was a strange man in many ways, but a man I came to admire. He was hugely talented with a great intellect. I am talking here, if you have not guessed, of one Sir Robert Jones better known to most Kiwis as Jonesy, or just Bob. In my bewildering life I have met many characters from all fields of endeavour. Bob is right up there with the best. He was a very formidable man as is evidenced by his success in life. He was a perfectionist, which for me was sometimes hard to take, as my nature has always been more to the creative side of things. I have always been prepared to look for, and unfortunately take, short cuts, for which I sometimes paid a high price. Not so with Bob, he was the most attentive to detail man that I have ever met.

On that fine spring morning Bob and I were driving about 80 miles south from Auckland to Hamilton, which lies in the Waikato province of the North Island. The area was known for its dairy farming, tough rugby players and a strong Maori heritage. Bob was attempting to purchase a Main Street building; from memory I think it was the Victorian Building. Our conversation at the time was mainly about the boxing scene in New Zealand. Our conversation turned to human behaviour; probably because of the problems which always come when dealing with professional boxers. I was probably moaning at the time about the hassles I was getting from the family of a fine Samoan middleweight, Battling La'avassa, who could have been going places if things had been left to us. He had great potential and in fact he went on and won forty of his forty-one fights, the later ones against very good opposition.

Of all the Pacific Island boxers I promoted, my

experience was that the Samoans and Tongans were the best, particularly the middleweights. All the Islanders had plenty of courage, but it just seemed that Samoans had that little extra bit of natural ability and aggression. It shows up in their rugby as well. They do not seem to have any respect for their own bodies, or those of anybody else when competing. I think the day will come when one of them, probably a Samoan, wins a major world title. To my way of thinking, it would be in the lower weight divisions and probably at middleweight. I think that is what triggered Bob's next statement. Bob had a theory at the time and if I understood him correctly, it was something along the lines that all things that happen to us in our lives are connected to the present, the past, and the future as if there are things that have to be in life and things you cannot escape from. If I use my own experiences of life as a measuring stick for Bob's theory, I would have to agree with him, it just took me longer to get there.

THE DARK SIDE OF BOXING AND
THE RIOT AT STANLEY STREET STADIUM

Riotous End As Samoan Keeps Unbeaten Record

By RALPH KING

Disqualification of the San Francisco boxer Jimmy Lester in the fourth round of his bout with "Fighting" La'avassa, the Auckland-based Samoan, produced a riot at Stanley St last night as fans stormed the ring and bottles and other missiles pelted into the arena.

Guilty of frequent infringements, including kidney punching, Lester had roused the ire of the crowd—which included many Polynesians—and police intervention was needed to restore order.

A cutting from the Auckland Star

The genteel black tie nights were the most enjoyable of our promotions. They were glamorous; they gave the opportunity to interact with the guests. I always used to throw a private party after the shows were over. These became a rather special sought after event. There were always plenty of Auckland's big noters there, showing off and buying champagne for everybody.

I have to relay a special night, which could have cost me my licence. It was a sold-out, outdoor promotion at the Stanley Street Stadium. In those

215

days that outstanding venue was a bit limited size-wise and was licensed for a bit less than three thousand seated patrons. My top draw card at that time was Battling La'avassa. He had fought fourteen times as a professional in his native Samoa and in Australia winning all of those contests. He had made it known that he was very keen to live and fight in New Zealand where he had family ties. The emigration route from the Islands into New Zealand was quite strictly controlled. There was a quota system operating, which was rigorously enforced.

One morning I was sitting in the 246 coffee lounge in the Kerridge Building in Queen Street, which might as well have been my office. I was chatting to Bert Clapham and we were arranging a game of golf for that afternoon with a contact of his. We were in a deep and quite heated discussion over handicaps. The game was to be for big bucks; with Bert, you could not be too careful. We were still debating it when this joker I knew vaguely by his nickname 'the tipster' sashayed up to the table. He was sporting a big sales representative's smile with his hand outstretched in overacted friendship. It turns out that he was the son of the manager of La'avassa in Samoa. He was a slippery customer and a gambler. He hung around on the edge of the illegal bookie fraternity, taking and making bets. He was that classic case of a hopeless gambler who operated on both sides of the fence; I knew of him as he also used to hang around the boxing gyms. As well as his bookie come betting activities, he ran an illegal tipping service for gamblers, hence the nickname. He asked if he could have a word when we were finished as he had a boxing proposition that would definitely interest me. I looked at Bert,

"Do you mind if I hear this? You can sit in."

Bert was a big buyer of tickets, sometimes a whole row. He used them to entertain his clients and agents. He ran his illegal betting racket like a polished business. Like most bookies and gamblers, he was a boxing aficionado. No harm could come from his being present and there could be a gain.

"Okay then, sit down and have a coffee."

I waved across to Val Lucas, the efficient manageress; she smiled and organized another round of coffees. Once the drinks arrived, I turned to the tipster and said:

"Okay what's the deal then? Let's have it."

The tipster got straight into the proposition. He started to give me the big build-up on La'avassa. I cut him short.

"That's not necessary, you don't need to sell him to me; I know all about him."

The Tipster was the son of La'avassa's Samoan trainer, Eric Beetham. Eric Beetham was also the father of Monty Beetham, another good Samoan middleweight, who joined us a year later. The tipster then put it to me that if I could arrange for La'avassa to enter New Zealand permanently, he would happily fight exclusively under the SPBA banner and sign a management contract with me. It sounded good, but I knew there was a deal still to be agreed. He wanted ten per cent of the purses La'avassa would earn to go to his father. I readily agreed; that was pretty much standard procedure. He then came up with the curly one. The tipster asked for a further ten per cent for himself. I was not happy with that. I thought about it and offered ten per cent for them to split as they saw fit. Alternatively, I offered to pay him a fee of 100 dollars every time La'avassa fought. After plenty of hot air and the usual 'I can go to the ABA they will pay it,' I invited him to do just that. He knew who was doing all the promoting and he reluctantly agreed to my offer.

That was how my major draw card for the next three years fell into my hands. It was late August 1971. We worked fast; I was able to arrange his entry successfully. He had his first fight under my management on October 21 in Sydney, where he beat a good performing, tough, Aussie country boy, Errol McIvor. He beat him in seven rounds with the ref stopping the fight. Over the next three years, La'avassa blazed a trail through all the Australian and New Zealand middleweights. He also fought and beat top English, Irish and American boxers. Two of the Americans had previously enjoyed ratings of 3 and 4 in world rankings. These were heady days. Not just for me and the SPBA, but also and more importantly for New Zealand boxing. It was back where it belonged. Not just because of La'avassa's efforts, but also a crop of top class boxers had emerged that could appear in any arena anywhere in the world and not be disgraced. They included the Santos brothers, Ali Afakasi, Monty Beetham, Eddie Wulf and Ben Compain (had he trained harder).

Before I took him on, I figured I should first get myself up to Samoa and check the deal and arrangements with La'avassa himself.   This turned into an idyllic week's holiday, as well as the completion of an important acquisition.   While there I enjoyed excellent hospitality. I found myself treated as something akin to McHale of the old TV show, *McHale's Navy*. I had asked Ali Afakasi, a very good Samoan light welterweight, to accompany me to Samoa to assist me in any negotiations that might arise with La'avassa and his manager.

While in Samoa on that first trip I met a very gracious elderly woman. The great reverence shown to her by all those round her was mightily impressive. She was a very interesting character. She was the famous Aggie Grey, the owner and founder of the equally famous hotel that bore her name. It is part of Samoan folklore that she was the inspiration for the outrageous character Bloody Mary in the fabulous Rodgers and Hammerstein musical and 1958 film, *South Pacific*. Aggie Grey's Hotel started its life as Aggie's Drinking Club catering for American troops on rest and recuperation from the bloody Pacific theatre in the Second World War. It stood in a unique location. It was a beachside *fale* (house) on the edge of an idyllic lagoon. It was apparently a pleasure Mecca for the service personnel based in Apia. Unfortunately I missed its glory days by about thirty years. However, the upside was I have always enjoyed the show *South Pacific* and its songs. Having known the real life Aggie always brought an extra and pleasurable dimension to the show for me.

Two great South Pacific and New Zealand Champions, on the left, Battling La'avassa and on the right, Ali Afakasi pictured with SPBA Chairman Bob Jones. I took Ali to Samoa to help negotiate La'avassa's contract. It was there I met the famous Aggie Grey of the Musical, South Pacific fame.

The trip to Samoa ended well. La'avassa confirmed the deal regarding management and his future boxing career. I had developed some very useful contacts in the emigration department by then. I seemed to be there arranging entry visas for various boxers almost weekly. I always took on this task myself. I always knew who appreciated a few prime tickets for the shows, plus entry to the well-publicised weigh-ins, drinks parties and receptions afterwards. I was always happy to spread a little good will; it can take you a long way.

La'avassa had a great career with the SPBA. We were good for him and he was equally as good for us. He was an amazing draw card. He was a sell-out attraction every time he fought in Auckland. The large Samoan community were boxing mad and could not get enough of him. Whether the promotions were indoor or outdoor events, it was always a full house. He won all his fights under my control. Many of these took place in Australia, some in the Pacific Islands. Unfortunately, towards what became the latter stages of his career, he suffered an injury. Whilst on holiday in Samoa he was hurt in a village fracas. We were told that he had been struck on the head by a stone thrown by an adversary in an inter-village dispute. His New Zealand trainer, a good straight operator George Cammick, a New Zealand legend, was a very experienced boxing man. He thought the world of La'avassa and immediately recommended that he should retire. I agreed with George and I advised him to retire as well, which he agreed to do. However, after a short time, like most boxers, he could not face life in the slow lane and returned to the sport. He made a comeback under new management. The bout was an elimination contest for the Commonwealth Middleweight Championship. I had been steering him towards that bout. He put up a good show, but lost comprehensively on points. That injury received in the brawl had blighted an outstanding career. It is to his credit though that he lost only that one bout, the last.

One of La'avassa's memorable moments was a bout with the American middleweight boxer Jimmy Lester who had reached a high world middleweight ranking of four earlier in his career. Jimmy was a very good American pro. He had mixed it with the best, though now on the slide and past his prime, he was a still a good test for La'avassa. The match was a 'catch weight' contest. I had set the limit at eleven stone nine pounds. The actual middleweight limit was eleven stone six pounds. We knew Jimmy had weight problems, so had included a penalty of two hundred dollars for every pound above the agreed limit. In the package, we had also included a good welterweight, Bobby Jordan, the Californian state champion. We had matched him to fight another popular and talented Polynesian boxer of ours, Si Nomura. This was an outstanding quality double bill that could have graced any of the world's top arenas.

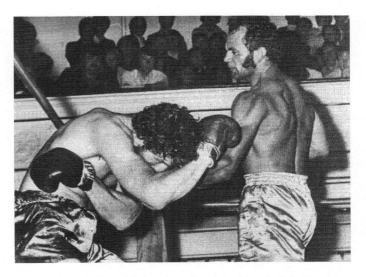

Gentle Ben claimed four knockouts on the riot night, one officially in the ring and three on the apron.

Amongst the preliminary fighters, we had the popular draw card Ben Compain. Gentle Ben was a popular, hard punching middle-to-light heavyweight. He was a great draw card in his own right. Unfortunately, Ben never reached his full potential due to an aversion to training. He compounded this failing with a taste for good times, women and drink. His manager was a shady character, Alan (Page Boy) Page. Alan shared Ben's taste for the good life and was somewhat of a hit with the women. He was a sometime antique dealer, but in reality an illegal bookie. Page Boy was an associate of Bert Clapham and worked closely with him.

Left to right, George Cammick, trainer; centre, Page Boy, Alan Page, Ben Compain's Manager, another Pommie seaman and Fetaiki Namoa, Tongan heavyweight.

It is quite strange in boxing that the best draw cards are not always the best boxers. Hard punchers who are themselves vulnerable to hard punches are the ones who put bums on seats. Gentle Ben was one of those. The posters were up, newspaper and television interviews had reached saturation point. Sports Line, the talk back show, was inundated with callers. I had been a guest on the show with Tim Bickerstaff and Geoff Sinclair twice. The prevailing opinion was that Jimmy Lester who was ranked 19 in the world was a good test for La'avassa and we should have a real fight on our hands. The promotion was the talk of the town. The box office ticket sales were flying. It was going to be a complete sell out. To increase the capacity of the Stanley Street courts, I had a meeting with the safety officers and the fire brigade. After much wrangling and negotiation, I got them to agree to four hundred extra temporary bench seats on the grass. I was praying for good weather.

The fight that caused the riot at Stanley Street Stadium; top American Middleweight Jimmy Lester versus Battling La'avassa.

The big day had come around. It was glorious weather. We had agreed to hold the weigh-in on fight day; this was to give maximum time to the Lester camp to make the weight. The weigh-in was to be a fateful one. It was a showy event in the opulent parlour of the Pacific Sauna. TV and radio reporters were there in numbers with their newspaper colleagues. Bookies, lawyers, cops, crims, TV and sports personalities were there, all enjoying the hospitality. Our very best girls were gliding around, smiling and serving free drinks. They were getting a lot of attention.

As soon as I had seen Jimmy working out and sparring in the gym, I knew he was overweight and we would be facing a problem. La'avassa was first on the scales; he looked really fit and tuned. Many fighters who came to New Zealand made the same mistake. They never realized how fit and well trained our fighters were. Our fighters, with one or two exceptions, may have lacked a little of the European boxing skills, or not been quite there with American guile and know how. However, they did carry a superb weapon; they were well trained, and as fit as it was possible to be. The longer the fights went on, the better that suited us.

"Battling La'avassa eleven stones five pounds, or one hundred and fifty nine pounds exactly," announced the chief weigh steward. He delivered the line with a show business flourish. This man was widely known in Auckland as Brownlee the Bastard. The name wittily bestowed on him due to his profession. Brownlee was a private investigator, specialising in snooping and gathering evidence in mucky divorce cases.

"Mr Jimmy Lester if you please."

Brownlie the bastard looked at me with a concerned look on his face.

"Jimmy Lester twelve stone, or one hundred and sixty eight pounds exactly." There was a gasp from the gathering. This was a huge amount of weight advantage. I immediately took Jimmy and his manager into the office; this discussion had to be in private.

Jimmy stood with his hands on his hips, a knowing look on his face; he was a wise old pro. He was tough; he was mean looking; a man you would not want to meet in an alley. He looked like what he was - an experienced well-travelled fighter, who would not be disgraced no matter whom he fought. He was the real thing, albeit past his best. The manager was a smallish, ferret-like character, and in fact 'the ferret' was the title we bestowed on him. He came complete with the American pork pie hat. It was always perched on the back of his head. He looked like he had just stepped from the set of the classic gangster movie *On the Waterfront*. He had piercing eyes. I think they had seen some unpublishable sights over the years. Even though he was from California, he had pale, pockmarked skin.

I realised that the faceless men in charge would only send a man worthy of respect to control Jimmy. Crammed into that little office with the two of them, I realised that this was not going to be easy.

"Listen up you two; this is a real problem for all of us. You know the deal was one hundred and sixty three pounds",

It was no use talking to them in stones and pounds. I turned to the Ferret.

"How much can you sweat off him? The sauna is on, get him in there. You're allowed four hours." They turned to go.

"You had better get serious; I will be calling the weight penalty." Whatever it was, it would be added to the La'avassa purse.

We stepped out of the office straight into the waiting throng. The reporters gathered around. La'avassa was very popular with the press. They regularly ran stories about him, his strong religious beliefs and Christian lifestyle made good copy. Controversy however sold the news and this was controversial. If La'avassa was beaten by a far bigger man I would get the blame and be pilloried in the press. Everybody wanted him to keep winning. He was good for Auckland sport, good for reporters and the public were with him. You can believe me, hometown decisions are not a myth; they can just happen. Woe betides the person who blew this gravy train. I did not want it to be me. I knew how quickly the public and the press could turn.

"You lads may as well have another drink; they have four hours to drop some weight. I have informed them I will be calling the penalty."

There was a rush to the girls and drinks.

An hour or so slipped by, I was chatting to Geoff Sinclair the well-respected sports editor of the Sunday news and Radio I. I felt a tap on the shoulder. I turned and there was the Ferret. He said they were ready and asked for another weigh-in. Brownlee the Bastard was hovering close by. I signalled him that it was okay. The Ferret disappeared in the direction of the sauna. After a few minutes, he returned with a sweating Jimmy clad only in his underpants. Brownlee motioned him forward. Jimmy stepped to the scales, at the same time shedding his wet underpants. He did not hesitate; he stepped onto the scales dressed just as his mother had brought him into this world. Brownlee who was not in the least embarrassed, leaned over him, fiddled with the scales and called out in his stentorian tones:

"Mr Jimmy Lester, eleven stones twelve pounds or one hundred and sixty six pounds". He had dropped two pounds according to Brownlee.

I signalled to the Ferret to follow me. We went into the receptionist's office. He sat on the desktop like he owned it and as if he did not have a problem. He didn't really, I did. I had sold every available ticket and more. I was not able to postpone as there was a tennis tournament scheduled to start the next day. If I went ahead and La'avassa lost due to the extra weight, I might as well emigrate. The Americans were there, ready, willing and able to fight and prepared to pay the penalty. I turned to the Ferret, but before I could speak he said: "That's it, I am not putting him into that fucking sauna again; it's too tough on him."

"Look we both have a problem here, you don't understand yours. Mine is this: the public will be mighty pissed off if La'avassa loses over your guy being too heavy. Yours is I will not pay the match fee due to your boss in the States, which I know he will blame you for. The thing is he won't be too happy and believe me, I know all about him. The other thing is your fighter Jimmy has asked me to pay the purse directly to him. I know you and your boss would not like that one bit, but if you don't make a real effort and get some more weight off him, I may do that. I may be forced to do that."

That last statement really galvanized him.

"Okay, okay," he said. He was uncomfortable now. "Whatever you do, don't do that. He owes me and he owes the boss nearly half of his purse. What do you want me to do?"

"I want you to go back to the sauna; try to lose some more, keep him in there for an hour. He can keep jumping in and out of the spa plunge pool. Then come back for another weigh and we'll call it a couple of pounds lighter, whatever it is. Get going, you must put him back in there."

My c'mon let's fix it attitude must have struck a chord with him. He turned to me with a cunning look. I wondered what was coming next

"Look Len, this may not be the problem for you that you think."

"Really," I said, "how is that?"

"How good is your boy? I've heard he's good, but is he?"

"Yes, he really is, but I think your guy's experience plus the extra weight will make it too difficult. La'avassa has a big heart, but you know the old saying in racing and boxing."

"What's that?" he asked.

"Weight will stop a train, that's what we think down here." I hesitated.

"Anyway what did you mean?"

"Well, it's like this, if your bloke is good, good enough to really mix it for four or five rounds and believe me Jimmy is still really good for those rounds. If your bloke is still there and making a fight of it, Jimmy will look for a way to lose. He will not fancy another 5 or 6 more rounds if he feels he can't win. He has that older fighter's mentality now."

He paused. If it was for effect, it worked.

"I suppose we can forget about penalties, huh?" he added.

George Cammick, our trainer, had La'avassa at maximum fitness. At that stage La'avassa had never been knocked down, let alone knocked out. All being equal, I believed La'avassa would win comfortably. He was on the rise and Jimmy was on the slope, which is the way that matches are arranged in boxing; it is often confused with fixing.

I didn't agree or disagree. I didn't know if he was on the level or not. I thought it wise to ignore it, and let things take their course. Meanwhile I carried on with what I planned. We stepped out into the lounge again and I spoke to the waiting crowd. "Lester is going back in the sauna; the final reweigh is in an hour's time". The Ferret led him back in the direction of the sauna. I knew the throng would disappear now. Arrangements to phone in for the result of the weigh-ins were agreed. Very quickly we were more or less on our own. I called Brownlee the Bastard over. I advised him to send his assistant home, as we didn't need to keep him there any longer. With that detail taken care of I casually said to him, "Allan wouldn't it be great, if Jimmy came in at a hundred-and-sixty-four pounds or close to it?" He looked quickly at me, nodded his head. I knew that would cost me another batch of tickets for no charge. In boxing, everything has a price.

THE STANLEY STREET RIOT

The large numbers of fans that turned up hoping to buy tickets at the box office surprised us. Most of the tickets had been pre-sold. I had persuaded the safety officer to increase the bench seats to five hundred, rather than four. They sold within half-an-hour of the box office opening. The crowds continued to build up and they were getting aggressive; they wanted to get in. They were mainly Samoans and other Pacific Islanders. They were not worried about having a seat, they just wanted in. We were worried they might storm the gates. There was a strange mood in the air.

There was still space between the bleachers and the bench seats. I took the safety officer out and showed him the angry crowd. I said to him:
"Do you want to tell this lot they can't get in?"
He looked at me with something near panic in his eyes.
"What about we let this last lot in, standing room only, come on it's the best thing we can do. We could have a problem if we don't do something," I said.
I watched him thinking about what to do.
"It's not we, Len; it's definitely you." He spat that line out.
"I'm going for a cuppa, when I come back I want these gates closed." With that he turned and walked briskly away. I followed the old principle of

a nod's as good as a wink to a blind horse and directed the stewards to lead the remainder of the crowd to the now designated standing area. They happily paid up the lowest ticket price. Everybody was happy and we got another two hundred joyous spectators in.

The promotion got away to a great start. The preliminary bouts were good value. Gentle Ben fought the main one of these, an eight rounder against another big punching Island boy. It had the crowd on its toes. Ben won with a knockout in the second round. He had looked likely to get KO'd himself. That knockout was Ben's first knock out of four that he would perform during the night. An unbelievable sequence of events lay ahead for us. So much so that it made the newspaper billboards in the States. It doesn't come much bigger than that. In the meantime, Page Boy was publicly dancing hoops. He rushed up to me demanding a bigger purse the next time Ben fought. I put it down to another incident of world champion fever. The excitement stayed at fever pitch; you could feel it in the air. Sometimes no matter how you try, the promotions are hard to ignite. Not this one, this one was buzzing; it had a life of its own. I'd introduced a new ploy into the evening's entertainment. For the first time Pacific Island music played over the public address system. Most of the material we played was Polynesian, mainly Samoan. I was attempting to introduce a carnival atmosphere (some carnival). I was thinking ahead to a couple of large, outdoor, summer promotions I was planning at one of the rugby football stadiums. I was really trying to whet appetites and milk the public and the press even more. What I had actually done was further stoke up the deep emotive allegiances of these islanders. The mainly Samoan audience lapped it up; there were bursts of laughter and cheering as various songs played. There was the odd outburst of island hula dancing. The atmosphere was electric.

The main entrée of this volcanic night of boxing had been well served by the Gentle Ben scrap. More large helpings followed with Si Nomura. His bout with the American Bobby Jordon was a classic contest between two very classy welterweights. The bout was very close over the opening five rounds, before Si who was right in it on all judges' cards, suffered a cut eye and had to retire.

A little more Samoan music and it was time for the main event. Mo Mersky, the ring announcer, took centre stage. The stadium lighting slowly dimmed. The music was faded out. Mo addressed the crowd; 'ladies and gentlemen' and then introduced the night's main event. He theatrically paused and pointed to the entrance to the arena. There was a rustle of excitement and anticipation from the massive throng. A beam of light shone on the entrance; there was a brief moment and Jimmy

Lester commenced his walk to the ring. Old pro that he was he milked the limelight and shuffled Mohamed Ali-like to the ring. Bevan Weir, the experienced referee, who had courageously resigned from the ABA and joined us, was now in the ring with the other officials. Bevan, like me, did not realise what a pivotal part he was going to play in tonight's events. Jimmy Lester was now shadow boxing and dancing in the ring. He looked comfortable and at home in that ring; he looked the real business. You could sense the apprehension in the crowd. He looked big and strong. He looked, and was, the epitome of a string of excellent American middleweights. The light beam went back to the arena entrance. As the light shone on La'avassa, the crowd erupted. George Cammick and his assistant Dave escorted the smiling Samoan to the ring. Bevan Weir, who was looking fit enough to fight still, took centre stage in the ring. He called the fighters to the centre of the ring and issued his instructions, then ordered them back to their corners. The atmosphere was somewhere above electric. With a grand flourish, Bevan signalled the timekeepers to ring the bell for the first round. It rang out, an ominous, shrill, but exciting, sound. Jimmy Lester's black, sweat-glistening body seemed to dwarf La'avassa. I felt very apprehensive. I thought to myself, this is it La'avassa, I need you to come through now. As that bell rang, the crowd rose as one to cheer on La'avassa. The only vestige of support for Lester came from his trainer and the lone voice of Bobby Jordan who had joined the Ferret in the ring as his assistant corner man. The frenzy in the crowd was contagious.

They touched gloves and Lester immediately bored in on La'avassa using his obvious weight and strength advantage. He pushed and mauled. He kidney punched La'avassa continually. He showed all his experience, tying La'avassa up on the ropes and fighting in bursts. His tactic was to tire La'avassa. Lester won the first round, but he didn't have it all his own way. La'avassa fought doggedly, back-catching Lester with some fine snappy punches. The referee, Bevan Weir, had to give two warnings to Lester before the first round was over for his persistent leaning.

Round two was a riotous one. Lester came bounding out of his corner. His idea was to cut off the ring to negate La'avassa's movement and it worked. Lester commenced leaning on La'avassa and holding, then bursting on the attack with a string of vicious punches. Bevan Weir warned him again for leaning. He replied by raining lefts and rights on La'avassa. La'avassa weathered the storm and came back strongly, landing good straight lefts, followed by his snappy left hooks and a couple of punishing body shots. La'avassa just shaded the round. I could see he was starting to feel confident and his heart was in the fight. The crowd were baying for Lester's blood; they were incensed by his illegal tactics. Not that it worried Lester one little bit. He had heavy shoulders and was well muscled. Under those lights his black body glistened with sweat. He looked the dangerous fighting machine that he was. Those bursts he fought in were classy.

The third round was a wildly close one. Lester was enraging the crowd with his brawling tactics, he was playing a dangerous game; he obviously didn't understand Samoans. La'avassa started to succeed in standing Lester off. He was scoring well in spite of the butting and holding. Bevan warned Lester again over his holding. Lester seemed to snarl at him and just bored in again without stepping back. This was becoming a real donnybrook. La'avassa, who was showing signs of real anger, was right in it, giving as good as he got, if not more so. Towards the end of the round, Lester showed some of his class with a burst of great boxing and punching, but La'avassa matched him. The crowd were on their feet and deliriously chanting La'avassa's name, again, and again. This was definitely a La'avassa round.

Sitting next to me was Fred Dickens, a good friend of mine. He was a committee member of the association and loved his boxing. As a young man, he had boxed as a heavyweight for the Royal New Zealand Navy.

"Christ Len, this is a good scrap. The punters love it, but the shit will hit the fan big time if La'avassa loses". He was looking at me with a quizzical look in his eye.

"Yeah, you're right. It is a worry. I have Tom's Security plus Ben Compain and the other prelim boys in the far aisle by the ringside. I got Tom to get them on standby in case of trouble."

"I think we're going to need them," said Fred.

"I think you had better get over there as well," I said.

He let out a startled yelp, "Me? Shit, this could be bloody dangerous." Old Fred was proud of being a committee member, which I had arranged. I think he went to sleep in the SPBA brown blazer with our badge on it; even his wife Margaret used to make jokes about it.

"Sorry Fred," I said," but it's down to you. It's your area, get over there and organize them just in case."

"Okay then, okay," grumbling as he stood up.

"Fuck me, Len, I sure hope La'avassa wins."

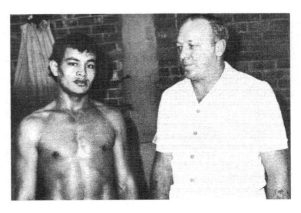

Fred Dickens, the 'Hero of the riot'!! Pictured here with Monty Betham, a talented middleweight who he managed.

The fourth round was nothing short of amazing. There had never been anything remotely similar in Auckland and probably San Francisco, if the newspaper billboards there were to be believed. Lester bounded out to trap La'avassa and cut off the ring again. They fought furiously; he rocked La'avassa with some good shots and then bored in again holding La'avassa on the ropes. Bevan Weir stepped in and broke them up. He pushed Lester to the centre of the ring and warned him again. He snarled something at the ref and the fight resumed. La'avassa really got in his stride. They traded punches and then Lester tried to head-butt La'avassa again.

"That's it, that's it," Bevan Weir jumped in and raised La'avassa's arm, in the traditional sign of victory, while disqualifying Lester. Well that was just the start of it. Lester began arguing with the ref and pushed him. La'avassa had his blood up now, as did most of the Samoans in the crowd. He then put himself between the ref and Lester and pushed him away. That turned into a fight again. They started throwing punches, Bevan joined in and started grappling with Lester. A mighty howl rent the air as a rain of plastic chairs and other missiles pelted the ring. Bobby Jordan, the welterweight, joined the fray helping Lester. Bevan Weir and La'avassa were now back to back rough housing with the two Negro boxers. We were lucky in that

Lester and La'avassa still had their boxing gloves on, that probably saved severe damage. All four were really slugging it out. Bevan Weir was more than holding his own. Bevan was an ex-New Zealand champion. Couple that with the fact that he was raised in the country districts in a large no beg your pardons Maori family; you had a man who was not averse to a bit off fisticuffs.

The fans were going wild; and a crowd of rampaging, rioting, angry Samoans was a frightening sight. They were surging forward, throwing missiles. Their intention was to join the fray and assist La'avassa and Bevan; they were trying to storm the ring. Make no mistake they were after Lester's blood. I think if they had made the ring, they would have killed him. Our security led by Ben Compain and four of our preliminary boys beat them to it. They were in a position of dominance up on the apron of the ring. The battles on the edge of the ring were titanic. There were bodies flying everywhere. Our boys and the security had a battle on their hands. Our lads were ruthless; to be fair, they had to be. They stood up on the apron of the ring, punching and throwing the invaders off. Ben's tally of knockouts for the night was four, which included the one in his official fight. It became a joke amongst us as to whether or not we could include them in his record.

It was dangerous. It was bad, very bad, but it

could have been a lot worse. There were a few sore heads and bruises, but they were tough people. There were no complaints from any of the combatants; they accepted their bumps, cuts etc., as fair enough. We were fortunate, as was reported in Radio and TV news flashes, that nobody was seriously injured, or worse still, killed.

The after fight party was a special one that night. We turned it on for the brave boys who had defended the ring, the ref, and the fighters and trainers in it. Ben and his team's efforts were the major topic of conversation. The main fight almost becoming an also ran. The riot was now the big attraction of the evening. The lads who had been up on the apron of the ring could do no wrong and did they milk it? They were the heroes of the hour. As the night went on the story became somewhat exaggerated. At one stage, Ben was in the middle of a circle of mainly female admirers, modestly claiming seven knockouts. On closer examination, by those in the know, he was awarded four. He claimed he had 'miscued' on the others. Brownlee was last seen scrambling under the ring clutching the official bell. He later claimed he saw it as his duty, first and foremost, to protect this important item of equipment. I must say from my elevated position in the press box I thought it a very wise self-preservation manoeuvre.

The riot had been an unforgettable experience.

Imagine if you will a flickering old western movie. One of those featuring a massive bar room brawl. One in which everybody became involved, whether they were just bystanders or angry combatants. The only thing missing was the brassy singer and band playing on through it all.

Whenever I think back on it, those clear images spring into my mind. It was as if a mass hysteria had gripped everyone. Those who could not get to the ring threw chairs. These and other missiles flew through the air. The noise from the shouting, screaming rioters; the panicked, shrill screams of the ringside patrons as they scrambled for safety, mainly under the ring, was ear splitting. The waves of angry Samoans attempting to get into the ring seeming more than happy to slug it out with Ben and the boys. Jimmy Lester, Bobby Jordan, and the Ferret looked on in sheer terror and disbelief. They were trapped like rabbits in the glare of headlights. All hell was breaking loose; it was now looking very dangerous for them.

Ben and the boys were tiring, the weight of numbers starting to tell. Then just as it is in the movies, the cavalry arrived. The relief came in the form of a phalanx of police officers, some uniformed and on duty, and others who were there off duty. These were mainly young constables who used to enjoy free tickets in return for stewarding duties. I think it was Senior Sergeant Les Higgins who ably led the rescue contingent. Les was a boxing aficionado, a good Kiwi bloke. He was someone I knew quite well. They joined Ben and the boys and took instant charge of the ring. Things quickly started to quieten down. The angry Polynesians were up for a fight if one of their own was in trouble. However by and large they were respectful of authority. The danger period was thankfully almost over. I called on the Reverend Sio. He was the moderator of the Presbyterian Church in New Zealand. He was the senior religious figure in the New Zealand Island community. Reverend Sio attended all of my promotions as my guest. He was an astute boxing fan and a valuable ally for me in any dealings I had with the Island people. I invited him up into the ring to address the crowd, which he did. He called on them to be peaceful and to make their way home and respect the police and the South Pacific Boxing Association, which they did. I breathed a sigh of relief. I allowed myself a smile when I thought of the huge gate takings and I realised the extent of the publicity that would be in store.

THE FIRST OF THE TWO GREAT FIGHTS, WON BY LA'AVASSA

Later that month when La'avassa was to fight the outstanding Maori boxer, Kahu Mahanga, for his New Zealand middleweight title, I felt it wise to have the Reverend Sio address the crowd prior to the fight. At that time, there were strong divisions between Maori and Islanders. It was felt that this fight could be the spark to cause open clashes between these factions. What we got however was a marvellously successful fifteen-round sporting contest between two fit and skilful, outstanding representatives of their races. Again, this high quality bout could have graced any of the world's great boxing arenas. The fight swayed back and forth, each man having times in the ascendancy. In the end, after fifteen hard rounds, three of the judges called it for La'avassa by the smallest of margins. The fourth, Bob Jones, controversially called it clearly in La'avassa's favour. That started another row, but that's a part of boxing. The crowd appreciating the superb sporting contest they had witnessed, had nothing but goodwill for each other and the contestants, dispersed very happily. I do however think the Reverend Sio with his pre-emptive speech earned his tickets that night.

Kahu Mahanga and La'Avassa,
Two international class Middlewieights – Mandalay Ballroom,
Auckland, August 1973, Fight promoted by Len Russell and The
South Pacific Boxing Association

Anyway, back to the Lester riot night. The remnants of the crowd were ushered to safety outside. The genteel tennis arena was cleared and restored to normality. The police had escorted the rattled Americans to their dressing room. I made my way there with Bevan Weir and Fred Dickens. We went into the room and there they were sitting glassy eyed and appearing to be almost in shock. Lester jumped up as we walked in.

"Fuck man, we could have been killed out there," he said wide-eyed. "I've fought in tough towns and clubs all over the States and these are the maddest, meanest, toughest bastards ever. I'm telling you man, these dudes down here are fucking crazy, they were definitely gonna kill me. I ain't going anywhere near those mad fuckers again. Get us our money and get us out of here and fuck your drinks party."

"Okay," I said, I turning to the Ferret who was now a shadow of the cocky gangster type of earlier. I handed him an envelope with the cash in it and asked him to count it and sign the receipt, which he did without a murmur.

"Well now, thanks guys, I am sorry you didn't enjoy your trip. Anyway have a nice trip home. Fred here will drive you to your hotel and pick you up in the morning and take you to the airport."

I looked at the ferret.

"Thanks for everything, maybe you'll come down here again with another fighter for La'avassa. Ask your boss to line another one up; I'll phone him about it."

The Ferret, who looked like he was in shock, had been stuck for words, but at last burst forth:

"Not fucking likely, not me."

With that, Fred, Brownlee and I joined the party in the Marina bar of Tom Madgewick's Station Hotel in Anzac Avenue. Everybody was enjoying the party. Free drinking tends to do that, but to me, as the man doing the paying, it was an investment. Our main draw card was safe. His record further enhanced. From the look of the assembled, inebriated, laughing journalists, I was confident that the publicity would favour us. After all, they had not only got a good story; they now had a great one. I looked around the room; it was all the usual free loaders, plus all the committee of the SPBA and their guests. I kept that small and tight. Fred, who stood far above the gathered throng, seemed to have grown a foot taller now. He was striding around with his chest out, trapping whoever he could and regaling them with his not so modest account of himself leading the troops on the apron.

The fight and the accompanying riot were a constant topic of discussion and scandal over the next few days. We later heard that the riot had featured in the American press. Knowing the introverted nature of their press, that is not easily accomplished. They were known for a lack of interest in matters outside of the USA, however, this incident was considered important enough to make the billboards.

There was one further issue; Fred turned to me and said:
"Len, why do I have to take those buggers to the airport?"
"Because Fred, you are now the liaison officer."
"Oh am I? I didn't know that. What else do I have to do then?"
Some people in life are never grateful. Much as you try, you just cannot please them.

In truth, Fred Dickens was an able administrator and a great bloke. Being an SPBA committee member had brought a new dimension into his life.

It was not just luck that I had Fred and a few like him around me in the boxing days. The committee of the SPBA was composed of a few handpicked friends. For a number of years, with their assistance, we made a difference.

A LITTLE HOMILY THAT SAYS A LOT ABOUT LA'AVASSA

An amusing incident that originated around La'avassa typified our relationship. It took place in Sydney just prior to one of his early fights; I seem to remember it was against the tough Queensland cowboy Errol McIvor. It was a bit sloppy on my part. This particular day saw us strolling around Sydney central; somewhere nearby to George Street. Sydney always held me spellbound. It was such an exciting place for us from quieter New Zealand. We were window-shopping in a large department store when we bumped into the pro golfer who always stayed with Mary and I when he played the NZ circuit. We were excitedly exchanging gossip; by this time we were outside on a comfortable wooden bench on the pavement.

My friend owned a golf shop just around the corner. He had been busily filling my head with information about sensational new golf clubs. Apparently, these clubs couldn't fail to make you hit the ball longer and straighter.
"Come and have a look," he said.
I agreed to and shy La'avassa said he was happy to wait for me there.
"Right, mate, I won't be long."
Every golfing treasure was there. Drivers, wedges, irons and putters all containing magic formulas to

make you play better. I had to try them all out didn't I? Then there was coffee and the usual information exchange with golfing buddies who came in. Well as you know, time flies when you are enjoying yourself. Before I knew it two and a half hours had slipped by. "Shit," I yelped and ran out of the shop, still with an expensive wedge in my hand. My friend with his twisted sense of humour ran out behind me yelling, "stop thief".

Well, that wasn't so bad, after all we were in Australia, nobody would interfere. Even though it was two hundred years since the convict ships were active; it was still built into their character to look the other way when there was a bit of law breaking going on.

Anyway, I make it back to where I'd left La'avassa; he was up on the balls of his feet dancing from foot to foot. I thought that's good he's doing a spot of training while he's waiting.

"Well done I said, doing a bit of training?"

"Where you been Russell, me not training, me want a piss."

He was agitatedly dancing, his face was strained, but he had waited for me on the exact spot that I had left him on.

"Russell, you bad man."

He was half running and holding himself from piddling, but I got him to the loo in the store just in time. You may wonder at it, but that is the way it was then. He didn't think to find somewhere to go;

not because he was dumb, he was far from it as boxers go. No, it wasn't that, he was just doing what I had told him to do. What a simple world it was then, where did it go?

TIM BICKERSTAFF AND
THE RADIO I ATTACK ON ME

Professional boxing, by its very nature, creates a rich breeding ground for jealousy, rivalry and envy. Minor slights and circumstances often don't end well, as is shown in this next event, which led me to the Auckland Supreme Court once again. In the early seventies I was often a guest on the very popular Radio I talk back show Sports Line. It was an interesting task and one that I genuinely enjoyed. It was also a heaven sent opportunity to promote our shows and by association the good old Pacific Sauna.

Jerry Clayton, Hughsie and me in Hawaii for golf. This trip was after the Bickerstaff court case; by then we were all friends.

The villain of this piece was a certain Tim Bickerstaff. Tim was the owner and a co-presenter of this very successful show. His fellow presenter was a very popular and fine sports journalist, who enjoyed a reputation as a straight shooter, Geoff Sinclair. The show never lacked callers. It was a depot for sporting complaints. All Blacks, selectors, referees, administrators, they were all taken to task by irate callers. No sport was sacrosanct; they could all come in for a pasting, and they did. It was an opportunity for the fan to have a say and vent his feelings. The show went out live in the primetime slot, between six and seven o'clock in the evenings. It was a very good show. It enjoyed high ratings and therefore attracted large sponsorship support and advertising. For a couple of reasons Tim had his knickers in a knot over me. I had briefly discussed with him a project I was contemplating. I had discussed it with him as I wanted an estimate figure on advertising and promotional costs. Tim, who was very excited about the project, either misread the situation or tried to muscle himself into it as a partner. That was not something I had contemplated or wanted. I could get myself into enough trouble. I did not need Tim's undoubted ability in that department. The problem started at a lunch attended by Detective Inspector John Hughes, known to friends and enemies alike as Hughsie, a well-known, in-your-face car dealer called Jerry Clayton, and Tim Bickerstaff.

Whenever Hughsie and Jerry Clayton got out together, things got over exuberant. They were both real characters and almost looked like twins. Hughsie In his younger days was a very competitive athlete. In his later days he specialised in ultra-distance running. He eventually won the Melbourne to Sydney ultra-distance foot race, something approaching six hundred miles. He had also been a talented amateur boxer. As a young man he won the New Zealand light-middleweight championship from 1955-1957. He was also a stalwart of the police athletic team, in the celebrated Inter-Services Games. He shone in those, winning a clutch of gold medals over different events. Hughie's record as a police officer was also outstanding. He had joined the force after a stint in the Royal New Zealand Navy. He quickly rose through the ranks from uniformed Constable to Detective Constable, Detective Sergeant, then to Detective Inspector. He was an old-fashioned thief-taker sort of cop. He built a fearsome reputation amongst criminals and the New Zealand underworld. If you were a crim, he was a man to fear. He was the last man you would want on your case. His exploits were legendary and sometime later, he became a great friend.

The other member of that boisterous lunch was Jerry Clayton, a brash Australian who used to front his own television and radio advertisements. He was a self-promoter par excellence, which was essential in the highly competitive Auckland used car sales market. Jerry's other speciality was gracing the latest restaurants and clubs, surrounded by sycophantic followers. Any new club or restaurant openings found him at the top of the guest list. It was a popular joke passed around about him that he would attend the opening of an envelope. For all this, and the problem he helped cause me, he was an outstandingly good bloke. He was also a very good golfer with a hugely competitive nature.

There was an obvious and overwhelming problem looming. Here we had three massive egos at the lunch table. The long, alcoholic lunch, resulted in the spawning of a plot in which I was the victim. For reasons best known to them, they conspired to attack me and the SPBA. It may have been that Sports Line needed some controversy for its ratings. More likely though, it was Tim's annoyance at me for not going ahead with the other project. Though to be honest, there could have been a bit of the 'he has got a bit too big for his boots' assessment and perhaps I had. The attack came in the form of pre-arranged slanderous phone calls to Sports Line that evening. The intention was to bring into question some of the decisions relating to bouts that I had promoted. The identity of a mysterious main stirrer was never disclosed, but I suspected the wounded hand of the ABA; that was certainly a possibility.

My first inkling of what was taking place was a

phone call from a friend. I was sitting at home in a lovely old colonial house in Jervois Road, Herne Bay, a very fine suburb barely ten minutes from the hub of the city. I was in a reflective, happy mood, having decided to forego work and spend the evening with my family. We were about to watch television, probably one of Mary's favourite soaps. We had just enjoyed a great dinner; it was one of my favourites - grilled New Zealand lamb chops, mashed potatoes, kumara (a delicious New Zealand sweet potato) with leeks, peas and onion gravy; my idea of soul food. The kids were playing and shrieking with laughter at a little kitten that we had somehow acquired. It was playfully teasing our dog Irene. The kitten was darting round and round the big leather chair that I was sitting in. Irene was chasing it and enjoying the fun. They were careering and skidding around the chair and having a fantastic time of it. The chase became so intense that you could not tell if the kitten was now chasing Irene. The kitten would screech to a halt, flick a claw at Irene and then reverse track as fast as she could the other way around the chair. We were all enjoying the fun; Mary's brother Johnny McGlynn and his wife were there. Johnny was enjoying a couple of Lion Browns. Sammy and Lenny, with their two cousins, Robyn and Abraham, were having a great time, the house was alive and warm and it was quality time. I was really looking forward to the evening. Though life in the boxing game and in the activities of Karangahape Road was enjoyable, it was also stressful. A rare night off with the family was a treat.

The phone in the hallway started to ring. I left my chair, walked to the hall and picked it up thinking it would be a problem at work. It was a problem all right, but not from work. The caller was Bert Clapham, the bookie. He was terse and his voice was urgent

"Len have you got Sports Line on?"

"No mate, it's a telly night."

"Well get it on, Bickerstaff and a couple of callers are on your case. It sounds bad mate, they're saying you're fixing the fights."

"Are you kidding me, Bert?" I said that with a laugh.

"Get the Radio on mate, I am not kidding you, they're killing you."

"Thanks mate," I said, "I'm on it." I hung up and went into the other room. I flicked the radio on. Sure enough, Bert was right. The trouble was Jerry Clayton and Hughsie; I immediately recognized their voices and their calls were drawing responses. Some of them questioning decisions, but equally as many supporting us and disputing the malicious claims. Their calls had prompted an avalanche of irate listeners wanting to have their say. The sporting public love a row and everyone wanted a piece of this one, particularly ABA supporters. What should I do? To be honest, I didn't think it through at all. I abandoned the family evening, jumped in my car and drove quickly up to Newton

Road and the Radio I offices. I had flicked on the radio in the car just in time to hear Geoff Sinclair saying he did not want any part of this and that there would be trouble and he left the studio mid-show. I arrived at the front steps and the security man who knew me just opened the door for me and waved me through. I went straight to the broadcast studio, opened the door and there sat Bickerstaff in one of those black leather swivel chairs. Tim was a big man, but tending towards fat. This was caused by his main hobby, which was drinking. In another life he had been a New Zealand billiards champion. As I burst into the room he had the headphones on and he was bleary eyed. A half-full bottle of brandy sat on the desk. He was just raising his glass for another drink, at the same time conversing with a caller. I didn't plan it; I just reacted to the anger in me. I punched him very hard while he was sitting there. I caught him just under the ear on his jaw. He went sideways out of the chair and down on the floor in a tangle of wires.

"Don't Len, don't hit me again. What did you do that for?" he yelled as he crouched on the floor.

"I thought we were friends," he yelped plaintively.

"Never ever, not in a million years," I said.

I stepped back, wondering whether to hit him again. I was a bit surprised at my action. I didn't hit him again; there was no pleasure in it. In fact, I was regretting it. I was not a violent person, but in this case he caught me on the wrong night. I usually thought things through and covered the angles when I had a problem; this had not been a very smart reaction. I should not have acted as I did and to have acted so publicly was just crazy. My next thoughts were damage limitation.

The station manager, a Mr Mason, burst into the soundproofed studio. Bickerstaff was still scrambling around on the floor. He was blind drunk; he couldn't get up. It wasn't because of the one punch; although, in the on-going telling of the tale it did get exaggerated into the perfect one punch KO. I must confess that not in keeping with my customary modesty, I didn't absolutely deny that.

"Get out of here, get out," Mason was yelling at me, like a man demented. His investors and board of directors would not appreciate this broadcast. It came out in a subsequent court case that Bickerstaff had other defamation cases against him and his insurance was likely to be withdrawn. The security man jumped between us. He was in a difficult position as he was generally on duty at my shows.
"Take it easy Len, you had better get out of here," he said.

Just as he said that the police invaded the room. Apparently, most of this fracas had gone out live on air and they had reacted fast. By now things were getting crowded. The broadcast studio was a Spartan sort of space. The main feature was the control panel; it was a long desktop running wall to wall. All the electronic paraphernalia, speakers, microphones, and flashing bulbs that provided the communication for the callers were attached to it. One of the bulbs excitedly flashing indicated callers still on the line. Two high back swivel chairs on castors squeezed up to it. One other chair was now lying on its side. In addition there was an overstuffed magazine rack of sports publications and two full-to-overflowing wastebaskets, one of them now upended, its contents spewed out on the floor. A few posters and newspaper headlines were blue-tacked onto the walls. Tim's glass was now lying in a pool of the brandy it had previously contained. The confined space had that unaired, smoky, smelly atmosphere, laced with alcohol and body odours, that pervades bars and clubs.

Mason was a picture of pent up anger, his face contorted with rage. He was shouting and demanding that the police get me out of there. The security man was helping the mumbling Bickerstaff to his feet; pandemonium reigned. The police Sergeant, whom I knew, led me out of the room. He was a boxing fan and a stalwart of the George Cammick boxing gym that La'avassa and other SPBA boys trained in. That fact would not stand in the way of his duty, but it did give me an opportunity to limit the danger of the situation. He formally recorded my details in preparation for later charges. He then left me with one of his constables while he returned to speak with Mason and Bickerstaff. He returned after a few minutes, "Okay Len, for the moment there are no charges, they just want you out of here straight away, but there may be charges later."

"All right, I'm happy to go, but I think you should impound the broadcast tape, as it will be needed in evidence and I think there is a good chance they may destroy it."

He thought about it for a few minutes, and returned to Mason and demanded it as future evidence. Apparently, Mason at first refused the request. He then made the grave mistake of telling the Sergeant he was acting for my benefit. The Sergeant insisted on having the tape and threatened to charge Mason with withholding evidence and obstruction. Mason mumbled about lawyers etc. but realised he was on a loser and agreed to comply with the request. It looked like the excitement was over for the night; two constables escorted me from the building. One of them gave me the Kiwi seal of approval.

"Good on you, Len, that Bickerstaff is an A grade prick."

"Thanks mate," was all I managed before the Sergeant came and gave me an official police warning not to return to the premises. He also advised me to be ready to attend at the police station if requested. I was allowed to go as fortunately Bickerstaff had refused to press charges at that stage.

I was back in my lounge enjoying a cup of tea within an hour of leaving it. It was only an hour in time, but the events of that night went on to dominate the town scandal and gossip in the bars and clubs of Auckland for the next few months. There was no way that this one would fade away quietly. My first job in the morning, after fielding a mountain of phone calls was to see a solicitor. At the time I had two or three excellent legal eagles that I was able to utilise. With solicitors for me it was always a case of different horses for different courses. With this delicate kind of situation I went for initial advice from the most conservative of them. I realized I could face charges of assault, or maybe worse. On the other hand, I was seriously considering and hoping I had enough evidence to sue Bickerstaff and or Radio I for defamation, damages and loss of future earnings. Therefore it was essential to get the right man for the job. It had to be one who had the genuine respect of any Supreme Court judge. I knew that in my suing them in a civil case they would have licence to have a real go at my character and any perceived bad elements in it. The right legal representation could help counter that threat.

I talked it over with my solicitor, Anand Satyanand, known affectionately as 'Satch'. He was a highly respected lawyer and went on to be the Governor General of New Zealand. We sat there in his office and mulled it over for an hour. I firmly believed that I had a good opportunity to sue. Satch being rather conservative agreed, but thought it wise to get an opinion from a Queens Counsel. I agreed and he immediately set up an appointment for eleven o'clock the next morning with a very eminent man and the one I wanted on this case, Lloyd Brown QC, assisted by a junior barrister, Roger McLaren who sat in on the meeting.

Lloyd Brown at the time was also the Charge d'Affaires in New Zealand for the French government. Lloyd was a heavyweight second to none, but an establishment man. With Lloyd representing me, I was confident about the battle ahead. I knew it would be a hard and dirty battle, particularly with Hughsie on the case. He was not only involved in the Police case. He was largely the cause of the event, so he had to cover his own backside. There was no mistaking the fact that Hughsie would be taking this very seriously. He had a win mentality; I truly believed that there was not much that he would not do to win. This was a champion boxer, a champion athlete, and a thief taker of extraordinary capability in the one body and a policeman who, shall we say, sometimes avoided the niceties of the law when gathering evidence. My true adversary was not going to be Bickerstaff; it was not going to be the battery of legal brains that his side would bring to the contest. No, it was not any of those; the man I had to overcome was Hughsie.

PUNCH A POM A DAY

A few weeks into the case and the interest had gripped the sporting public. It became so high that the locals were betting on the result. Apparently, the public sympathy lay with me, mainly because of Bickerstaff's unpopularity and the Kiwi's natural sympathy for a rebel. Having said that, Hughie's reputation and his involvement had made his side the favourite. Bickerstaff, an inveterate gambler, was betting large sums on himself to win. Bert Clapham and his agents were covering most of the bets. Bert, who disliked Bickerstaff to an amazing degree, was up to his neck in it, offering whatever assistance he could.

I had another advantage. About a month or so before this furore Bickerstaff had bought other troubles on himself. It had emanated from some callers to his show that had annoyed him. The annoying callers were 'Poms' and the calls were related to a failed English sporting team's poor effort. Remember, this was in the seventies and Poms were not that popular. It is fair to say that they and the Aussies were equally prized scalps. Because of the difficult dialogue that developed between the Pom-supporting callers and Bickerstaff, he had decided to launch an anti-Pom promotion. Part of this promotion had him making scathing attacks on English sportsmen and Poms in general.

However, Bickerstaff being Bickerstaff, he went over the top. His *piece de resistance* in this campaign lay in the t-shirts he had manufactured that he then either sold or gave away with much ceremony as prizes for winners of the sports quizzes he ran on the show. Not too much wrong with that you might well think, but actually it was a massive problem for Bickerstaff. It sat badly, very badly with the large English population in Auckland and the surrounding areas. The brightly coloured t-shirts bore an interesting, antagonistic logo and message - a gnarled, brown clenched fist with the immortal words inscribed in large type below it 'punch-a-Pom-a-day'. He certainly knew how to lose friends and alienate people. This had to have a bearing in the skirmish to come.

Because of the anti-Pom promotion, my attack on Bickerstaff had elevated me to an almost iconic figure in the English resident's minds. Though in truth that had not been a factor in the escapade. I literally had them stop me in the street to congratulate me. Many came up to Karangahape Road to meet me. The applications to join as members of the SPBA and the private sauna club tripled. What was that about an ill wind? It took about two weeks for the infighting to start. The public understanding about high profile court cases only comes from what they see or read in the newspapers. This all comes across in a highly sanitized and civilized manner. They, like the jury, are shielded from the actual cut and thrust of evidence gathering. They are unaware of the deception, the backstabbing, the wheeling and dealing which goes with the territory. With Hughsie running the opposition show behind the scenes, this was going to take some winning. Every trick in the book was to be brought to bear; this was 'game on'. The first salvo was fired in Sydney.

IN THE BLUE CORNER, ERNIE MCQUILLAN

I became aware of it through a phone call from a legendary character in Australian boxing called Ernie McQuillan. I had met Ernie through the *TV Ringside* shows. They were boxing nights, promoted, and beamed out live every Tuesday evening by Channel 9 Sydney, from the South Sydney rugby league club in Newtown. Ernie was their matchmaker and I acted as their agent in New Zealand. It was my job to keep Channel 9 well supplied with boxing talent from Auckland.

"How are you son?" I recognised the Sydneysiders' drawl of the caller, it was Ernie.

"Ern, how are you old mate, what's new?" I enquired. I knew there had to be something important going on. Ernie was notorious for not wasting money.

"Don't worry about how I am son; you've got a few worries. I've rung to mark your card."

"Fire away mate, what is it?"

"I have had a 'jack' (Aussie slang for a cop) over here asking questions. He didn't say he was a jack, but you know me son, I can spot them a mile away. I heard you were getting some flak from that arsehole on the radio. I always told you, don't ever trust those journalist pricks; they always turn on you. Anyway, this guy was asking all sorts of questions. He wanted to know if I thought you were organising a few stews." (Downunder slang for a fix.)

"I told him straight, I told him he was barking up the wrong tree. I said to him you were a breath of fresh air in boxing and New Zealand boxers have never had it so good. I told him we did a lot of business together. I told him you always paid up and looked after the fighters and trainers I send over there and that it hadn't always been like that."

"Thanks for that mate. I think the guy was a jack called Hughsie." I described Hughsie to him.

"Yeah son, that's him. I don't know if you have been up to anything, but be bloody careful."

"Okay, thanks Ern, I'll keep you up to speed. Make sure you keep Ron Casey calm."

Ron was the boss of sports for Channel 9 and had a lot of power. Something like this could spook him. He had flown over to meet me in Auckland some months previously and we had negotiated an exclusive two-way deal for the following twelve months that guaranteed a minimum number of fights would be booked through me. This consolidated my position with the boxers. Casey and McQuillan in turn had first call on my fighters for Australian bouts. It also gave me access to any European or American boxers they imported to fight in Sydney. It gave me the opportunity to feature them in an extra promotion in Auckland before they returned home. The great advantage to me was that the fares to bring them downunder and the expenses involved were already paid. These were often more costly than the fight purses.

"Nah, no worries there mate. He thinks the sun

shines out of your arse; shows ya what a fuckin mug he can be," he said that with a belly laugh.

Ernie was a real old-fashioned, Sydney character from the inner city suburb Marrickville. This man was your genuine city survivor and he had survived and brought up a family while engaged in one of the toughest of businesses. It was good to have him standing behind me and Ernie had made sure that Hughie's trip to Sydney had drawn a blank.

Meanwhile all sorts of wild rumours were flying around Auckland. There was talk that there were threats against Jerry Clayton. There were rumours that his cars were to be damaged, maybe sprayed with paint, or even torched. In any event the threats had not come from me. It was my belief that the Bickerstaff camp were behind them in a crude effort to present me to the court in a bad light.

Through all this, my main worry was the Pacific. I had developed a very real fear that the Pacific, Ray and I would become justifiable targets for increased police activity. Never forgetting who was guiding the opposition.

THE LIGHT WENT ON

One sunny Monday morning found me out on the Chamberlain Park Golf Course. I was having a game with one of Karangahape Road's main characters. This was Rainton Hastie, the strip club king. Rainton owned the Pink Pussy Cat strip club, situated next door to the Pacific Sauna. He was a noted boundary pusher and had recently served time in Mt. Eden Prison over his strip club activities. This was for so-called offences that would not attract even passing interest in today's world, let alone justify a prison sentence. They simply involved his striptease artists exhibiting too much movement. If the police hounding and the subsequent jail sentencing had not been so draconian, the situation would have been laughable. The trouble was that back in the late sixties and early seventies New Zealand was still in the grip of a very conservative, religiously dominated society.

In my early days in K' Road there was a time when things between me and Ray and Rainton were difficult and looked to be heading for an explosive confrontation. Good sense prevailed and we realised it would have been a battle with no winners. So instead of trouble we collaborated and opened a massage parlour together. It carried the dubious, but very marketable title of 'the Swank'. It certainly fired the imagination.

Playing golf with us were two of his managers. One of them, Shane Kelly, was a champion boxer and a well-known street fighter. He later won the Auckland Boxing Association amateur lightweight championship, while representing the SPBA.

Our other companion was a likable, but ne'er-do well character called Mo Mersky. He also worked for me as the ring announcer on our boxing nights. He had a background in show business and entertainment. Shortly after this golf game we lost Mo's services. This was due to his having to serve a longish prison sentence as a consequence of his part in organising an armed robbery of an illegal gambling club just off Karangahape Road called Cream. Well-heeled punters and bookmakers patronised this successful, but shady, gambling club. They were the type who carried large wads of cash, as Mo was well aware. Some were quite dangerous men in their own right and were capable of extracting extreme revenge, which they swore to do.

This goes some way to demonstrating the criminal ambitions and capability of the New Zealand crime scene at that time. It was about this time that the foundations of New Zealand's biggest, most dangerous and successful criminal group with international connections came into being. This was the infamous Mr Asia Crime syndicate. A group of ruthless New Zealand criminals controlled this organisation. They were hugely successful in their field for a number of years in the mid-to-late seventies. They were responsible for many murders of people they felt were informers, at least ten and probably many more. They started out in New Zealand; but success on home turf, initially selling cannabis from Asia and then heroin, led them to seek the bigger, more affluent and booming market for their products in Australia.

They started operating in Sydney. Through their ruthless tactics, coupled with corrupt contacts, they became dominant in supplying heroin to that market. They spread their tentacles throughout Australia and for a couple of years they lead the pack, eventually became victims of their own success. The murders and mysteriously missing persons could not continue to be covered up indefinitely. By this time a public clamour was developing. There were heavy hitting journalists after their blood in Australia and New Zealand. This pursuing group was led by a determined Auckland Star reporter, Pat Booth. He, with his newspaper, was instrumental in the exposure that led to the downfall of this highly successful syndicate. The pressure and public opinion was such that a Royal Commission of Enquiry with sweeping powers was set up in New Zealand and Australia. Their brief was to examine the whole episode and lay bare the corruption that had played such a major part in the success of Mr Asia Syndicate.

The authorities were starting to close in, so they decided to move their operation to the UK. Once in the UK there was an internal dispute. It resulted in another murder and it was the one that brought the Syndicate down. Terry Sinclair, the syndicate leader and hit man, had ordered one of his original partners, a certain Marty Johnstone, killed. The task was given to a long term syndicate member, an Englishman called Andy Maher, who had been Martin Johnston's original partner in the early days in Auckland. Maher, with an associate, duly accomplished this bloody task. Johnston's body was then crudely dismembered in a council house shed and dumped in a former stone quarry, now a lake called Eccleston Delph in Lancashire. The body, which two hobby divers discovered a couple of weeks later, led to the arrest of Sinclair and his remaining associates. This final murder brought about the demise of the infamous Mr Asia syndicate. This ghastly murder grabbed national attention in the British press and unmasked this dangerous downunder group's activities in the UK.

Terry Clark, the syndicate's acknowledged leader, was a criminal who hailed from the town of Gisborne, situated on New Zealand's east coast. The same town that had produced Kimball Johnson. He had successfully evaded the Australasian authorities for a number of years, but his luck ran out when he based himself in England. Terry Clark was arrested and stood trial in the UK. A jury found him guilty of murder and other crimes. He was to serve his time in a notorious prison on the Isle of Wight.

Even in death he stayed true to character and continued to make waves. His death, reputedly caused by heart attack, to this day is thought suspicious within New Zealand. Those who supposedly had inside information firmly believed his death was at the hands of the IRA. It was a commonly held that they had hatched a plot to break him out of jail for a very large fee. Somehow this plan had gone wrong. In any event I believe that the Mr Asia syndicate and its activities were a significant turning point in New Zealand criminal history. The murderous actions of Sinclair and the corruption that allowed him to operate as he did were a major reason for the formation of a Royal Commission of Enquiry into organised crime. It was a first in Australian and New Zealand legal history, as it was empowered to sit and deliberate in both countries with full and unfettered authority in both of them, particularly with reference to its ability to call witnesses and force them to testify.

For now though it's back to the golf course and Mo Mersky's indiscretion. There is some good in every activity if you look for it. Mo's subsequent arrest eased my travails. His audacious robbery, in which many of the underworld's hierarchy were victims, dominated the gossip in the bars, clubs and dives and for a while that mercifully took the rumour heat off us. We in our turn did everything possible to keep the rumour mills going on Mo and the Cream Club hold up. While strolling down the fairways Rainton and I were chatting about our woes. We were both experiencing pressure from the vice squad. I was rather miffed as at that time Ray and I had just completed a successful series of Parliamentary meetings with a government statutes revision committee looking at regulating our industry. We thought it not quite cricket to be hassled whilst the committee hearings were in progress. This committee, with a forward looking brief, was required to investigate and then to introduce measures to licence the industry and bring it under some sort of control. We, as prime movers within the industry, were invited to make submissions on behalf of an operators group we had formed. This was the Sauna and Massage Parlours Association Incorporated. This high falutin' name had brought forth gales of mirth and derision from a certain section of society. However, the powers that be had recognised us as the official representatives of an industry that was somewhat beloved of Kiwis. We had almost manoeuvred ourselves into a position of acceptance and respectability. We had learnt that the best way to fight back and defend our position was through legal channels. We were growing up; we just needed the establishment to do the same.

As Rainton and I walked onto the seventh green,

both talking and neither doing much listening, I suddenly had a eureka moment. I remember it well as at that moment Rainton had just yelled and almost performed a cartwheel on the green. He had just holed a thirty-foot putt for his first ever birdie on that treacherous par five.

"Great birdie, mate," I said.

Rainton insisted in talking me through every stroke, and thought he had had in making that birdie; sadly, that is a cross we golfers have to bear.

"Mate, I could stand and talk to you for hours about the birdie, but I have to go, I have just had a very important thought, I need to act on it as soon as I can."

"Shit, mate have I scared you off? We're only playing for a tenner a hole."

"No, mate it's not like that, I have to go, but I'll play on until the ninth, double or quits. You're two up now aren't you?"

"That's a bet, get your money ready."

He was up for it; I just wanted to get off the course and pursue my stroke of genius. We played the final two holes, in which I managed to scramble two halves. My mind was elsewhere so it finished with my having to pay Rainton twenty dollars. The real pain was the on-going verbal banter I had to suffer. It was the usual stuff, along the lines that Rainton had hit a patch of form and I had created a reason to do a runner. That was all part of the cut and thrust and had to be accepted. For me it was a cheap exit fee to allow me the freedom to address a major problem.

This, of course, was all taking place before the advent of mobile phones. I just wanted some time to sit down quietly, marshal my thoughts, and figure out the best way to proceed.

I GO TO ASSISTANT COMMISSIONER
GRAHAM PERRY, HUGHIE'S BOSS

How to make this scrap a level playing field? That was my mission. What I was planning was very delicate; I knew that I would only get one shot at pulling it off. I had to get it right first time, as it could rebound with difficult consequences. I thought that I would get another opinion, so I made my way to the Pacific to talk over my plan with Ray.

I parked my car in the alleyway behind the sauna and slipped in by the back door. The lounge was full of all the usual suspects, most of them just clad in towels or dressing gowns. Picture the scene. Subdued, hidden lighting, coupled with the sound of soft music. Add a gentle lapping, splashing and bubbly sound coming from the plunge pool. See the scantily dressed, very pretty girls sitting with the punters. This ambience of pleasure created a scene of hedonism that would have graced any ancient Japanese, Roman, or Greek bathhouse. This however was Karangahape Road, Auckland 1974. Try as I might, I could never quite understand what it was that the authorities were trying to stop.

Val, one of our original girls, was talking to big Jim. He was one of her regular punters. Jim was a bearded farmer from South Auckland. Jim's weekly visits were always welcome as he invariably staggered in with great bags of fresh fruit or produce for the girls. Val was by no means one of the younger, nymphet type of girl. She was the more attractive 'yummy mummy' sort. I suppose that supports the old theory that variety is the spice of life; or perhaps that there is no substitute for experience. Whatever the reason, whatever her secret, and she definitely had one, Val was one of the most successful of working girls. At the last count at that time, she owned six houses, and I understand she went on to own many more. Such a pity she had lost her way in life.

"Len, if you're looking for Ray he's upstairs, training a new girl." I might have guessed.

"Thanks Val, is everything okay here?"

Foolish to ask really; we always had the place running like clockwork. I helped myself to one of our big fluffy towels, slipped into the changing room, showered and made for the sauna. Let me tell you, even though the primary function of the sauna is to induce sweat, it does have far greater properties. One of those for me has always been the restful feeling it creates. That darkened small room, the warmth, the dim red light all seem to provide an atmosphere of security. Many relate it to a return to the womb. That may be so, but for me it was the perfect thinking space.

Hughsie's visit to Sydney really had me on my toes. I was acutely aware that he could ramp up the pressure on the Pacific. I had to try to defuse the situation a bit. Ray was still busy with his tiresome training session. He really suffered for the business; such commitment! I didn't bother him. The time in the sauna had clarified my thoughts. I wrapped my towel around me and slipped out of the sauna. I went up the stairs to the little private office and picked up the phone.

"Auckland police station, can I help you?"

"Yes, could you put me through to Mr Graham Perry please?"

"One moment sir, while I check to see if he is available, who is speaking?"

"It's Len Russell."

"One moment, please Sir."

"Len, how are you, what can I do for you?"

"Graham, I'm okay thanks mate, but I better get down to it. I would like to have a chat. I think it's in all of our interest to do so. There's an unnecessary problem developing that nobody needs. Can I come down and talk it over with you before it gets out of hand?"

"That bad is it?"

"Well it could be, but a chat might fix it."

"Okay, can you come down now?"

"I am on my way."

I dressed in a hurry. I left my car behind the sauna and walked there. I strolled along K'Road turned into Pitt St, down past the fire station and down to Cook Street, via Vincent Street to that grey, uninviting building that was Auckland Central. I suppose that image was deliberate. Graham Perry at the time was the Chief Detective Inspector; he went on to become the Auckland Assistant Commissioner and he was Hughsie's direct boss. He and Hughsie were good mates. They had served in the navy together and had fought on the same boxing teams. They were part of a New Zealand navy crew sent to England to pick up the Black Prince; an almost obsolete Royal Navy cruiser that the New Zealand government had bought rather cheaply. A friend of mine, Fred Dickens, who has already featured in these pages, had also been on that trip and had told me about it. While the Kiwis were in Portsmouth the Royal Navy issued a challenge for an inter-services boxing tournament. The challenge was naturally accepted. The Kiwis were a bit short on capable boxers, apart from Hughsie and Graham Perry. They had to fill the team with lads from the rugby team. Fred Dickens, who fought as the heavyweight was a good rugby boy, a front row type, but definitely not a boxer. Apparently, the Kiwis put up a good show. Hughsie and Graham won their fights. Poor old Fred got a pummelling, but went the distance. His account of the fight had the result getting closer and closer as the years and the telling went on. He may even have won it by now.

So I knew Graham from the boxing. He was a keen fan and attended most of the shows. We often enjoyed a chat at the after fight soirees. I was taken up to the sixth floor and shown into Graham's office. He was sitting behind a large desk, looking very comfortable.

"Hi Len, what's new on the boxing scene?" was his friendly opening gambit. We talked boxing for a few minutes, and then he moved the conversation to the matter at hand.

"Okay Len, what is this about?"

"Graham, what I want to talk about is this Bickerstaff and Hughsie thing."

"Go ahead, I'm all ears," he said.

"Well it's like this, as you probably must know, Hughsie has been to Sydney trying to dig up some dirt on me. The thing is, is it official police business, or is he working on behalf of Bickerstaff and Radio I? You may not wish to, or be able to, tell me, but I have a very good reason for asking."

"Go ahead, what's the reason?"

"Look Graham, I am going to win this case and a lot of shit could come out, which is no good for anyone. My lawyers are pressing me to call Hughsie to give evidence and I have refused to let them. I don't want to involve him, or the Police in this. I quite like the bloke. He is ten times the man that Bickerstaff is, but it will look like he is doing his dirty work. If he is called, we will probably need to know who paid for his trip to Sydney. It would be to show whether it was official or not. If it was, it will look a little strange, as he was one of the telephone callers that night. When push comes to shove, as it surely will, he won't get any support from Bickerstaff or

Radio I. You know we have the tapes of the phone calls and Bickerstaff has named Clayton and Hughsie as his drinking partners all that boozy day leading up to it. It won't look good that those two made the phone calls; it will look like a jack up. I could extend the action and claim damages from him and Jerry Clayton as well. The thing is I don't want to do that. I'm not a fool; I know you could turn the heat up on the Pacific and me even more. Look Graham, you know that Ray and I are appearing in front of the government select committee on saunas, and co-operating. Our lawyers are joining with the government departments, including the Police and Justice Dept, to draw up a code of practice, which will tighten things up for everybody. Let's not ruin a good thing."

I stopped for a few seconds.

"Graham, I swear to you that I don't want to put Hughsie any further into this; he's doing that himself. It doesn't make any sense."

I then told him of the rumour mill, the threats etc. we were supposed to have made. I pointed out that any fair jury would see right through them, and realise where they came from. Now the thing is that Graham Perry was a do things by the book type. He was well respected everywhere. He was successful and very careful about his career. He would not allow any risks to it from his own actions or those of his staff. He had received the George Medal for bravery; he was a man's man.

While Hughsie was also very successful; he operated by a different set of rules; his own. Everything I had said to Graham was correct. I really was not going to call Hughsie to give evidence, no matter what. However, I needed to slow him down and for him to see I was not his enemy, not in this instance anyway. In retrospect it was a very wise move. It had a startling effect on the forthcoming case and had a far-reaching effect on my future. It provided me with a couple of great friendships that I had never thought likely. At the time that I went to see Perry it transpired that the police had successfully inserted an undercover man into the criminal cadre who frequented the Pacific Sauna. He was well entrenched, not only with the crims, but also the Pacific girls. It turned out that the police had bigger fish to fry. The Pacific had become a vital listening post for them. So there we have it, it would have been counterproductive for them to move too heavily against the Pacific.

This was a time of major change in the criminal culture of the city. The drug scene, which was exploding around the world, reached New Zealand. Auckland easily provided the biggest market for any enterprise in New Zealand. Massive changes took place in criminal society. Ruthless men who had previously been bank robbers, stand-over men and armed hold up robbers, quickly rose to the top of the drug distribution chain. Fortunes were there waiting to be made, provided you were willing to risk huge sentences if caught. There were plenty who were. The chief operators in it were now the main target of police activities. As far as drugs were concerned, the fact was that Ray and I suffered from the growing drug problem. It was very bad for us and we had to combat it to a certain extent. We had girls who had been reliable and keen workers enjoying their jobs. They were the girls who attracted many punters, not only by their looks, but also by their friendly outgoing personalities. They were changing before our very eyes. Heroin and LSD were taking a hold on them. They had previously been keen marijuana smokers, which in all honesty seemed to enhance them and their personalities. Strangely, considering other moral stands taken in New Zealand, marijuana was not seen as a major problem. In fact it was considered by many as a good alternative to alcohol, which I agree with, and a blind eye was turned to its use.

In a way, it answered a lot of questions. The cops having a man on the inside had the effect of lessening the police pressure. They didn't want their actions to start a flap that would cause their targets to stop meeting there. There was a suggestion after the undercover police officer was discovered that the sauna room had been bugged. If so there would be a few red faces around. The pressure dropped off and the odds on the result of the Bickerstaff case swung heavily in my favour.

However, as the old saying goes, 'there 'ain't a winner, 'til there is one.' Don't hold your breath Lenny boy.

DID I FIX THE FIGHTS? THE BICKERSTAFF, RADIO I COURT CASE

The big day arrived. The case was due to start. I find myself once again in the Auckland Supreme Court. I had arranged to meet Lloyd Brown QC there at nine o'clock for a briefing. Lloyd and the assisting barrister, Roger McLaren, arrived together. I watched them stride through the palatial, castle type entrance of the old Court building. Observing them from my shielded position, I was very impressed by their confident and easy manner. They appeared very much at home in this, their natural habitat. I felt a real glow of confidence. I knew I had two of the very best representatives of their profession acting for me. I also knew they were committed to winning.

This case and the result would be extensively publicised and discussed. Not just in the media, but as importantly, over many dinner tables and in the bars and restaurants. The winners would get the accolades. In those days the legal profession was not allowed to advertise; consequently winning was very important to their careers and standing. In addition we had a further opponent to deal with, the ABA who had their own axe to grind. They would join any crusade against me and did so, mostly in the guise of expert witnesses. Their main thrust was to prove that some of the fight results

293

had been fixed. They went to extreme lengths to do this. They called various members of the ABA. They made some amazing claims, most of them inaccurate. They made claims against our official timekeeper. The main one centred on a sell out South Pacific Middleweight Championship between our man La'avassa and the previously mentioned New Zealand middleweight champion, Kahu Mahanga at Stanley Street Stadium. It was a fifteen, three-minute round championship contest. It was also a showdown between the two associations, the establishment and the SPBA, the new kid on the block. From a promotional point of view we had the added lustre of a Maori against a Samoan, a certain high octane draw card in Polynesian Auckland. We had two skilful, internationally recognised, gutsy fighters. Kahu was a household name. He was highly thought of, not only by the Maori community, but by all sport loving New Zealanders, as most were. He lived with his wife and family in Tokoroa, a quiet provincial timber mill town and generally only ventured out of it to box top rated international opponents, mainly in Melbourne, Australia. His fights were always top of the bill. He was a great draw card in his own right. Kahu was so explosive and so willing to make a fight of it with whomever was in front of him that whenever he fought the house full sign was always out. His style and his combative nature won him many fans. So much so that at his peak he polled as the highest-ranking personality in the popularity stakes on all

Australian TV programs, not just the sporting genre.

La'avassa was well respected and he was also a household name in sport and boxing circles. He was a religious, family man who attended his local church every Sunday. He lived very simply with his aunt and extended family in Grey Lynn, an inner city suburb of Auckland. Neither of them lived the flamboyant life style that they could have. La'avassa was unbeaten; Kahu had only been beaten by the best international fighters. What combatants! What a promoter's dream! And I had it in my hands. That night I realised I had travelled a lot further than the thirteen thousand miles from Rickmansworth, England to Auckland, New Zealand; a whole lot more.

There are always complaints about decisions in good fights that go the distance. Our man La'avassa had won on all four judges' cards; a fact sportingly acknowledged by Kahu Mahanga. There were some however, who disagreed. Bob Jones, who was one of the judges that night, came in for some criticism. He had scored the fight by a much wider margin to La'avassa than the other judges. Bob robustly defended himself; maintaining that La'avassa had won every round. However, the criticism aimed at him was meaningless as all the judges awarded the fight to our man.

In the court case they came at us down a far

more insidious track. They attacked us with the old long count, shortened round allegation. La'avassa had suffered a knock down, late into the fourteenth round. As the referee was applying the count, the bell rang to end the round before the count was completed. The championship rules at the time allowed that a boxer could be saved by the bell, anytime apart from the last round. Well, the bell had rung to end the round. La'avassa, who had been knocked down and stunned, recovered in his corner. He came out and won the last round, which all agreed was a great one. It should be noted, that there was no official complaint laid at the time.

Bickerstaff's lawyer, Mr Hillier QC, dwelt on this alleged action. He was adamant that it was deliberate cheating and that we had shortened the fourteenth round out of necessity. He called ABA officials to testify that in their opinion the round had not run the full three minutes. He charged that we had used that manoeuvre to make sure that our man La'avassa could not be counted out and therefore lose the fight on a KO. If that were provable, they would be a long way to winning the case.

The next claim drew ripples of laughter from the public benches. This was the amusing assertion that I used the Pacific girls to provide sexual encounters for the boxers. The accusation was that these favours interfered with the boxers' performance.

Particularly, as it was claimed, that this service was only provided the night, or afternoon, prior to a fight. Most fighters I knew did not need any help from me in that department and in any event fighters like La'avassa and Mahanga were genuine in their religious principles and their commitment to their families.

There were attempts to paint me as a thoroughly bad person, prepared to use violence and threats to achieve my ends. These were easily disposed of as I had no record or convictions for any such offences. In an effort to support that, they did drag out a bitter ex-manageress come masseuse, whom Ray had sacked. Her allegations were so unconvincing that they were easily disposed of.

The Bickerstaff team took a couple of days and then it was our opportunity to prove our claim and refute their allegations. Their claim regarding the fourteenth round and La'avassa's knock down needed rebutting because if this were true, it would be strong evidence that I was fixing the fights. Supreme Courts can be scary places. The statues looking down seemed to glower at the participants. The imposing podium seating and desk for the judge were set in an elevated position. The dark stained brooding timber seating, the stark witness box; all left no doubt as to who wielded the power. The wigs, the black cloaks, the authoritative demand of 'all rise' on the entrance of the judge added to the impact of the place. It was 1975 and not so many years since the black cap had been worn by judges handing down the death sentence. The last one in New Zealand had been in 1964. However, even with these dour components, people being people, flashes of humour and wit shone through. Fortunately I had the benefit of experience, having had previous appearances there, but even with this background I still felt a degree of nervousness as I waited to take the stand.

I heard my name called, but I was so deep in thought that the sound of the usher calling me seemed to be a far echo in the distance. I quickly returned to the present. My natural thespian tendencies took over me. I consciously changed gear as I entered the witness box. I went through the oath taking and then Lloyd led me through a series of questions on the SPBA, and its formation. He also called upon me to answer questions as to its activities, method of operations, viability, number of promotions, and its potential. This was all standard stuff and quickly dispatched. No matter who cross-examined me on those matters, the outcome could only be positive. The high number of promotions we had delivered was a matter of record, as were the vastly increased work opportunities created for the boxers. My evidence was later supported by a number of well-known boxing trainers, who had been called to give evidence. To a man they praised the work of the

SPBA. This produced clear evidence of current success and future potential earnings. We needed this to support the claim for damages.

Lloyd then questioned me on the events of the night of the fracas in the studio. I related them exactly as they had occurred, knowing that I would be castigated for the violent part of it. It was no use denying it; it had happened and it was common knowledge. Much of it had been heard live on air. Lloyd having finished with me, it was the turn of the opposing QC to try to break me down. You will have seen this sort of tactic on TV court cases and believe me, if you have not been there, that is how it is. The usual stuff about the use of violence and threats was levelled at me. I parried this by denying it and pointing out there were no previous court cases or arrests to support that allegation. He soon tired of that and moved to some of the fights and the decisions given. I answered them all as best as I could, but his lack of knowledge about boxing made some of the questions laughable. He kept getting the fighters and or promotions mixed up. As an example of this, I was questioned closely about an alleged unfair decision in a contest in the Intercontinental Hotel between (as they said) Joe Santos and Steve Nikora. Mr Hillier pressed me to admit that the decision reached in this contest favoured the SPBA man Santos and had in fact drawn much criticism. I could not help smiling. My disposition brought a rebuke for me from the judge.

"Mr Russell please treats these proceedings seriously and also is it necessary for you to preface all your answers with a speech?"

"Yes it is Sir, most of the time it is necessary."

"On what do you base that rather arrogant assumption?"

"Your honour, with due respect to you and the Court, it seems that on these questions about boxing matters, I am the only one here who knows what he is talking about."

I think the judge wanted to say:

"That's a bit rich," but I think he suspected that I was largely correct. What he did say was:

"Mr Russell, explain yourself and if you cannot, please desist from this conduct; you must respect the Court."

"I do respect the Court, Sir and I value the chance to explain. To do so, I will give you an example. Take the last question regarding a claimed bout between Santos and Nikora. Sir, it never took place. However, they did both fight on the same bill that night, but not against each other. One of them, Nikora, is a light heavy weight, which has a twelve stone seven pounds limit; the other, Santos, is a light welterweight with a ten stone limit. It should be obvious that they would not fight each other. Sir, there have been other similar questions and that's why I have had to make the short speeches, I would rather not have had to."

Well you know how it is, the establishment stick together and to save any further embarrassment for

Mr Hillier QC the Judge adjourned the Court for lunch.

I went to the dining room of the old Central Hotel; it was just down the hill from the Courthouse. It was a pleasant easy walk down the palm tree lined street which ran alongside a picturesque little park. It was particularly so if your case was going well, as ours was. There is a cost in everything; it is not quite so pleasant a walk back up the hill with a full tummy. I tried to join Lloyd and Roger for lunch, but Roger advised me that as I was still under cross-examination they were not permitted to talk to me.

The room was full of lawyers so I had lunch with Peter Williams and Kevin Ryan. Kevin was one of four robust down-to-earth brothers, all good rugby league playing Catholic boys. An interesting situation arose one time with Kevin. This short story not only well illustrates the mettle of Kevin and his brothers; it also shows the Wild West side of Auckland in those days. Unfortunately for Kevin, he had in some way that he knew nothing about offended a vicious Auckland criminal. It was Mad Dog Shaw, who had been involved in the notorious Basset Road machine gun killings I have mentioned in Book One.

Kevin had a problem; Shaw was making threats, and spreading bad and unfounded gossip about him to the effect that Kevin was a police informer, which was fatal for a criminal barrister. Kevin tried to ignore it, but Shaw would not let up. The police are often no use in these matters, particularly if you are dealing with a nutter. Kevin won the admiration of all who knew what was going down and that was most of Auckland, by what he did. At that time, Shaw and other Auckland desperados gathered for drinks on Friday nights in a pub called The Occidental in Vulcan Lane. It was one of Auckland's oldest pubs, built in 1870 by an American sailor, Edward Perkins who allegedly deserted an American whaler operating in New Zealand waters. Vulcan Lane sported two very busy small pubs, a couple of restaurants, a coffee bar and shops. It had a colourful past. What we had here was a very public place for a showdown. Not many 'professional types' would choose this location for a straightener. It was usually teeming with shoppers and drinkers who spilled out of the pubs into the lane. Mad Dog Shaw bossed things there, but he was just another bully. Kevin had decided enough was enough. He and his brothers decided to confront Shaw in his lair.

When you take into account that Kevin was a barrister, that one brother went on to be a Mayor, another Gerald a successful accountant, who later became the president of the New Zealand Rugby League, it was a surprising thing to see them facing down a dangerous crook in public. And Irish Catholics of course were never known to be a hot headed bunch. The Ryan brothers went into the pub and Kevin went right up to Shaw and offered to discuss the matter as a means to resolve it, or if he had to, he would fight him outside on a one-on-one basis to put a stop the gossip and threats. The brothers were there to keep it fair in case any of Shaw's dilly mates wanted to get into Kevin. Shaw ranted and raved, but did not take up the offer. Kevin said: "If you don't cut this crap out Shaw, I will come down here every week and call you out in front of everybody."

Shaw huffed and puffed and he came up with the usual, I will get you routine. The thing is he did not. The story quickly spread and old Machine Gun Shaw suffered an alarming loss of reputation. Generally, from then on he became only a nuisance drunk. Kevin became something of a folk hero over that bit of theatre; Shaw was quite mad and it could have had a far different result.

The lunch break over, I wended my way up the hill, a bit slower than I had strolled down. It was back to the business in the Courthouse. My time in the box ended and I was relieved it was finished. Our main thrust now lay in an effort to rebut the accusations of the long count, short round charges. We had discussed it and thought our best tactic was to call the timekeeper and the referee who had officiated in that bout. We were very confident that their evidence and above all their character and previous experience, when known, would stand us in good stead. Lloyd called Bevan Weir the referee first. He cleverly drew Bevan on his experience and unblemished record. He had officiated in many Auckland and New Zealand championships and international contests, including Commonwealth Games bouts. Lloyd drew out evidence of his long tenure as a qualified leading referee for the ABA. Bevan confirmed that the president of the ABA had threatened to have him barred from ABA and New Zealand Boxing Council promotions should he ever officiate for the SPBA, with whom Bevan had bravely thrown in his lot. Bevan, an ex-New Zealand welterweight champion, was very much his own man. It speaks volumes about the lack of judgement by the ABA to threaten such a man. Bevan's interest lay solely in the progress and growth of New Zealand boxing. It became obvious that in his previous vast experience there had never been any criticism laid at his door. He gave his account of the events on the night in question. There was now someone in the court besides me, who knew exactly what he was talking about. I am sure that was in the mind of the Judge and jury.

Lloyd called the timekeeper next. By this time, I was thinking this was a belt and braces exercise. The timekeeper was an absolute pillar of the community, also that rare thing, particularly in the boxing community, a gentleman. This was Charles Linden, a well-known Christian leader and teacher.

He was a director of a major Auckland building company. I think he was also a Councillor. He was a man of good works. He had offered us his services in the interest of furthering boxing. Lloyd took him through his background. He then questioned him on his previous boxing and timekeeping experience. He had officiated in ABA and NZBC promotions, and national championships. It was plain foolish to intimate that wrongdoing was present in this man's nature.

There were two more points of interest and a dash of courtroom humour on which to dwell. One of them astonished me completely. It concerned Hughsie. Later in life after we had become friends, I understood his capacity to astonish. People had many and differing views on him, but however you viewed him, he was a real man, operating in a hard world.

It happened like this, I had slipped outside and was standing in the arched entrance when all of a sudden; Hughsie appeared in front of me.
"Len, I appreciate the fact you didn't drag me into this, they did. If I can, I am going to fix this."
"Well mate, I haven't come after you or Clayton, just Bickerstaff. He's a slag and he's screwed a few other people besides me. You probably don't know it, but there are three others queuing up to sue him. We can't all be wrong."
"I don't know anything about that mate, anyway,

good luck, have to go," he said as he strode off. I went back into the court and took a seat at the back, trying to be discreet. The usher called 'Detective Sergeant John Hughes'. He would have called that name out a few times over the years. In cross examination Lloyd questioned Hughsie on his job as a detective and his knowledge of boxing. He then moved on to the SPBA. What a surprise lay in store. Lloyd's questioning brought some stunning answers from Hughsie. He declared that he could find no evidence of wrongdoing within the association. He went further by confirming that we exceeded the standards required for the health and safety of boxers. He also confirmed that the officials who officiated at our fights were beyond reproach. Well that just about settled everything. It only remained for the judge's summing up. That was the only area that could now hurt us.

The summing up by the judge on the issues was clear and to the point. Then he addressed one of the areas that I thought might be tricky. Another surprise was in store; in fact, he brought a humorous edge to the proceedings. It was on the allegation that I had provided the Pacific girls for sexual favours and intercourse for the opposition boxers prior to their bouts. In addition, that I utilised the pretty staff of the Pacific Sauna to effect that. You may recall that the defence had called a couple of ex-employees to testify to that. However, the judge's wit on that subject finally introduced some laughter into the proceedings. His dissertation on this subject went something like this: "With respect to the allegation that Mr Russell provided the opposition boxers with sexual favours with the intention of handicapping them in some way; and the inference that those favours weakened or in some way interfered with their performance; I find no evidence, scientific or otherwise, that the sexual activity referred to, would in fact interfere with performance, even should it have taken place. There were no boxers brought forward to support that claim. The only evidence offered in support of it were the allegations of a disaffected ex-staff member, who under cross-examination denied that she herself would have taken part in such activity. I am also somewhat surprised and a little disappointed, that there hasn't been a bevy of these girls paraded through my court to give evidence in support of that contention."

Those remarks caused muffled chuckles from reporters and the public who were present. The jury were out for a very short time and they found for me. The damages were set and were generous. Costs were awarded against Bickerstaff and Radio I. The celebration party went on in the Pacific until the early hours. I had won and was pleased with the result; it had been a hard fight. Bickerstaff had more irate litigants to face; he had brought himself plenty of trouble. I had a substantial sum awarded, but I was pleased it was over.

After the gruelling months leading up to the court case, then the court case itself, it was time for some relaxation. It was summer time and the pool at the Pacific beckoned. I could think of no better way to unwind.

A SUNNY AFTERNOON BY
THE PACIFIC POOL

Two of the lovely Pacific girls, 1975-ish, see what I mean! Nice
casting couch, eh?

Not everyone who turned up at the Pacific had the
street smarts to thrive there. Ray, in a rare moment
of wine-induced generosity, had invited a somewhat
nondescript chap, a neighbour from the suburbs, to
call into the Pacific if he was passing. I can only
assume that Ray had an undeclared motive.

Once invited Mr Suburbia, our hero, could not get
away from his wife and work and come to us quickly
enough. He was a nice bloke but a real straight
John. The afternoon that he had decided to man up
and exercise his invitation found Jimmy, Ray and me
having a self-indulgent time by the pool. We were

chatting and listening to Jimmy's tall tales, laughing, having the odd swim and a drink. The girls were happy to join us and enjoy the company in between punters. That meant that there were always at least three cracking topless girls lounging or doing the honours with drinks and smokes.

Ray's guest had joined us by the pool. At first he was quite shy, in fact very shy. That however, did not stop him slyly ogling the topless girls. He started to enjoy a few wines. As the afternoon wore on he became more relaxed. With every drink and bit of encouragement he became more confident. One of the girls started showing a particular interest in him. This was probably on Ray's sneaky suggestion; he was only being a good host of course. Our hero was convinced he had pulled. He kept sucking in his tummy, he was intoxicated and it was not just by the wine. The lady who had become the object of his desires enticed him into the pool; she was topless, which was the norm. They gambolled about, splashing and playing in the clear cool water. I swear he thought he had died and gone to heaven. That was quite understandable really; she was a nineteen-year-old nymphet. After a while she slid slowly and sexually out of the pool, glistening in the late afternoon sun.

This fulsome woman was of the type that inspired Paul Gauguin, the French artist, famous for his paintings of Polynesian female, nude or near nude

subjects.   Even a cursory viewing of Gauguin's classic works, and his novel *The Gold of Their Bodies* would clearly illustrate the reason for our hero's panting obsession. This beautiful Polynesian female could have stepped out of one of Paul's canvasses.
Gauguin, after spending many happy years in the Polynesian Islands, eventually died in 1903 of a heart attack. He now lies buried in Tahiti, still with a smile on his face; on that I would be prepared to wager.

That afternoon she came to represent release from all of his pent up desires and perhaps the means of his escape from twenty years of boredom and suburbia. At the same time she also became his greatest disappointment and the source of his downfall.

Her long, dark hair was down round her brown shoulders; her fully exposed figure was beautiful. Meanwhile, our hero who was now transfixed and had eyes only for her managed a scrambled, ungainly, panting exit from the pool, flopping unsteadily onto the tile surround. The close combat exertions that had taken place in the pool were catching up with him. However, he had become completely protective of his girl. We did not appear to be visible to him. His concentration levelled solely on the dusky maiden was such that we hardly existed. Ray was amazed and almost peeing himself with laughter. This was not the same person, who nodded to him from his gardening and weekend car cleaning chores. We now had a situation similar to a rampant stag invading our territory in the rutting season. Jimmy and I were laughing and teasing Ray. "He's your mate Ray and what a lovely bloke. Are you going on holiday together this year?"

Ray was not sure what he had got himself into. Our hero brandished his wine glass and uttered the immortal words: "Christ, this is the life; I knock my balls out every day working, I must be a fucking idiot." He got that right.
Right at that time he would have traded his three bedroom house, tidy garden, sensible car, wife of twenty years, the nine-to-five job and everything he had aspired to in life for what he found here on this afternoon. His brief border crossing into the smut strip of Karangahape Road was a life changer for him. More and greater temptation was looming. The obliging, giggling nymphet pulled out another joint and lit it. A delivery of high-class Buddha sticks had just been unleashed on the Auckland streets by the Mr Asia gang. She took two very deep throat drags and offered it to him. There was no holding back our hero; this was the life and he wanted to try it. He had become a new man in the space of two hours. He was determined to show her, and us, how cool he was.
"Like this, darling" the nymphet said, motioning him to come closer and kiss her. He enthusiastically responded with his mouth open. She took another

deep drag, moved in as if to kiss him, but instead of that, she exhaled the smoke in his mouth and down his throat, which soon produced devastating results.

"Ray, your mate is having a ball," observed Jimmy.

Ray, who by now was getting slightly annoyed at the constant references to his 'mate', burst out with,

"He is not my fucking mate; I keep telling you he is just my fucking neighbour. Give it a rest with the shit."

Jimmy, never one to let go lightly, said, "I don't know how you can be like that Ray; he obviously thinks the world of you. I suppose his wife will too, being as you have been so hospitable to him. Yes, mate, of course she will. I can see it now; I bet she comes over the fence to personally thank you tonight."

"Fuck off," said Ray, "it's not my fault if he's such a mug."

By this time, our hero was in a wonderland world of his own. He had wandered off hand-in-hand with the nymphet to the sauna. I don't think he knew or cared where he was. The affair ended with our hero passing out in the changing room. Ray had no alternative but to call for the fallen hero's wife to come and collect him. She took one look at him lying there on the changing room tiles, with his privates exposed and then with an icy stare at the surroundings and the girls, who were floating around, turned to Ray and announced he could keep him. With great determination and looking straight ahead, she strode out into Karangahape Road. Meanwhile, our hero was spread-eagled, out cold on the floor with a couple of towels over him. In his stupor he kept mumbling the nymphets name and smiling, blissfully unaware of some impending changes to his domestic arrangements. I don't know how severe they were, but Ray did comment that he wasn't invited over for afternoon tea ever again. Sad that.

MEETING JOE FRAZIER

It was about 1975 that a benefit of my move into boxing transpired. Through it we at the Pacific were privileged to meet and host the famous world heavyweight champion boxer, the great Joe Frazier, while he was in Auckland. He and his party fell in love with the Pacific Sauna; they came in every day and relaxed. One of their pleasures was eight ball pool competitions amongst themselves. There came a time that they challenged us and in doing that they had bitten of more than they could chew. On one famous occasion Joe challenged Jimmy to play for a bottle of champers per game. Jimmy won eight straight games before going in off the black to lose the last one. I think that was Jimmy's way of letting Joe off the hook. Joe's competitive nature, blazed through. Although he was hopelessly outclassed, he just wanted to play on. This was all taking place before his last fight with Muhammad Ali, the titanic world championship battle, the 'Thrilla in Manila' which many aficionados of boxing claim to have been the greatest heavyweight fight of all time. It was going to be such a showdown; the worldwide publicity and build up was amazing. The fight seemed to be on everybody's lips, whether they were fans or not. They had already fought twice at that stage and had a victory each. There were other major rumblings around it. This was probably the most controversial fight in history and it was between two great champions at the height of their powers.

Naturally, the journalist wanted to interview Joe and you did not have to be a detective to work out where he was. It didn't take long for the rest of the Auckland sporting public to figure out where to find him relaxing and enjoying himself. The Pacific was packed out daily with sports fans, journos, cops, crooks and boxers, all eager to meet him. Once again, Ray and I found we had many old friends we had never heard of. It was an incredible time and as was usual, some amusing incidents' took place.

Joe was a very nice person. He had suffered a hard upbringing in the ghettos of Philadelphia and New York, where he had moved to at a very young age to advance his boxing career. We had a few chats about his life and times over games of pool and sometimes in the sauna having a sweat. Like most boxers he came from a tough background and boxing had been the way out for him. His life experiences had brought about in him some forthright views. One of them causing the very real problem that existed between him and Muhammad Ali and his associates, the Nation of Islam movement. Joe explained it to me that the problem was not a promoter's publicity stunt to sell more tickets for their fight. There really did exist between them a deep chasm in regard as to how best to address the prevalent racial problems in America at that time. A huge and dangerous by-product of this had been the very public verbal abuse of Joe by Ali, who had labelled Joe an Uncle Tom and the white man's champion, which was as bad an insult as could be levelled at such a proud black American as Joe was. Joe was also angry for another reason. He had been a staunch supporter of Ali in the battle to get his boxing licence back, even to the extent of financial support. As the world knows, Ali's licence had been taken from him for refusing to be drafted into the US army. Joe felt betrayed, and hearing the story from him, I think he was.

They fought three epic battles, the last one being the famous Manila bout, which was for a lot more than the title and money. It was a very personal feud, but fought out in public. It was also for the biggest prize in sport, the heavyweight championship of the world. Although Joe was well schooled by his management in how far to go when talking in public, he was very open and forthright with me. Most days he came in with some of his entourage and they made a beeline for the pool tables, then the sauna and then the swimming pool. Our pretty staff members were always happy to entertain them. I think Joe's party may have thought they had died and gone to heaven and maybe our girls thought so too. For his part, Joe was enthralled with Karangahape Rd; he loved it there; not just us, but the cafés, shops and colourfully dressed Island people. At night it was a hot, rippling, neon bright, entertainment area, rather than the poorly lit, run down street that had existed before our involvement and investments. We enjoyed having New Zealand's top strip and dance club, the Pink Pussy Cat Club, next door to the Pacific. The two businesses obviously complemented each other.

Diamond Jim Shepherd, one of the best. Jimmy's greatest claim to fame? He beat Joe Frazier ... at eight ball.

One Friday night, Ray, Jimmy, Joe and I were having a quiet drink and chat in the bar, when Joe said he would like to go into the strip club next door, but was worried in case he was recognised on the way into the club. This remark caused Jimmy, Ray and me to burst out laughing. Joe was perplexed and good naturedly said "Hey you guys what's so funny?"

"Who's going to tell him?" I asked. Joe at that stage had not spent any time at night with us and therefore had only seen K' Road in the daylight with its normal mixed daytime business crowd. I think it was Jimmy, who being half Maori, was best equipped to answer, and piped up with:

"Joe, this is probably the best street in Auckland for a black man to go unnoticed at night." We took him outside; it was about ten o'clock at night, and Joe just looked at us, looked at the heaving mass of largely Polynesian males and had a good laugh at himself. We took him into the Pink Pussy where Rainton turned on the VIP treatment. Joe by this time was not caring who saw him. He was happy to be spotlighted with us. Rainton introduced him to the audience who greeted him with great show stopping cheers of appreciation. Joe willingly shook a few hands and signed a few Pink Pussy napkins. It was a treat for everybody there, though I suspect most of the chaps would not have been able to go home and show the wife their autographed napkins, nor tell of meeting Joe Frazier in the Pink Pussy.

While we enjoyed Joe spending time with us, we also scored great PR out of his association with the

Pacific Sauna. We'd been busy and now we got busier. Joe told me how much he had enjoyed the trip and in particular the hospitality we had shown him. He asked me if there was anything that he could do for me, in return. I asked him for two things. The first was to tell me the inside story on the animosity between him and Ali, which I have previously outlined. There was some upside however; a well-connected American promoter later told me that the magnitude of their great last fight caused them to reignite respect for each other, although it didn't entirely heal Joe's deep wounds. Anybody who saw that titanic contest, which went beyond courage, would well understand Joe and Ali's feelings afterwards. Though Joe lost, it was a great battle between two true warriors. That night, they cemented their place in the annals of history.

The second request provided a night to remember for all those present, but particularly for me, Ray and Jimmy. Just before Joe and his party were due to leave, I had had a call from a friend of ours, Martin Joiner, a well-known character and sportsman who owned a very good downtown nightclub. Martin asked whether we could bring Joe and his party down to the club. If so, he would arrange a fabulous complimentary night for our party. It sounded a good idea. I checked it out with Joe and he was very much up for it. What a party and what a night. Martin truly turned it on; it was champagne all the way. We were all having a great time, so I asked Joe if he would do me a favour. I knew that Joe was also a rock singer and had his own band called 'Joe Frazier and the Knock Outs'. I asked him to perform for us. He readily agreed. He was great. He must have been on stage for forty minutes or more. He sang some popular rock numbers, but the *piece de resistance* was when he sang a special version of the Frank Sinatra's great hit *My Way*. Joe's version was a special one written for him by Paul Anka, who had written the original version for his father-in-law at the time, Frank Sinatra.

Joe sang it brilliantly, it was fantastic, but that was not the end of it. He called for me, Ray and Jimmy to join him on the stage and publicly thanked us for the hospitality he and his party had received. Joe was a real man. As you go through life, sometimes nice things happen; this was one of those and it truly was a time to remember.

MY INTRODUCTION TO ELIZA'S,
A LEGENDARY SYDNEY RESTAURANT

I now need to take us back a few years to 1972, to the early days of the boxing promotions. We had done so well that Ron Casey, the man in charge of sport content for Sydney's Channel 9 TV had flown over from Sydney to see me. His purpose was to negotiate an exclusive deal that tied my fighters to his successful Tuesday night show, *TV Ringside*. Ron Casey visiting was a bit like boxing royalty dropping by in those days. Because of this meeting, it became necessary for me to pay a return visit to his offices in North Sydney. On this trip I had Scotty with me. Although Scotty and I had become involved in a couple of deals, his involvement in boxing was only in an advisory capacity. Anyway, after the meeting with Ron Casey in the Channel 9 offices in Chatswood, on Sydney's North shore, we were escorted around some of the Sydney hot spots by one of their PR people. I must comment that his job must have been one of the most pleasant in the world.

Eliza's restaurant in Double Bay was an amazing, fantastic place. It was patronised by politicians, businessmen, detectives, bookmakers, TV stars, rugby league football stars, pimps, crooks, and wannabes. It was alive and throbbing with excitement and had an element of mystery - who were the cops and who were the crims? Who were the lawyers and who were the pimps? It was as if they all morphed into one.

"Len, come over here and say hello to John," said my host. I was introduced to and exchanged pleasantries with John Singleton, Australia's equivalent to England's David Frost or Sir Michael Parkinson. More introductions followed. I met an Assistant Police Commissioner, detectives, property developers, businesspeople, bookies, horse trainers, and a couple of unassuming looking people I was later informed were A list crooks. The wine flowed, the food was great and everybody was having a great time. This was Sydney at business and at play. No lords, no ladies, no snobs. It was a constantly changing merry-go-round, founded on what you could do and what you could bring to the table. I looked across the room from my position near the main bar and felt the exhilaration. These people felt they had the world readily available. They were positive, and anything was possible. An air of confidence pervaded everything; a spirit of 'can do' that I found so intoxicating down under. They found a reason to do, instead of a reason not to do, and to me it appeared that the leafy luxurious Eliza's was their Camelot.

Part of this regal treatment found me and my colleague propping up the bar one afternoon in a beautifully appointed Sydney massage parlour as VIP guests. Our host had designated a well-known

Sydney character to look after us and he seemed to have the run of the place. They just could not do enough for us; I put it down to market research. You have to hand it to the Aussies; they do not hang around when they want something. I picked up some tips that would prove useful later when I joined the sauna parlour business. I had been invited there to finalise our deal. The TV Ringside program used to go out live from the famous South Sydney Rugby League Club (the Rabbitohs) in Redfern. The show had become a victim of its own success and developed an insatiable appetite for preliminary and main event boxers. It was struggling to find enough skilled and entertaining boxers locally, to maintain its quality and content. Ron Casey, a certain high-powered Channel 9 TV executive had realised the control and influence the South Pacific Association, in other words me, had achieved in the boxing scene. Because of that, he was doing his level best to tie our supply of quality boxers solely to his TV station. He was acutely aware, that I was being courted by a rival Melbourne TV channel, which also ran successful weekly boxing shows. It was nice to be courted like this and we did a very good deal. I headed back to Auckland, but something had changed. Seeing parts of Sydney like Double Bay, which to my mind is one of the finest suburbs in the world, and the exuberant lifestyle at places like Eliza's, had me hooked. I was going to have a part of this world, I knew that my boxing involvement opened the door;

it was an entry into another life and I resolved to exploit it.

ROGUES GALLERY

This picture shows Ray Miller (with cigar) and some of the crew 'on the lash', in the Top Dog Bar in Panama. It features a young John Prescott, one of the boys (centre, hooped shirt), who went on to become British Deputy Prime Minister and the owner of two Jags, apparently.

The Three Amigos; Three shifty Auklanders, Marty Slade, left, Ray Miller and Bruno Belton, right. Founder members of the Boundary Pushers Club.

Steve Bell, left and Zac Ratana, onboard my boat, the Amalfi.
Two good guys.

Rainton Hastie, strip club king and me on his Gin Palace boat in
the bay of islands, one Christmas

Top man Steve Bell on the oars, with Pete Maderatz and his wife, Sue.

Steve Bell rowing again, one of life's good guys, no longer with us, with me on a holiday cruise.

PUSHING BOUNDARIES,
THE PACIFIC SAUNA PARLOUR

That memorable visit to the Sydney massage parlour was the catalyst for me to get a similar operation underway in Auckland. My plan was to establish a gym in the upstairs of the Karangahape Road premises that I had purchased earlier. The gym was initially a smoke screen, a manoeuvre to provide the legitimate cover I would need to get the necessary planning permission. If I had applied as a massage parlour it would have been stopped stone dead. I thought I needed the smoke screen for Auckland's police and the wowser population. Meanwhile I would be getting the massage parlour underway downstairs, which would have a separate entrance. I thought that would be confusing for the authorities and add a bit of a comfort factor for the punters. You can imagine this scenario. A punter comes home all shiny and smelling nice and clean,
"Just been to the gym darling, trying to lose a bit of weight, had a great work out."
"Oh, that's so good, keep up the good work, darling, and you will be able to get back into that nice business suit of yours." Well that was the plan.

I was careful to introduce the massage part of the business after all the relevant permits were granted and the gym was operating. The great advantage was in having a genuine gymnasium and sports massaging complex operating at the same time as the more in demand topless type. The punters could always claim to be there for the legitimate side of things, if for any reason their visits were exposed. Many column inches in the press were devoted to this enterprise. I had a good understanding with journalists and they were always welcome at the very happy Pacific Sauna. And Karangahape Road was the perfect site for us. It has been said that the 'hape' in the name certainly was appropriate as most of punters went home happier than they were when they came in. Maybe some see that as a sad commentary on society, but it is very true; all we did really was fill a demand. The paying public are the true barometer of society's needs and boundaries.

Rainton Hastie was the owner of the neighbouring premises. Rainton had learnt his trade in London whilst working for London's famous strip, porn, and peep show king, the owner of Raymond's Revue Bar. Rainton had suffered under the draconian laws and attitudes so prevalent in those days. He had been under intense pressure from the Police and so-called moral groups. They agitated and petitioned to close his venues down for exhibiting shows less saucy than those which are now featured on prime time TV or readily available in films or DVDs. In the end the public have quite rightly decided the issue and this form of entertainment is now a part of the fabric of life in most cities of the world. And the original Pink Pussy Cat marches on forty years later.

In the early days in Karangahape Road, Ray and I saw Rainton as an enemy. We soon realised after a confrontation or two that we would be better off acting in tandem. We sat down in a peace meeting as a war between us had nearly broken out. This had been a tense situation as Ray and I had deliberately moved further into his territory and business. Though we were a lot stronger, there were guys lining up on either side. Winning may not have been worth the price we would all pay. Our businesses were complimentary to each other; anyway, he was a guy we came to like.

Auckland at the time, the early seventies, had a real Wild West aspect. There were no Marquis of Queensbury rules; you did what you had to do. Later, we joined together in opening another massage parlour in a prime position in K Road. We rather overdid its upmarket decor so needed a name to reflect that, consequently, it joined the stable as 'The Swank.'

Unfortunately, the name upset the wowsers as apparently it conjured up other images. Try as you might, that old saying was proven to be true, 'you can keep some of the people happy, some of the time, but you can't keep all of the people happy all of the time', Even on K Road.

THE RUN IN WITH THE PTA

New Zealand in the mid-seventies was still a conservative, arguably puritanical, type of society. As an example, there had been no Sunday papers allowed until the mid-sixties. There was no weekend trading until the late seventies. There were restricted drinking hours. The pubs used to have to shut at six o'clock, which gave rise to the New Zealand phenomenon known as 'the six o'clock swill'. Add to that the tight liquor licensing regulations; licensed restaurants were rare. They only really got started in the early seventies and even then, they had to close at ten o'clock. So the opening of our pleasure palace had surprised a lot of people, particularly some members of the religious establishment that was so prominent in New Zealand affairs then. We had the pleasure of engaging with an individual who represented the parent teacher association of the local girls grammar school. He had appeared and opposed us in the Select Committee hearings. To be fair the school he represented was about five hundred yards from our front door, but on a side road. It appeared that his major problem was that the school girls chose to wait for the bus at a bus stop which was only yards from our front door. This particularly energetic person had also opposed me in my initial town planning applications. He had written to newspapers trying to generate opposition to us on any front. He was a right wowser! For the benefit of Brit readers that probably translates to something like a real miserable bastard and a jobsworth of the worst order.

The next thing I knew was that an investigative TV journalist from a popular current affairs program had become very interested in the row that was developing. This journalist, who was acting on a tip off, had a nose for a hot story. He invited us both to join him to debate the issue live on air with him stoking the fire. Well, we did appear and he did stoke the fire.   Once I had received the invitation I started to think through the possible consequences. I was immediately aware of the great exposure we would receive as the program went out nationally and the New Zealand public was no different from the rest of the world when it came to a bit of scandal. This was a Godsend, handled correctly. I wanted it both ways; I wanted to show the gymnasium and boxing aspects and the community benefits of the facility; but I also wanted to get the other naughty, under the counter message across as well.

After a weekend's thought on it I figured out that Mr Wowser would be so pumped up to show me in a bad light and the Pacific as a den of iniquity, that I would best leave him and his messianic approach alone. Nothing would get my message across better than appearing to be the tolerant, rational one of the two of us. The next tactic I decided on was to invite Mr Wowser to inspect our establishment. I rang him and offered the inspection tour, which he hesitantly agreed to. We fixed a day and time and I set about preparing the scene. I arranged to have the gym busy with boxers and a couple of obvious street kids getting tuition from the immediately recognisable Bobby Dunlop, the just retired Commonwealth light heavyweight champion, who was now acting as the gym's trainer. I walked him through the downstairs naughty section. I made sure that a couple of the attractive girls were highly visible and barely clad. I had really committed to getting him so irate that he did the publicity job for me. He looked at me incredulously as if I had shot myself in the foot. I hustled him through the softly lit massage section, making it look and feel obvious that I was rushing him through it and led him upstairs to the gym, where it was a picture of health and happiness. There were a couple of pro boxers working out with Bobby Dunlop the trainer. Then there were also two leading amateurs working with a couple of obviously novice street kids. It would take a truly embittered man not to see the upside of the gym.

The big day of battle arrived for Mr Wowser and me. We were ushered into a lounge and offered tea or coffee, which we both declined. I thought it strange that we were left alone together for a short time. It resulted in a brief, but bitter, exchange, which I came to believe was manipulated and was overheard; then an assistant came in and advised us what to expect. The interview would be going out live in the prime time slot. However, due to a technical hitch, there would be a five-minute delay. I don't think this bothered Mr Wowser and it certainly did not worry me. I just saw more exposure. A production assistant escorted us into the studio, showed us to our seats and made us comfortable. The host settled us down and gave last minute instructions. Somebody counted down and we were live. The host introduced us by name and outlined the situation for viewers. I now understood why they had delayed the start by five minutes; it was to give them more time to promote the interview. They were obviously expecting something good. Fortunately, for me the host gave the first opportunity to Mr Wowser and he did a good opening job for himself. He started rationally explaining his position and concerns. In reply to the host's questions, he did not dispute that perhaps a certain section of society might want the services that he suspected were provided in our premises; although at that stage he was being circumspect as to what they were. As he continued on, with the occasional prod from the host, he struggled to contain himself. He made vague statements and great use of innuendo. He became increasingly heated; he maligned the Council for letting us operate. He regularly mentioned falling standards in the country. He magnanimously disclosed that I had invited him to inspect the premises. He then launched into describing the downstairs as a dimly lit and plushly appointed lounge; definitely not a normal gymnasium. His description of the upstairs gym was cursory, but accurate, as had been his description of the downstairs area. He then launched into his main obsession; that schoolgirls had to wait for the bus at the stop outside our premises. Well if this was the problem and morally bad for them, how come was it that literally thousands of shoppers who used this area regularly and enjoyed shopping and socialising there never complained; in fact they got quite friendly with the girls when they sometimes sat out next door in the coffee bar. Many of them happily joined the queue at the same bus stop, some with their children. Incidentally the area was well served with alternative bus stops; there was another one only three hundred yards away. His tirade finished with a remarkable statement that 'the sauna should at the very least be moved far away from a bus stop'.

The host turned to me and asked me whether I wanted to refute the assertions and asked whether there was there any room for negotiation. Happily for me most of Mr Wowser's complaints and accusations had been pretty much what I'd wanted him to say. I was not going to go down the road of flatly denying them, but I had to appear to defend myself. I also realized that there could be a backlash if I ridiculed him. I started chatting to our

339

host and included the Wowser in the conversation. The first point I made was that the main tenant of the building was the South Pacific Boxing Association. This was a properly constituted body with a committee compromising various well-known personalities and sportsmen. I dwelt on the fact that the gymnasium was available to all sections of society. I stressed that there was no charge for youngsters to use it. In fact they could be there as much as the amateur and professional boxers who trained and operated with the SPBA, plus they got free tutelage from the boxers and trainers.

While I was saying this, Mr Wowser kept mumbling about 'that other business'.
"Yes what about that," said the host. This is where he wanted the discussion to focus; he was not interested in my good works spiel.
"Okay then, what is it that you want answered?"
Mr Wowser looked a bit more comfortable. This was his moment. The first one he hit me with was:
"In reference to the statement that the masseuses are scantily clad and young and pretty, could you explain that, or the need for that?"
What a beauty I thought. In that instant, that one statement conjured up such a powerful image. I could see hordes of new punters slipping in through the back door no matter how I answered it. Ray and Jimmy later told me that they were in hysterics when he asked that. With all the seriousness I could muster I looked at them both.

"It's very simple; it's largely due to the heat generated in the small massage rooms. Add to that the fact that the masseuses splash a lot of oil on their clients and lots of it seems to settle on them, it seems so much more practical to wear a bikini. They usually wear the same ones around the pool, so it's not that unusual, is it?" I immediately carried on in answer to the second part of the question. "And why are they young and attractive? I thought that would be self-explanatory. It's a bit like airlines; the flight hostesses are generally young and attractive."

In those days young and attractive actually outweighed all other considerations in the selection of airline staff.

"If it's against the law to employ pretty girls I am certainly in trouble as I confess that we do employ very pretty girls as our masseuses and I think the customers prefer it that way."

The host was looking at me with a quizzical glint in his eye, but I think he was happy with what he was getting. However, I thought I had better change tack.

"There is one other point I would like to address," I said to the host.

"What is it?" he asked with a smile.

"Well, it's the question of the bus stop."

"Oh yes," they almost said in unison. I carried on in a cooperative manner.

"I suppose it might not be a suitable stop for the girls to use, I can definitely see your point on this."

There were serious nods all round now.

"I think it is entirely unreasonable to expect us to move, but there are two solutions easily possible."

"What do you suggest then?" said Mr Wowser.

"It's simple; why don't you ask or instruct the girls to use the other stop, the same distance down the road. On the other hand, as an alternative, ask the council to move the bus stop, that would be easier than us moving, don't you think?"

Then very graciously, I said: "I will support any application you make to the Council."

Mr Wowser looked a tad perplexed and unhappy at this commonsense suggestion, which completely shot down his ill-conceived complaints. The host was not sure if he had what he wanted, but he knew he had a good show. I was very sure it could not have worked out better for us. This interview had supplied us with the sort of publicity that you could never buy.

Our time was up; twenty minutes had flown past. The host expertly brought the proceedings to an end. He thanked us for our time etc. He gave a short summary pointing out the usual good and bad points of either pitch and stated that he hoped the interview would help to heal our differences. I said I hoped so. Mr Wowser struggled with that a bit. For a while after that I had people stop me in the street or in a bar or restaurant and say how much they'd enjoyed it and what a laugh it gave them. And you know what? They never moved the bus stop. Though the interview was of great benefit to the business, it did not present itself so well at home. Things had started to get difficult. I realised that the publicity that I was getting, good or bad, was making things untenable at home. Something had to give.

THE BATH HOUSE ASSOCIATION

There was massive wowser hostility to the Pacific once it was underway which we were never able to completely overcome. We managed the situation as best we could. We figured that we had to improve the public's perception of us. This included undertaking a sponsorship deal with the Ponsonby Rugby League club, which certainly helped our image, but not with the wives and girlfriends, I'm afraid. Ray and I realised that we were exposed and set about protecting ourselves legally. To achieve this we set off down a legal path to initiate a licensing system. To do that we did the time honoured Kiwi thing when there was a problem; we formed a committee, which in turn grew into an association. The South Pacific Sauna Parlour Association was born. It was a title and it gave us a platform, a dollop of legitimacy and more importantly a claim to speak on behalf of a national body. Naturally, I was the President and Ray was the secretary; that kept it nice, close and controllable. This format achieved phenomenal success. We called in some favours, which resulted in our being invited to make submissions and to appear in person in support of them in front of a government select committee set up to control this emerging industry. I loved it when they used that term, on behalf of the new 'industry'. As soon as they started using that term I knew that we had them, whether they realised it or not; it was recognition.

A few months after the hearings, our solicitor representing the Association received a select committee letter. The letter thanked us for appearing and providing valuable input. The letter then advised that they had taken some of our submissions on board and weighed them against other counter submissions. It was agreed that it was in the best interests of all parties to include some of our recommendations and have the industry licensed. This measure, along with others, was accepted as the best way of controlling the industry and keeping out undesirables. Can you believe it; it was a case of making the poacher the gamekeeper, all over again. We were invited to recommend requirements for, and be involved in, the licensing process, as the committee had been very impressed with our knowledge and genuine interest (you bet we had that) in legitimising the industry. Coincidently, the first license ever granted was issued to us, the Pacific Sauna.

The upside was that it took many of the risks away from us, and placed it on the girls. It was a fact that we were not involved in taking money off the girls; we had never gone down that path. Our income was solely from the exorbitant entrance fees and the bar; yet the police and the wowsers would never accept that fact. The boys on the vice squad down in Cook Street were well peed of by the outcome and the decisions of the select committee, as they had been making counter submissions. They had been looking to cause us some problems. A common tactic was using undercover cops in an effort to implicate us and build a case against us for living on the immoral earnings of the girls. They could never have made that stick if they played by the rules. They knew that was not how we made our money, so they used to try to get the girls to fit us up by giving false evidence, which fortunately they never did. So we had spiked their guns for a while at least, but they would be trying another tack, that was for sure.

We had a celebration of our new legal status in our upstairs private bar. It started out as just a quiet drink with a couple of friends and the legal team that had helped us. At that time we had just finished the outside pool and decking; you can well imagine what that lent to the party. More and more people arrived. The alcohol flowed, the party got wilder and wilder. The pool and surrounding decking was a mass of inebriated bodies male and female. There were so many they looked intertwined, some were, but who cared? The moment and the euphoria had taken over. None of our girls had gone home and I do not think Ray or I were worrying too much about customers. After a while, we just shut the doors and had our own 'Caligula' night, which is probably the best description I can give of it.

The Ponsonby Pacific Ponies rugby league team were all there. Their captain Roger Bailey, one of New Zealand's greatest ever centre three quarters had become a close friend of mine. Through this association had come about probably the first real hands-on sponsorship for a rugby league club in Auckland. It had become a great publicity move for us as the deal had given us naming rights for the team.   The Pacific Ponies grew to be synonymous with the Pacific sauna, which gave us further legitimacy and great publicity. It was beneficial for the club and not just financially; the sponsorship resulted in their being besieged by top players wanting to join the Ponies to enjoy the facilities and be part of the brand. The Ponies had just become the New Zealand club champions. Our girls had tended to become camp followers for the Ponies; I suppose that could have been considered an unfair advantage, a net to attract their players. It caused a bit of squealing from some of the clubs. Hey ho, all families have arguments. Although it appeared it was plain sailing now, the next story illustrates the unofficial difficulties we faced.

RAY'S RUCKUS

Late one Friday night, while I was home trying (unsuccessfully) to improve my situation with the wife, the phone rang. It was quite late and I sensed urgency about it. It has to be a problem at the Pacific I thought to myself. It was; it was Ray and he was steaming. Now Ray is normally a cool sort of bloke who thinks things through. This time he was not; he was white hot angry. Ray had called into the Pacific after being out to dinner. Upon entering he was surprised and mightily pissed off to find three tipsy young detectives who had been out on the town. They were throwing their weight around and had invaded the receptionist's office. One was sitting with his feet up on the desk! In addition, they were harassing the girls. Ray was not the kind of person to take that, police officers or not. He ordered them out, but they were not taking a lot of notice. They were attempting to stand over him. Ray realized they were probably trying to push him into throwing the first punch so they could then arrest him and probably bash him, while claiming assault and resisting arrest by him. A standoff developed and after verbal threats by them to tuck him up and arrest him again on illegal bookmaking charges, they noisily left. It was not a good look for our punters, particularly the married ones there; they were always sensitive as to who was around, in case they were recognised. So overall, it was not a good night for us.

Ray and I sat down the next day and discussed our options. I thought it best left, as I doubted there would be a repeat performance. I also thought we would bring more problems on ourselves if we pursued it. I had a very good high-level contact in the Police with whom I played golf. I had called him on an unofficial basis and run the incident past him. He said he would have a word and try to sort it out. Ray however was having none of that. He wanted to take it as far as possible. As he had suffered the problem, it was his right to respond as he thought best.

Ray was a big man, with a determination to match his size. He was hopping mad and was prepared to settle it with a straightener in the back alley with them one at a time. There had been a few straighteners out there in the alley behind the Pacific. Knowing each of those three detectives, I would have to say, that solution would have suited them as well. Young Auckland detectives were no shrinking violets; they would not have lasted if they were. If that had been the chosen option, regardless of the result, that would have been the end of it. There would have been no complaints from either side. Auckland detectives had to be, and mostly were, tough hombres. A lot of them were top-level rugby league or rugby union players. Some of them played for the very good Mt. Albert

Club in the same competition as our team. Consequently, because of these and other long held grievances, when they met on the field, there were no beg your pardons. It was not only get even time, to a degree it was might versus right, cops versus robbers and the cops were up for it too. Rugby league officials estimated that there were thousands more spectators present, whenever the two teams clashed.

My partner, Ray Miller, another Pommie seaman. You can see he was big enough for a straightener.

The Pacific sauna was not the official clubhouse, but it was the premier team's clubhouse of choice for socializing and relaxing. All of these things added up and there was a bit of jealously thrown in, particularly if you had not been selected for the Saturday game. Consequently, things sometimes boiled over and the back alley was the venue of choice; the OK Corral without guns one might say.

Going back to Ray's ruckus; he decided to make an official complaint. This choice of action was probably the best, even though I was against it at the time. We were hoping that an official complaint would ease the situation a bit as most of the problems we were suffering were coming from these young macho detectives, not always acting officially. The funny thing was that the young detectives seemed to like coming to the Pacific. If they were cruising in K' Road, or looking for someone, they tended to drop in. They certainly weren't wowsers; in fact, they were just the opposite. I thought about it, but I don't think they knew about the undercover cop that had been secreted into our midst, as one of them was sweet on one of the girls and that could have had repercussions.

The undercover detective the drug and vice squads had infiltrated into our midst was named Andy James. He had worked his way into things as a big spending client. He was a young, good looking, dressed for the part guy, spending lots of cash, the taxpayers' as it turned out. He was passing himself off as a marijuana dealer; which he was actually doing. The girls all loved him. He spent all his time at the Pacific and through some contacts there had worked his way into the company of some major dealers and dangerous crims.

One day he was in the sauna spending up large with the taxpayers' money again and going from girl to girl. He was obviously very stoned. By late afternoon he had passed out in the upstairs lounge. The girls had not been able to shift him, so they asked Ray, who was on call that week, what they should do. We were supposed to take it in turns to be there, but it was such a fun place, neither of us could keep away. However, on this occasion it was Ray who was on hand to help the girls. In no time at all Ray threw him out with some choice advice on his future behaviour if he wished to spend more time at the Pacific.

By an amazing coincidence, Andy James' house was burgled that night. Interestingly the burglar had targeted Andy after a tip off about his extravagant spending sprees in the Pacific; it was probably by one of the girls. Well, it was this tip off that brought Andy down. The burglar discovered documents which clearly showed who Andy really was and more importantly, who he was undercover to trap. The burglar, realising how important this piece of information was, immediately referred it back to some very interested parties. Some of them were recent friends and acquaintances of Andy's, and had been involved in marijuana deals with him.

I will not say there was panic amongst the troops, but quite a few faces went missing. Within two days raids were taking place not just in Auckland, but all over New Zealand to apprehend certain parties.

Journalists homed in on the Pacific from all over the country. It had become public knowledge about Andy's activity and his time spent meeting various crims there.   You may think that all this was damaging for the business, but the fact was that the publicity caused a fresh wave of interest and we had a new crop of customers. It was unique; we now had would-be villains, wannabees and nosy members of the public rubbernecking. K' Road and particularly the Pacific were becoming places of interest. A place to maybe catch a glimpse of real villains at the place they hung out. Had it been a promotional gimmick, it would have been a good one. We cashed in.

At this stage, we had no great reputations to protect, so we surreptitiously fanned the flames, mainly through our contacts with the press. I had a great one with a Sunday news reporter, who was an absolute nut on boxing, and had a background with South Island crims. He was invaluable.   In the light of subsequent events, covered further along in this book, 'fanning the flames' may be an unfortunate turn of phrase.

The eventual outcome of all this action was some arrests, but mainly of lower order crims. The main men walked away and this proved to be an acute embarrassment for the police. They had missed an excellent opportunity to limit or infiltrate the growing Mr Asia syndicate, as the leaders of the syndicate were nearly all involved in meetings at the Pacific. They had met and mixed with 'Undercover Andy', as he was promptly nicknamed. Had he been able to stay undercover for another six months, it is quite possible that huge heroin and Buddha stick importations into Australia and New Zealand might not have happened. More importantly, a minimum of eight murders in Australia, probably twelve, may not have taken place.

MARRIAGE DIFFICULTIES ARISING

Looking back, we continually had to deal with people who had difficulties accepting the existence of the Pacific Sauna. Ray and I could handle it, but some of the fallout caused problems of a personal nature. The main casualties were our marriages. Considering the environment we were in; I suppose that was to be expected.

Mary, sadly and unfairly, was running into problems which were not of her own making. Other women on a school committee she was involved with had started to treat her rather badly. It was not a good state of affairs; it worried me, Mary was becoming more and more unhappy with the way I was living my life and who could blame her?

Although I owned property and the Pacific was doing very well, I was financially over extended, property wise. The boxing enterprise was starting to pay off, but I was juggling financial balls. I had committed myself to long range property plans which included hefty mortgage repayments on the K' Road property. The situation I was in was good, but to hold it all together I had to keep going. I had to squeeze as much out of the Pacific and other deals as I could. I certainly couldn't change direction.

Taken whilst guests of Peter Williams and Eb Leary, this picture is of me and my beautiful wife Mary, at the annual Law Ball in the Town Hall, Auckland, late 1960s.

Mary had no input into the way I ran my life or business affairs and she had no input into my activities, other than being shocked and opposing them. She was a decent Kiwi, a Freemans Bay girl who found herself in a foreign and confusing situation. In all honesty, I fell into the trap of believing my own publicity. I was enjoying the playboy lifestyle that had landed on my lap and all the female attention that went with it. Some would say I was weak, and they may well be right. Experience showed me that most of the friends and neighbours who turned on me blamed pressure from their wives. The majority of those who viciously fanned the flames between Mary and me and adopted the morally indignant position were people in regular jobs. I felt sorry for the poor sods, nine to fiving as they say, or worse. They were often in brain-numbing jobs, alcohol usually providing their Nirvana. They were the people whose lives allowed for little exposure to the opportunities I had. The husbands in these relationships were our best Friday nighters. Through observing them and the sneaky married daytime customers who regularly enjoyed the services available, I came to believe that morality and opportunity are very closely linked. I continually hear people say: live your life hard; you're a long time dead. My experience invariably has been that many can say it, but not many have the balls to do it.

The plan I had come up with to overcome any objections to establishing a sauna massage parlour by first establishing a regular gymnasium with a slant towards boxing worked. I had started building the project in about August 1973 and the gym opened for business in October. By late November I had the first section of the massage parlour open. From there on the Pacific Sauna was like Topsy; it just grew. This was an exciting, but very dangerous business and I felt that all my previous activities had been merely an apprenticeship for the parlour industry.

Ray joined me in March 1974. He needed a new interest after falling foul of the police, who had arrested him for illegal bookmaking activities. They continued to persecute him in annoying little ways until after the incident with the three young detectives at the Pacific sauna. Ray was a very capable and good partner in all areas. His merchant navy background fitted in nicely. Ray had been around a bit, running with a Teddy boy gang from Woolwich; he knew how many beans made five. Ray took charge of the admin, banking, rosters and staff hiring and training side of things. He was very conscientious in these duties and he made it his business to learn different eastern massage techniques; both the theory and the practice of them. He would then teach our pretty trainees these techniques including his famous 'effarage' and the 'Thai body slide'. It was a tough job, but somebody had to do it. His sense of duty was such that he would not hear of anybody else assisting him in this Herculean task. In spite of the many offers he received, he was adamant, but that's the sort of guy that Ray was. What a sacrifice!

Over the next couple of years, the Pacific gradually dispensed with any pretence of actually being a gym and grew into a fully-fledged sauna and massage parlour occupying the whole of the two-storey building. At its height, it employed thirty pretty, young masseuses. It needed every one of them as we were now operating twenty-four hours a day. We had installed Cleopatra double baths in all the rooms, an outside swimming pool, and our own VIP bar. The place was a huge success; the punters were like bees around a honey pot. We kept it true to the boxing agenda that started it. We received TV and newspaper coverage by having the official weigh-ins for the boxing promotions in the main lounge. As these often featured overseas name fighters, there was always a media scrum to cover them. We laid on drinks, always served by our scantily clad masseuses, who expertly took the opportunity to drum up more business. It worked for everyone and everyone was happy; isn't that the way the world should be?

Where Ray had his particular strengths in the business, I also had mine. I occupied a front of house role. I knew most of our clients and made sure they felt welcome and safe. We took every precaution we could to avoid prosecution, but it was a very thin line. We had a code of conduct contract drawn up by our solicitors that all the girls had to sign before commencing work at the Pacific. It contained all the usual terms that you would expect to find, but a major clause strictly forbade any sexual activity on pain of instant dismissal. The girls all happily signed it and acknowledged that they had received a copy and had had independent advice as to its requirements. The girls all had their own methods of protecting themselves as far as possible. The main thing was that Ray and I earned our money from the charges for the massages and the entry fee. Because of the excellent facilities and because of the top class girls we employed, we could and did charge like a wounded bull. We were very careful that tips or any other payment were down to the girls and we did not interfere.

In many ways, it was a bit of a joke. When we first opened, we sold normal massages; then we extended it to topless massages. As we grew more confident we sold full nude massages. As each new boundary pusher of a massage was introduced, we just got busier and busier and hiked the charges accordingly. The real secret to the higher charges was as follows - a beautiful young masseuse massaging then bathing with you in a Cleopatra bath with strategically placed mirrors. The punters willingly paid the higher charges for the facilities that a top of the range nude massage brought with it. I imagine it proved very tempting.

You have no idea how many of the punters at the check in area complained about a sore neck or stiff back. "Oh that's awful," said the pretty receptionist. "Not to worry, I have just the girl for you. She'll be able to help you with any problems you're having with stiffness. I suggest you book Sheryl, that's the pretty girl sitting over there. Now, how would you like this treatment, Sir? You can have it full nude with the very soothing Cleopatra bath, or just a standard massage."

And like Marc Antony in ancient Alexandria, they generally found the Cleopatra hard to resist.

To understand the impact the Pacific had on Auckland, one has to measure it against what was acceptable at the time. The Pacific unleashed what had been readily available overseas. It was like unshackling a great storehouse of frustrated, embittered, Kiwi males and letting them live out their fantasies. Freedom comes in many forms. Probably the most important is freedom of choice. The Pacific gave them that.

In any business success brings competition. There were soon attempts to copy us. Mysteriously they seemed to be very careless and one or two suffered fires, which was rather disappointing, as they were all nearly ready to open when this misfortune struck. These fires caused the insurance companies to become very wary of covering any new start-ups. Without insurance, no property owner would rent his or her premises out for such a venture. There were investigations and interviews and a couple of news reports full of innuendos, but they were inconclusive. It was widely assumed that Ray and I were at the bottom of it. We of course denied it. There could have been other parties with their own reasons. Perhaps it was the Chinese. At about that time the Chinese Tongs were starting to establish themselves in Auckland.

The Tongs traditionally operated in the area of clubs, parlours, gambling and the like. The different Tongs were fighting amongst themselves for control. We, as upright citizens, felt it was our civic duty to point this out to the detectives, who questioned us on this epidemic of arson. Strangely they showed no appreciation at all of our civic mindedness and efforts to assist them. In fact one rather unkind detective, loudly and pointedly suggested that the arrival of the Tongs was very convenient for us.

Things stayed that way for a couple of years. Overly ambitious criminals or naive types not familiar with the difficulties that lay ahead sometimes chanced their arms, invariably with the same sad results. Then suddenly the accidental fires stopped. This may have been because the Sauna Parlour Association that we had formed was welcoming a limited number of new members to operate in certain areas not proximate to the Pacific. The Association advised them how best to operate safely and assisted them with insurance placements. We had become the respected elderly statesmen of the Industry; there I said it again.

WHY DO GIRLS DO THAT JOB?

The constant question that was posed to me in conversations whenever my involvement in the industry become tabled was, 'tell me about the type of girls who come into the business'. Next was always 'why is it they take up this profession?' I confess to having considered it a great deal. It's a question of interest to many, not just psychologists and social workers.   In the early days of the Pacific all the girls who came to us were generally as new to it as we were.   They were young, eager, very pretty and chasing money.   Our girls found the wealthy clientele very intoxicating.   Most of the girls who came to work there were friends of girls already operating for us. I think in those early days we only advertised once for staff.   We never had to persuade girls to come there. At the end of their working shifts the girls would hang around swimming or using the sauna. Invariably their girlfriends loved coming in to meet them.

We had one golden rule though concerning the girls; it was no husbands or boyfriends allowed on the premises; that invariably brought trouble. One day I received a telephone call from Dawn, not the Dawn of publishing fiddles; this was a new Dawn. She was a woman, with whom I was on nodding terms.   She was a very attractive, aged about forty and had four children.   She had separated from her husband and was making her own way. She was wonderfully well spoken, a quality in a woman that I hold dear. She was highly thought of in our neighbourhood; she fitted in and was popular. She surprised me by asking for a position at the Pacific. I thought she would be great, so I arranged it. She sailed through Ray's training program and turned out a big hit, soon developing a retinue of regulars. She was constantly booked out on her shifts, mainly on Sundays. Surprisingly, after about three months with us she left. She came in one Friday evening as a visitor with a couple of her girlfriends whom I recognized as other near neighbours. They were intrigued and had obviously been looking forward to this visit. After a couple of drinks in the bar they really partied. It was a case of clothes off and into the spa-pool in knickers and bras at first, but they soon came off. These suburban mums really let their hair down. It was as if years of pent up frustration were let go. I had previously only seen them in their normal pram-pushing role, so I got a surprise. No more needs to be said on how it finished, though they now knew what the inside of a massage room looked like!

Dawn took me aside and gave me the news; she was leaving to marry a very wealthy South Island sheep farmer, who just happened to be a regular and valued customer of ours. He used to fly his own plane up to Auckland twice a week and spend a fortune with us. It may sound very much like that classic film *The Lady in Red,* but this really happened, and if my memory serves me right, it was prior to that movie being released. The last I heard was that she was living in style with him and that they travelled the world in school holidays with her kids.

As for the other girls, some of them just drifted out of the business after making enough money for an overseas trip, or a deposit on a house. One girl was working to pay for an expensive wedding. There were many who used it as a means to an end, or until they met a special boyfriend. On the other hand there were some who stayed in it for many years and did well. Two of them came out of it owning quite a few houses. However, they were intelligent girls who would have done well in whatever field they had chosen. At the end of the day, the answer to the original question, what made the girls do it is a simple one, in a word, money.

One of the safeguards Ray and I implemented, in an attempt to protect ourselves, was that we had the girls sign an employment contract. That contract expressly forbade and sexual activity with the customers. So you can see, we tried hard to keep them on the straight and narrow, but you know how naughty these girls can be.

A harder situation to understand was the number

of married punters who actually fell in love with the girls. They were usually straight Johns. Many of them carried on the affairs while the girls continued working. Who knows how they rationalised it to themselves? It would need a Doctor Kinsey to probe that one.

As time went by hard drugs hit Auckland. The girls were prime targets for the dealers as they had the money and, as it turned out, the inclination. Their attitudes changed; they would cross the Tasman to work in the Sydney and Melbourne parlours; they came back much harder and life weary. They were never quite the same again. In all honesty, there were some hard cases amongst them. They were the type who would have had troubled lives whatever their jobs were. However, the majority of them came from ordinary, but good, homes. They just chose another way. I do know that after working for us they could never settle in to nine-to-five jobs, and who could blame them for that? Certainly not me, I could not have either. I suppose to an extent the lifestyle caught up with them, but most of the girls who started out with us ended up married, or living with partners; often they were same sex partners; but that was their business. Generally, they were okay and often came in with new babies to show them to the girls still working there. I liked the fact that we always maintained a good relationship with most of them, often still seeing them around the town and having a humorous chat about old times.   It was a great experience for all of us and I do not think it caused them any problems. When they looked back, like us, generally they would not have changed much.

THE AMAZING JEZEBEL,
A REGISTERED NYPHOMANIAC

Jezebel was the name she wanted to call herself. The girls all worked under assumed names, which they chose. It could say a lot about them. Jezebel was about thirty and she was strikingly attractive in a wild sort of way. She had a full figure but wasn't fat. She was a looker. She had come to us via the direct route; she just walked in one day and booked a sauna. She then sat around chatting to the girls and punters. At first, we thought she may have been an undercover cop; they were always trying something different. This mysterious woman, still with her large towel draped around her full figure, sashayed across to me in the small reception office. Then with a smile like a sunburst, she enquired about a job. She immediately qualified it saying she could only work on the day shift. She claimed to be fully experienced in many massage techniques and offered, with another smile to prove it there and then.

It just so happened that our good friend Jimmy had called in for a sauna. He had been sitting down quietly observing what was happening while he checked his weekend betting sheets. Jimmy at that time was an illegal bookmaker covering the whole of New Zealand. There was no such thing as legal bookmaking apart from the government owned

Totalisator Agency Board, the Tote, which was not always convenient and this created a vast market for illegal telephone and pub betting. Jimmy, a clever gambler and card player, had a share of that business well and truly cornered. Ray had also been very successful in that field, until constant police activity against him had made it untenable.   He always mentally and jokingly thanked the Auckland Police for hounding him into this superb new business, though I doubt they shared his views. Ray, who usually handled all staff hiring and firing, was not there that day so I might have had to step into the breach. Fortunately Jimmy, who had silently sidled up to join us, volunteered himself for the task. I considered phoning Ray, but felt I should leave him in peace and let him enjoy shopping with his wife. Jimmy was adamant that was the right thing to do. Jezebel went off with Jimmy for the great massage technique test. As they sauntered across the lounge Jimmy was heard using terms such as therapeutic, effarage, comfort zone, in an attempt to establish his credentials. They disappeared into one of the downstairs massage rooms just off the lounge. About three-quarters-of-an-hour went past and the door burst open. There was Jimmy, towel around him, hair dishevelled, wild eyed, blinking furiously. Now Jimmy at the time was a super fit sportsman. He had recently retired as a first grade rugby league half back and was in great condition, but he looked like he had just suffered a great shock.

"A drink mate, I need a drink," he croaked.

He took me to one side and whispered conspiratorially, "Len you must employ her, you absolutely must."

"Jesus Jimmy, that must have been a good massage, you look knackered."

He looked at me, still wild eyed.

"Mate, I haven't had the massage yet. But I'm going back in."

Jezebel was employed, and as she requested, worked only on day shifts. It turned out that Jezebel was what many men dream of finding and then they regret it when they do. She was a full blown nymphomaniac. I do not suppose there is any other sort. Like an alcoholic, you are one or you are not.

Jezebel reigned with us for three months. In that time she built up a huge clientele; but all good things end. Jezebel was married and her husband accepted her for what she was and knew what she was doing. She was a truly amazing, free spirit. With my twisted sense of humour I always thought it would have been funny if they had put in an undercover cop and charged Jezebel with prostitution. She would have been a great witness. I picture the scene as this, "Yes, Mr Crown Solicitor, I did have sex and several times with the young Constable. But I just did it because I enjoy sex so much. He left some money on the table, but I assumed that was just a tip for the lovely massage I gave him and I certainly didn't ask him for money."

"But the Constable has given evidence that you didn't give him a massage and that you engaged in sex with him almost immediately."

"Oh, I didn't mean a traditional massage. I meant I had to massage that little fella of his to get things under way. I had to get that Policeman's helmet out from where it was hiding, under his foreskin."

"I think we've heard quite enough about your sexual antics, Ms Jezebel."

"I know what you mean, Mr Crown Solicitor. Even the nice man at the private clinic in Remuera who is treating me for these nympho urges of mine, says I go on about it a bit too much. And now that I think about it he always gets me to leave money on the table after the therapy sessions, so I guess that everyone's doing what they're good at for money in one way or another."

Unfortunately, we never found another Jezebel, but there you go, even a wild pig finds acorns sometimes.

THE FAMOUS MADAM,
THE FLORA MCKENZIE INCIDENT

This gem came about in 1977 at a time when I had a couple of new parlours coming on stream. One of them was named Flora's, which caused an outburst from a certain well-known Auckland madam. Through the years, commencing in the fifties, this woman had operated a very successful knocking shop in the rather elite Auckland suburb of St. Mary's Bay. She seemed to have a charmed life and over the years she had become an institution. Just about, everyone knew about her and her business. 'Flora's' was a byword for illicit sex. She was reputed to have client list that included many of the city's moral leaders. An excellent brand name I decided and I embarked on what could also be termed an early case of identity theft.

I was trying to think of a name for the four-room, intimate parlour in Pitt Street I was doing on my own without Ray. I thought the Flora association was too good to pass up. I played around with 'Flora and Fauna' and pictured naked fauns dancing around the walls, but Fauna quickly drifted off into 'Faunacate' – you know how it is in this business – and I settled for Flora's. I knew it would cause a furore, I also knew it was a winner. Above all, that one simple name cried out everything that I surreptitiously wanted said.

Flora was outraged. In a way however, she was hoist with her own petard. Every report we got from her customers was to the effect that she constantly complained about the theft of her 'good name'. If she had sued me for that, the lawyers and judge would have a problem on their hands. I think the humour of the situation would have been too much for them. I was looking forward to her trying that one on. The publicity would have been as good as the wowser TV interview. It was my first exploitation of a brand name. What a start. I have to say the phone never stopped ringing with her clients coming in. We would pick up the phone when it rang,

"Is that Flora's? Is she there?"

"Yes it's Flora's. She isn't here now, but she will be soon."

"Great, I'll come in now."

"Okay, see you soon, please hurry." They invariably did.

A FAVOUR FOR ELTON JOHN

There was a lot happening in Auckland at this time. One event in particular had Aucklanders very excited; it was the pending, completely sold out, Elton John concert. I had not expected that it would involve me in any way, but surprise, surprise, it did.

I was sitting in the Pacific Sauna reciting to myself my version of the famous old nursery rhyme, *Sing a Song of Sixpence*:

'The King was in his counting house counting out his money. His maids were in the Parlour earning bread and honey,' when out of the blue I received a phone call from a friend of a friend in Sydney. The caller was involved with a major Sydney music promoter who had a big, big problem. It centred on none other than Elton John. The caller, whom I had never met, nor would, was justifiably frantic. The Elton John tour to Australia in 74 also took in New Zealand with a concert in Auckland. The Elton party were staying in a very nice hotel in leafy Parnell called the White Heron, which had spectacular views over the Auckland Harbour. The tour so far had been successful playing to a full house at the Western Springs Stadium, a wonderful outdoor venue. There was the usual after show party held prior to the group leaving New Zealand for the concert in Australia. It was rumoured that there was a massive 'coke' and booze fest going on. Unsurprisingly, given the circumstances and the party fuel an incident occurred that was to have great bearing on the future of the tour and possibly the later coming out of Elton. An angry exchange took place between John Reid, Elton's manager and 'companion' and an Auckland reporter journalist David Wheeler. Reid, who was famous for his volatility, took exception to Wheeler and king hit him knocking him to the ground and then kicked him. He had been raised in a tough area of Paisley in Scotland. You don't get much for free from a Scotsman, but they will often put a boot in without charge. Elton apparently joined the fray, tearing Wheeler's shirt.

The reason given for the incident was Wheeler asserting that Elton was gay. Sometimes stating the bleeding obvious can get you into a pile of crap. Think about poor old Galileo pointing out to the Pope that the world was round. 2013 has Elton and his bloke and their babies on the cover of Hello magazine but 1974 was not ready for Elton to be tinkling John Reid's ivories. I suppose that the seventies rock culture was the beginning of the dreaded celebrity culture that is now thrust upon us. I also suppose that there are many places in the world where celebrities get away with such antics, not so in New Zealand or Australia. Frank Sinatra found that out to his chagrin when he was taking a break in Australia after a taxing Far East tour. He abused and insulted some journalists who were pushing for a press conference. He called them a pack of 'fags, pimps and whores'. It resulted in a national blackballing campaign and a general strike by Aussie transport workers, waiters and journalists. He found himself unable to leave Sydney unless he apologised. The President of the USA tried to intervene by contacting the Prime Minister of Australia, all to no avail. He could do nothing to lift the Union imposed blackball. Bob Hawke, the union leader who later became Prime Minister, supported the strike. Eventually he arranged to get the parties together; a generous settlement was made, and Sinatra was able to leave Australia.

John Reid and Elton were arrested over the fracas. They appeared in the Auckland Magistrate's court, charged with assault. John Reid was found guilty and sentenced to serve one month in Mt Eden prison. Make no mistake; this was as tough a jail as there is. Fortunately, Elton was found not guilty and discharged. It appeared that Reid had taken all the blame to save Elton and possibly the tour. However, that was only the start of the problem. The caller was frantic. He told me that Elton was really spitting the dummy and having fits about having to leave Reid to face the music. He was beside himself over what could happen to his companion in that jail full of sex starved tough men, especially when it was known who he was and what his sexual persuasion was. Elton was apparently out of control and had declared he could not, or would not, go on the stage and perform in his present worried state. The Australian concert he was associated with was a sell-out.

Bobby Dunlop, British Commonwealth Light-heavyweight Champion. He was in charge of security at the Pacific. He was the go-between who arranged for Elton John's Manager to be protected in prison.

We got through the pleasantries and how he had been put onto me and then he got down to it.
"Well, Len, it's like this, I am a part of the syndicate promoting Elton's concerts and he's saying he's not going to perform. He's worried about what may happen to Reid in the Mount. Some smart bastard

has filled his head with a truck load of shit about what the Maori gangs will do to him."

"Okay, but what do you want from me?"

"I've told Elton about a friend in Auckland, you, who might be able to guarantee Reid's safety in there, Lindsay thought you could; can you help?"

As I have previously said, involvement in the boxing world and the nightclub world puts you in touch with plenty of crims and the underbelly which exists in all cities, whether you want to or not. It so happened that one of our door attendants, who was also a retired Commonwealth Champion boxer, Bob Dunlop and his psycho partner, whom you have previously met in Book One, were able to exert some influence. One of them arranged a visit to the prison the next day. He was well connected, he got the safety assurances we needed from a senior gang member; it was that easy. There was a promise of assistance for the gang in another area given in return and the problem was taken care of.

The Aussie promoter phoned me that evening as arranged. He nearly wept when I gave him the news. He assured me of his, Elton's and Reid's gratitude and said I only had to ask if they could do anything for me. I said maybe one day I would call on them; I never did. When I did think about it much later Reid and Elton had split up and were at each other's throats, so the wedding invitation for Elton's latest liaison seems not to have found its way to Rickmansworth. Should you read this and feel the need to say hello Elton, my contact details are on the back cover.

When I look back and think of these experiences, the people I met, the politicians, sportsmen, entertainers, criminals etc. and compare that to the quiet life I now lead, I sometimes find it hard to believe that I came out of it in one piece. I have to say I get some strange looks sometimes, particularly if I drop the odd story in a gathering of friends and acquaintances in a local coffee bar or pub. They probably think it's the ramblings of a show off. What matter? I lived it and I am still here. In those halcyon days I met many interesting people, one of them who impressed me greatly, as he did most of the world, was David Frost, the British TV personality. He came to Auckland to film a TV show called 'The Making of a Champion'. I was flattered to be selected as one of the panel members on the show.

My invitation was down to my boxing endeavours and being the President of The South Pacific Boxing Association and being prominent in rugby league circles. The show was filmed in the Marina Lounge of the old Station Hotel. David Frost was an agreeable sort, not at all snobby; he just seemed a regular guy. He spent a bit of time with us, his guests, I suppose. My contribution when asked what it was that I believed made a champion, was to say that when all things were near enough to equal, that is ability and fitness wise, the hungriest one, or the team who mentally wanted to win the most, would eventually win, that quality was so important in a champion.

New Zealand sportsmen and women were doing well internationally at the time. They were excelling in rugby; athletics, motor racing and Sir Edmund Hillary had climbed Mt Everest. It seemed amazing that such a small under-resourced nation of only three and a half million people could do so well internationally. That fact was the underlying reason for David Frost's show being shot in New Zealand.

THE FIRE BOMB, IT'S TIME TO
TELL THE STORY

Jealousy is one of the worst of the human emotions and it manifests itself in many ways. It was a driving force behind a firebomb attack on me. Readers of Book One will remember my references to a psycho that I dealt with on a number of occasions. He was a very dangerous, violent man. You may also remember a favour I did for a friend, an old shipmate, Tommy Adderly. Tommy and his partner Dave Henderson had upset the psycho by having to bar him from their club. Because of this perceived insult, the psycho and his accomplice, a Liverpool hoodlum and ex-merchant seaman, another dangerous individual, were threatening Tommy and his club, Grandpa's. Tommy was at his wits end. He came to me to see if I could sort the problem. Though I was reluctant to get involved, I was able to help at the time. I had some leverage, as the psycho was the assistant to one of my boxing trainers. He also did odd jobs helping with the boxing promotions. I knew it was a dangerous move to get involved, but Tommy was an old friend so I didn't have much choice. I expected that it could end in trouble for me, as he was so unpredictable.

The psycho had made many enemies and was not popular or accepted in the murky underworld of

Auckland of that time. To make matters worse, I think there were other elements stoking the fire behind the scenes. One in particular, was a very jealous individual. The situation had become complicated; this individual had fallen in love with the daughter of family friends of mine. They were unhappy about the liaison as he was married. They were a very straight family and it was causing friction as the individual and the daughter were spending a lot of time together around my house.

At the beginning of this chapter, I referred to the evils of Jealousy. Looking back on my life and its various problems and confrontations, I find it was rare, if ever, that that scoundrel wasn't present when trouble was looming.

For those who haven't read Book One, I include here my account of the firebombing.

"Whoosh!" was all that I heard, followed by the sound of breaking glass. I was a light sleeper and had just joined Mary, who was asleep in the upstairs bedroom. The kids were sound asleep and tucked up in their rooms. None of this had woken them. I jumped out of bed and ran to the front window. My instincts were kicking in. This was dangerous; this was no accident. I had an empty feeling in the pit of my stomach. I wrenched the window fully open and looked down at flames licking around the downstairs window. A petrol firebomb had

exploded. It had been thrown from the front lawn and had smashed on the wooden wall near the main lounge window. Luckily, it had missed the glass. Had it smashed through the window the curtains and soft furnishings would have served as an accelerant and the position would have been so very, very different.

With Mary in Herne Bay house that was fire bombed.

"Wake up Mary, get the kids and take them downstairs, there's a fire on the outside wall of the

house". I tried to play it down, but I didn't need to. Mary was great, she didn't panic. She brought the kids down and sat them in the TV room. I had rushed down the stairs and outside. I grabbed the garden hose, which fortunately was nearby and played it on the flames. The cascade of water quickly doused them. The house was a lovely two-storey wooden dwelling in Jervois Road, Herne Bay; a desirable property in a desirable suburb on the edge of the city centre. Neighbours had come out on hearing the commotion. They had called the fire service and the police. Even though the immediate danger had passed, it was still a nerve-wracking experience.

Fire, the very word itself conveys clearly what I am sure is the most dangerous and scary of all the elements. In its place, it has provided warmth, security, and comfort down the ages. On the other hand, when it is used as a weapon, when it is indiscriminately used to terrify and to injure or kill, it takes on a completely different character. That was the nature of what was perpetrated on me and my family that night.

I instinctively knew who and what was behind this cowardly attack. My mind went first to protecting my family, then straight to revenge. I knew what I had to do; I also knew that I had to take care of it myself. The police would be of little use in dealing with this character. And he had to be removed permanently from the scene."

His attack on me stemmed from two major incidents. The first one emanated from a situation within the Pacific Ponies rugby league team. The villain of the piece, the psycho, was a very good player, a second row forward. Had it not been for spells in prison and his attitude problems he would have gone far in the game; but he was so disruptive. He was a member of the premier team squad before my involvement; so in a way I inherited him. Because of the problems with him, I had banned him from the Pacific. He had been there one Sunday after a game and a fight had started between him and another of our players who was a real character and not averse to a bit of law breaking himself. This was the legendary Craig Brown. He was a six-foot-four, sixteen stone, second row forward. Craig could walk the walk and talk the talk. He was another of those men you would be foolish to cross. Animosity had built up between them and in the fight; the psycho came off worst, which was a real dent to his pride. In looking around for somebody to blame he picked on me, alleging that I had caused the fight as an excuse to bar him from the Pacific. So there it was; he believed that I was also standing in the way of his selection in the first team. That was so wrong; selection was something I had no control over anyway. In his twisted mind, I was now also effectively cutting him off from not only the club but also the Pacific. I think those were the circumstances that motivated the psycho to bomb my home. I was dealing with a dangerous combination, of jealousy, revenge and an unbalanced unpredictability.

It's quite amazing how things work out in life. Sometime before the firebombing had taken place, Mary and I had decided that our marriage could maybe work if we got out of Auckland, where all the temptations and the hedonistic lifestyle were. It was a crazy, but well-meant initiative. I had decided in one of my saner moments that I had to make an effort. Mary for her part was willing to give that a chance for the sake of the family. She had a big heart. We had been looking around for a couple of months and had bought a ninety-acre property we'd found in the idyllic country village of Kaukapakapa. It was a fabulous piece of land looking out over the Helensville Harbour. We were waiting for the house renovation to be completed. Then we were going to start a new life in the country, the firebombing occurred while we were waiting to move in. Naturally it pushed the moving in date forward.

This move and the change of environment were superb for Mary and the kids. They soon integrated into the local community. Mary joined various church and religious groups and the kids enjoyed the hayrides and country festivals that seemed to continually run. I could see how happy they were and how well this new life suited them. I tried to fit in, but it was very difficult. I stayed away from the parlours. I spent time at home trying to make this new clean living life work. Unfortunately, it didn't work for me. I had played in the streets of Gomorrah and Kaukapakapa, for all its appeal, couldn't hack it for me. The local god-fearing community saw me as some sort of a pariah. They were generally nice people whose families had lived in the district for decades. Their forebears had broken in the land. They had fashioned the place to their ways over decades. It was not quite an Amish type society; but not far from it. There were occasions when I would call into the village shop, or sometimes the pub and the conversation seemed to stop. They definitely did not roll out the red carpet for me. These folk were not weekend hippies; they were more Deliverance types.

There was a quaint little church on the corner and its cemetery boasted headstones with names and dates going back to the earliest settlers. This for me was reminiscent of Erskine Caldwell's famous book *God's Little Acre* and I did not fit into it. In fact I was probably an embarrassment to Mary. The village, the farms and the local community were dominated by a couple of local farmers who saw themselves as the guardians of morality in the area.

Whatever its drawbacks for me, Kaukapakapa in the mid-seventies, held a great attraction for Mary and the kids. For me it was nothing less than a nightmare. The second shadow was darkening its hue. I needed the bright lights, the cut and thrust. I needed to be in the action. It became obvious that this move, though beneficial in many ways, could not save the marriage and in fact it had compounded the problems. Our lives were going different ways. A break-up was now inevitable; it was a case of how best to manage it.

I took the plunge and leased a beachside flat in the very desirable suburb of Milford. This was supposed to be a prelude to the final parting of Mary and me. I had thought deeply about the situation. There was an underlying important reason in my deciding to move on and finish the marriage. I really wanted to protect Mary and the family from any more danger. Even though the marriage held nothing for either of us by then, protecting my family was a contributing reason and I felt it justified my moving away. I don't think the family realised that at the time, but it gave me some peace of mind.

WHAT GOES AROUND COMES AROUND

A considerable time after this upheaval in my life, some exciting news rippled through Auckland's underworld. There were media reports of an attempted shooting in Point Chevalier. Two shots were let loose at a certain individual as he lay sleeping in his bed. The shots, fired through a bedroom window had missed the sleeper. There was much speculation in the underworld as to whether it was intended as a warning, or whether bad light had caused the shooter to miss his target. The target was the psycho's right hand man.

There was much speculation about the reasons for this shooting and the firebombing of my house was at the forefront of this. At the time the psycho and his mate had plenty of other enemies. They had annoyed people by some of their actions and a drug turf war was developing. As expected, I did get a visit from the Police, but it was cursory. My detective friend came to see me, but did not seem unduly concerned. Cook Street would not lose too much sleep over this one. I had it on good authority that they would have preferred it had the psycho been the target. The upside was that the psycho's main man decided to leave town. One down and one to go some people thought. So, many were very pleased by the incident. Sometime after the shooting the psycho ran into a spot of trouble, for which he was sent down for five years. Oh well, what goes around, comes around.

My life at this time was a curious mix of highs and lows. The business side of things was good. However, by this time, my marriage was well and truly over. Like others in that situation, I suffered great pangs of guilt, leading me to over compensate with the kids.

The stress I suffered from the marriage break up, the firebombing and other difficult situations my life attracted had caused me to become a Valium user, initially under prescription. I found that in the short term it had some benefits, but it hid problems that really had to be addressed. I eventually realised the dangers of long-term addiction to it and managed to kick it after six months. I was then able to function and attempt to sort out the problems that were plaguing me. One was a very difficult relationship that I had foolishly let grow.

Even with my problems, I was enjoying my life in Milford. Some friends owned a great Bar Bistro, called Killarney, where most of our crowd converged. It was a great meeting place for the North Shore contingent of characters. It was probably Auckland's answer to Eliza's in Sydney. It catered for a similar clientele. It was a boon for me as it was five minutes walk from my front door.

However, as was the norm with me, there was a

complication. It was a clinging, stalking, on-and-off girlfriend. This was a fatal attraction; it was not in any way love. It was far from it. I believe it was a classic love-hate relationship, with hate mainly in the ascendancy. It was a volatile, dark affair that seemed incapable of extinguishing itself. We, the actors in this tragedy, were unable to bring a sane ending about. It was the foolish attraction of an older man for a young, lithe woman. I met her when I was thirty-eight and she was under twenty. She and her sister had come to work for us in the Pacific. It was the biggest mistake of my life and up till then and I'd made a few big ones. I paid a huge price for this weakness in loss of family and some friends. It ranks in my mind as the one thing I would change in my life, given the chance. Unfortunately, that luxury is never available, though often wished for.

The real answer to my problems started one Sunday morning when I went out to buy a paper. There standing in the shop was my old pal Jimmy. He had moved to Aussie and was home for the weekend. He was staying in the Mon Desir, an upmarket hotel on Takapuna Beach, a few hundred yards from where I was living. There were all sorts of rumours flying around about Jimmy. They included stories of how he had shifted his bookmaking operations to Sydney. There were tales of his involvement in the race fixing which was rife in Sydney in those years. On top of this, there were the rumours of a New Zealand crime and drug syndicate muscling its way into the Australian market. You could take your pick; there were stories galore and as usual, there's seldom smoke without fire. It was at this time that salvation via Jimmy presented itself. Strangely, I was at my most vulnerable and was seriously questioning my way of life.

It later transpired that he was indeed making big money in fixed races. It also later transpired that Jimmy, sometime interviewer of sauna parlour nymphomaniacs, had risen to become the number two man in the infamous Mr Asia Drug Syndicate. Its principal was a nasty piece of work, Terry Clarke, a ruthless New Zealand criminal. I had the displeasure of having to meet him at a drinks party Jimmy threw at his luxurious waterside apartment, on my arrival in Sydney. I had been introduced to him in the Pacific, sometime earlier; neither of us, each for his own reasons acknowledged that. I am not sure, but I don't think Marty Johnson was there. He was the unfortunate partner that Terry Clark arranged to have killed in England a couple of years later. It was the final killing that he ordered; it was also the one that brought down the Syndicate.

Clarke projected coldness from within; he was a full-blown psychopath. He murdered or arranged the murders of at least eight, probably twelve, people who he felt had become a danger to the syndicate, or had transgressed in some other way. I hasten to point out that all but two of those took place prior to Jimmy moving to Australia and he had no knowledge of the other two. Anybody who knew Jimmy was aware that he was quite capable of extreme violence against persons, generally criminals attacking him. However, he was not like Sinclair, capable of planned cold-blooded murder. In fact, it later transpired that Sinclair had planned to murder Jimmy. A point I should make here is that Sinclair did commit most of the hits himself. The ones that he didn't were done by a Melbourne hit man, associated with the infamous Painters and Dockers union and a somewhat notorious New Zealand hit man who crossed the Tasman for the occasional mission.

Another of the guests attending that night was a famous Aussie/Italian criminal, Robert (Bob) Trimbole, the acknowledged leader of the Griffiths Mob. They were a feared gang of Italian marijuana growers and distributors. They operated on an industrial scale. Although this man came across as an absolute gentleman, he was allegedly behind the sensational, very public, murder of Donald Mackay, an ardent anti-drug campaigner and also a Griffiths Councillor. Mackay was making a politically inspired stand against drugs and was causing major problems for the Italian growers. Trimbole later died of a heart attack in Spain, where he had been successfully evading the Aussie authorities who were trying to extradite him. They wanted him in connection with that murder and his connection with the Mr Asia Syndicate. For all of the syndicate's success and for all of the incredible amounts of money and luxury lifestyle enjoyed by the senior members, they all eventually paid the price and fell one way or another. Most were either murdered or jailed for very long terms. When I met these characters none of the information that I have recorded here was the common knowledge that it later became. I knew that some of those present at the Darling Point party were heavy-duty crims, but they hadn't emerged as, or been referred to as, the Mr Asia syndicate at that time. That all came out later when they were christened as such by the intrepid Auckland Star editor, Pat Booth. In any event, for better or worse, these were the characters in Jimmy's circle that I met and got to know quite well. Strange to say, but I found Bob Trimbole to be a very personable, pleasant guy, who was great company, although that's a hard concept to understand bearing in mind his alleged history. However, probably the most unforgettable of them all was the pre-mentioned Roberto Fiona. With Jimmy, he owned that great restaurant, Tati's in Paddington. It was a meeting place for the whole New Zealand crew. Roberto was an Argentinean national with a very shady background. He was an international fixer. He had all the leading trainers and jockeys in his pocket. They were all regular habitués of Tati's, along with a fair share of Sydney's police, the finest that money could buy. Having said that, I spent many an unforgettable night there. It came with the territory

Jimmy recently wrote a very good book, which comprehensively covered the events of those years. It is a very good read entitled *Last Man Standing*, which in respect of the Mister Asia gang, he certainly is. I believe it is a testament to his resourcefulness that he survived that and other problems in his life. He now spends a lot of time talking to young criminals attempting to turn them round. If anybody knows the arguments in favour of that, it has to be my old pal Diamond Jim.

I looked at Jimmy and that old psychic warning system of mine kicked in. The antenna wiggled, but I didn't want to listen.
"Mate, how are you?" said a happy looking Jimmy sticking out his hand,
"Jimmy, it's good to see you. Christ mate, you're looking prosperous."
I could not help but notice the Rolex watch he was sporting and the large diamond ring on his finger. We chatted for a while, exchanging information and laughing over past events.
"Lenny, I wanted to get hold of you, can you come up to the Mon? We can have breakfast. I have a proposition for you."
I knew Jimmy well enough to know that this would

not be a time waster.

"Okay mate, I'll be there at about nine, I want to go home and have a swim first. Then I'll wander along."

He headed off and I sensed this was a life changing moment, even though I didn't know what lay in store. I don't think either of us saw anything ahead but sunshine, but as it happened a great storm cloud lay behind it.

The Mon Desir at that time had a dining room with an outside terrace overlooking the beach. I found Jimmy ensconced at one of the better tables. It was a lovely, warm, breezeless summer morning. The ocean waters of the Hauraki Gulf were sparkling and there were already groups of people launching boats and pitching chairs and tents on the clean warm sand. It was an idyllic scene; it could have graced a Monte Carlo or Cannes travel documentary.

On a large bamboo table that was laid up for a lavish breakfast was an ice bucket holding a glistening bottle of Dom Perignon. A smiling Jimmy, bedecked in a white linen suit, looking like a Greek shipping magnate, was sitting there with a very beautiful companion. My mind flashed back to my first meeting with Jim in the old Robbie Burns pub in Freemans Bay where we had both started out, back in the early sixties. In surveying this scene I could not help but think that although we were sitting less than two miles from there, in reality, this situation was a thousand miles distant; a lifetime away from what surely had been an apprenticeship for where Jimmy was now.

This setting was my introduction into the fantasy-like, but dangerously real world that Jimmy now inhabited and would be inviting me to join. We had ideas for establishing a bathhouse massage complex, similar to our Auckland ones, which were vastly superior to anything in Sydney. His plan was to invite me to establish it as his partner. There were also other plans discussed in relation to a plan to export New Zealand Kauri hot tubs to Australia and the USA. I could not resist it. My present domestic circumstances were so tangled, another path was required and this chance, but somehow fate-induced, meeting was a needed deliverance.

I do not believe that we always have the luxury of picking and choosing where our lives are heading. My built-in warning system was signalling me that real danger was lurking ahead, but I was semi-addicted to that condition. The champagne and the Eggs Benedict breakfast in those luxurious surroundings won the day. I was easily tempted and I grasped the opportunity offered and embarked on a perilous path to Sydney. It took me back to that vibrant city where my Antipodean journey had started twenty-one years previously.

"Len, I've got a couple of good things going on over there," Jimmy said with an expression that implied - don't ask too many questions.

"The thing is, I'm well connected and can organise a free go with a parlour and bath house over there."

By 'free go', he meant that he had the problems of police and criminal interference sorted out. That being the case, it was a great opportunity to get into the business there. Sydney was a high rolling, hot town and a lucrative market. It was always a target for any ambitious Auckland entrepreneurs. Whatever their field, they would want to expand there. However, this particular field of endeavour was historically closely controlled by the very heavy local hoods and bent police. They did not take kindly to strangers popping up and thinking they could operate there. Many an ambitious, but naive, New Zealand wannabe had suffered badly trying to do that. They either tended to end up permanently on the missing list, or badly injured.

To my knowledge, only one had succeeded there and he was a tough and resourceful guy. He was a member of a heavy family connected to rugby league and pacing racing in Auckland. He was a friend of Jimmy's. His operation was in Kings Cross, the bustling red light district. Circumstances require that he remains nameless; he was a trusted guy, who gave back up to Jimmy in a number of dangerous situations in that ultra-violent world. I shared many a drink and meal with him, Jimmy and sometimes Scotty, in Eliza's restaurant in Double Bay.

"It's like this Len; I have a stash of black (meaning black money) to clean up. I need someone to front a couple of companies for me. I'm buying into a couple of land developments at Noosa Heads and the Sunshine Coast. I need a clean skin to front it. If you take it on, I'll cut you into a corner on that. The other thing is I want to set up a top bathhouse in Sydney between us. The way I see it is this, I supply the cash; you do the business. We'll be in it fifty/fifty partners; what do you think?"

I thought those stories of how well he was doing on the horses must be correct, this was a lot of money he was talking about. He had made big plans, they just rolled out from him; he had really thought this through. "Come on Len, you'll be a hit in Sydney. None of the operations over there are as good as you've created in Auckland."

He paused to let that sink in. Although I was flattered; he was right.

"Jim, it all sounds good and we'd have the advantage of my Auckland connections. We could pull the girls from Auckland over for two month spells."

There were many other obvious advantages that could be exploited through a cross-Tasman operation. I had my eye on a New Zealand guy who was making Hot Tubs using kauri timber; I could see an opportunity for exporting them to Australia. There were all sorts of opportunities opening up. This was a good proposition. Jimmy assured me the finances were no problem. On top of this he offered me what was called a 'golden handcuff'. It was a large cash incentive to make the move. Moreover, when I say large, I mean large. Remember, I was used to lots of cash.

SO HERE WE GO AGAIN

So there it was, another step on my journey, but this was a big one. A fair comparison would be playing sport at a high club level and then making the leap to international competition. As they say, at the top everything happens faster. The rewards are greater, so can be the punishment for failure. It's swift and unrelenting. Keep your guard up Lenny boy, was the thought foremost in my mind. I was in. I took the golden handcuffs and there was no turning back now. I had a distinct sense of inevitability. Even had I been able to have a look into the future, to the trauma, to the danger and violence that lay ahead, I would still have made the move. I have to confess, I would also have seen the hedonistic and luxurious lifestyle that went with the territory and would have wanted to be a part of it. Sydney here I come.

I find myself on an early morning flight from Auckland International airport to Mascot in Sydney. I am enjoying a champagne cocktail in the upstairs business class of a 747. Another cycle of my life was unfolding and a thought struck me like a thunder flash. My mind slipped back to the hasty retreat from my hometown of Rickmansworth in 1958 and here I find myself in a similar situation twenty years later. This time, though I am travelling in style, but similar circumstances prevail. I am on the move again and not completely by choice.

I spent two years in Sydney and I stepped straight into the maelstrom of the final Mr Asia years. I was lucky. The thing was, I was not directly in it. However, through Jimmy, I was as close to it as you could get. Unfortunately, when it all collapsed, that made me fair game for the cops and the heavies when they turned and by then Jimmy had departed. The cops wanted any Kiwi who was near to the action. There were no, 'beg you pardon, Sir', they needed collars to blame and they didn't really care if you were in it or not. It was a dangerous time and a dangerous game.

Jimmy had fled to the USA. He was a very resourceful man, but even so, he was eventually captured. He was deported back to Australia, where he was convicted and sentenced to twenty-five years in jail for his role in the syndicate. Sinclair stood trial in the UK where he was convicted on drug and murder charges. He deservedly died in jail on the Isle of Wight. Lives fell apart; fortunes had been made, fortunes had been lost, and the Antipodes would never be quite the same again. I narrowly made it back to Auckland in mid-1982, which is a story for another time, but I was a changed man.

The magnitude of the police corruption and criminality surrounding this mainly New Zealand

Gang had drawn the attention of the highest levels of Government in both New Zealand and Australia.

A decision was taken that a thorough investigation was necessary. To facilitate it, the Stewart Royal Commission was constituted with the power to sit in both countries with equal power in both. This was a first; it was a very serious step to take. The commission sat in Australia first; it then came in all its glory to New Zealand. If summoned, you had to appear. The thing was that with Royal Commissions, unlike a normal court, you had to answer questions put to you under pain of arrest if you refused.

Many people, some in high places, were very nervous, including me. The big question was; would I be called to appear? You could put your mortgage on it; there was nothing surer. The thing was I was relieved to face things in New Zealand rather than Australia. However, all these events were two years in the future; in the meantime I had a life to live.

The final book of this trilogy will start as I exited the baggage claim area of Sydney airport. I met up with Jimmy that evening at the drinks party he threw at his upmarket waterside apartment in Darling Point. The same party I previously described where I met 'Aussie Bob' Robert Trimbole, Terry Clark/Sinclair and various members of the Syndicate. It was the start of an amazing two years.

To this day, I sometimes wonder if I dreamt it, but no; it was all real, very real.

EPILOGUE

Writing this second book, *Dancing In The Shadows,* reminded me of the deep-seated urge we humans have to take a peep into other people's lives. We love to step outside our lives and have a burrow around in someone else's. This is a blessing and a curse for the writer. A blessing because without that curiosity no one would read his book; a curse because you can't control the degree of burrowing your readers get up to. Autobiographies are generally interesting if they are controversial, if they reveal secrets, or if they show a side of life that the reader may have wished for, but not experienced. In writing an autobiography the writer must have a story to tell that is largely beyond or outside the life of his readers. In many cases he or she must bare their soul. This can be viewed as brave or stupid. I suspect my efforts are somewhere in between these two, but I have tried to lay my story out with as much honesty as I can muster and have only withheld information when there was a need to protect someone.

Inevitably it is the failings and misdeeds of the writer that attract the most interest. All the writer can do is to record history honestly and ask the reader to suspend judgement. And why expose yourself to censure by telling your story, partly because it is therapeutic to investigate your past, to own up to it and to leave a record of it for your descendants. Perhaps also there are stories that it would be a great pity not to tell. And inevitably, because it never occurs to the peacock that his plumage was meant for anything other than public display.

My first book, *A Man Who Cast Two Shadows* enjoyed very good sales locally and the feedback I have had from readers has shown me how dissimilar my life was from theirs. The people of my hometown who I grew up with, the seamen I sailed with, the people I lived my life with in New Zealand and the people I have met since coming back to Ricky, have almost all been tremendously enthusiastic and supportive and not a little bit surprised by my writing efforts. It has been all of them who have encouraged me to write this second book in what I hope will become a trilogy.

So, my kind readers, I have bared my soul again. I've told some tales about some legendary figures recalled from the past and sometimes from the grave. Above all, I have tried to capture the flavour and essence of a time now gone by in a land at the end of the world, where all was seldom what it seemed. I hope you have enjoyed this tale and will join me for the final stage of the journey in book three. In the meantime, here is a poem I wrote about New Zealand shortly after my return to England in 1996, a time when I was confused, having to restart my life. Writing the poem had a therapeutic effect on my thoughts and helped me to settle. I hope you enjoy it.

A memory of Aotearoa (Land of the long white cloud.

I know a far off little country
Where for a lifetime I was pleased to be.
I lived there through many changes,
All its ways and cultures so well known to me.
I found the kiwis warm and friendly, with their cry
of "She'll be right".
Showed confidence in their future;
Their faith in their land so bright.

New Zealand when I arrived there,
A hardy and ready place.
Blessed by a caring culture
And the friendly Maori race.
Side-by-side Maori and Pakeha progress together;
Past grievances argued and overcome.
Though there have been problems,
This land's a racial lesson for some.

The Kiwis of the sixties;
A farm boy open and strong.
How quickly it now changes
As to the cities they all do throng.
They moved on from their cow towns,
From Northland to the Bluff,
Flooding inner city suburbs,

Of country life they'd had enough.

By their warmth and friendly bearing,
When I arrived there I was struck.
Few snobs or class supporting social climbers,
I could not believe my luck.
That was Kiwi life in the sixties,
Life so simple and full of trust.
Kiwis still thought Britain the Motherland,
Though her turn to Europe, nearly sent them bust.

Kiwis spilled their blood in Gallipoli.
They were there in the two world wars.
Volunteers; loyal allies; brave partners;
Though later they were still shown the door.
The lessons of life down under
Is of brave and independent hearts.
A roll call of immigrants
Shows most came from British parts.

This tiny country and population
Spawned achievements worthy of note.
In politics, social conditions, science and sport,
They also led with the women's vote.
Their soldiers fought with distinction
For freedom and democracy.
When measured against their numbers,
They claimed many honours, were awarded many
VCs.

Of their achievements to speak up I feel free,
As they themselves too modest,
But the facts are well known to me.

I feel I was so lucky
To live in the land of the long white cloud
And now of my Kiwi offspring,
I think and feel so proud.

I wonder at the ingredients
Required to mould this Kiwi type.
A people of resource and action,
Not easily fooled by spin and hype.
Perhaps the blending of races,
From immigrant spirit and wanderlust,
Not of those who know their places
But those of snobs not fussed.

My memories are of space and clean beaches,
Sparkling oceans and sandy shores;
Of fern covered green hillsides
Coloured houses, all with open doors.
That easy way of life now changing,
"She'll be right" now in danger I fear.
Isolation and distance no saviour,
Technology and eTech, now bring all so near.

The rat race now overtaking
This far flung independent strand.
The pace of life now overwhelming
A beacon to better ways, making a last stand.
Let the politicians remember traditions, on which
this nation was built;
Embrace the new ways and prosper,
But let not the spirit of fair go, waiver, fall or tilt.

I remember good cobbers and places

From Cape Reinga to Dunedin and beyond.
Many faces stored in my memory,
Matching to names of which I am so fond.
Cold wintry afternoons at the footy,
A drink from a bottle under the stand;
We sang 'Hoki Mai' and 'Pokere' together,
With respect, white shook brown hand.

Len Russell 1996

Pakeha is the Maori word for white European
'Fair Go' is a valued Kiwi expression = To give a
man a fair chance. It was one of the earliest of
lessons drummed into me by Kiwis.

ACKNOWLEDGEMENTS

I have been lucky enough to have many supportive friends who have put up with me and my perfect personality that did not always behave as it should during some of the frustrating times that writing can conjure up. Not in any particular order I acknowledge the following individuals and groups.

First and foremost are the three people who have really made publication possible through their unstinting support and efforts. My son-in-law, editor-in-chief and dedicated nagging critic, which is intended to bring out the best in me, Dan Witters; Ken Balneaves, a talented writer who has suffered the setbacks with me. Without Ken I doubt my books would have seen the light of day. Writing is one thing, preparing for publication another. Ken never once let me down, answering every call for help. No problem was too hard to solve, he is truly a great friend. Then there is Ray Freed, a man of many business and artistic talents with much patience who always has time for a friend; his support, friendship and advice have been invaluable.

Also, the Ricky businessmen who saw something in my writing and have been a great support team, Ray Freed, Geoff Simms, Gary Eaton, Ken Balneaves, and Ivan Toscani; you are all really appreciated.

I also acknowledge the support and encouragement of the Bugler boys, a well-known and respected Rickmansworth family.

There are also the Ricky High Street gang, mainly good old Mill Enders and others; they all know who they are. Thanks so much for your support. I think from what you have said that you not only appreciated the book, but appreciated it was one of your own who wrote it.

Then there is the rugby crowd in the Druids pub, faithful as ever; good lads all. Allan the Taffy (Mr Rugby), the owner; Pat, the original 'sports nut' (who would get up in the night to watch Tiddlywinks, providing it's England); Tommy Russell, no relation, even though he claims to be and good old Robbie and the noisy Chess Valley rugby boys and the Ruislip Rugby Club. Also, Phil, Neil (England forever!) and the constant Kiwi, Nathan.

And there's the coffee bar contingent; Gerrard O'Connell, John Gompers (the Strolling Minstrel), Richard (Storky) Bowden, Dave and Pat, also I must include Kim and Sarah, long time supporters, as is my good friend, Bushey Kat. Also, the old Mill End crew from the Pensylvania, they know who they are; thanks.

Now for the Kiwi brigade, again in no particular order I acknowledge all the following all who have featured in one or other of the books.

Ray Miller, a great partner that I shared both good and dangerous times with; Sir Robert Jones, or Bob as he is known in Kiwi land. Bob and I pushed a few boundaries, a real character who made great contributions to New Zealand in many areas; and Allan Harris (Rambo), a good and loyal friend and supporter.

Last, but not least, 'Diamond Jim Shepherd', an amazingly resourceful man. In any other time in any other situation, he would have been a war hero or something similar. I take my hat off to him, not many could have survived it.

Len Russell

<u>Books by the same author.</u>

A Man Who Cast Two Shadows

Dancing In The Shadows

Gigilo's End

(To be published December 2013)

Also,

Look out for the final book of the Shadows trilogy in the summer of 2014.